The Natural Order

B.H. Miller

Published by Centaurea Publishing
B H Miller
Bhmillerbooks.com

Book Cover by B.H. Miller

ISBN: 9798864418178

For all of those who were told they weren't enough.

You are. You change the world every day without even knowing it.

"In the very depths of Hell, do not demons love one another?"
- *Anne Rice*

Chapter 1 - Marie

I saw him well before he saw me. The larger of the guards flanking him stayed behind at the closed door that separated the visiting room from whatever lay beyond. Dirty orange cloth screamed at me from across the room like the caution signs construction workers used to warn you that the journey ahead was going to get super fucking annoying if you kept going.

Maybe that's why jumpsuits were made that way—as a last-ditch effort to warn idiots like me that they were about to make a huge mistake.

In the wild, some frogs had neon colorings to signify to predators that they were poisonous.

The man who sat in front of me was something much worse than poisonous, if the media was to be believed. He looked at me as though I was a ghost, come to haunt his remaining days.

Hulking dividers spanned the length of the room, so thick that looking through them coated everything in a slight haze that threatened to make me dizzy if I focused too hard on any one thing. Before they let me enter the room, an officer who seemed equal amounts bored and irritated assured me that I would be safe, and made me sign a waiver stating that I wouldn't sue them if anything happened to me.

Seemed pretty counterintuitive.

"Why?"

I was startled by the question, mostly because I'd planned to be the one asking it. And yet, it fell from *his* mouth as he took in the sight of me and pressed the phone to his face.

Jesse.

Truthfully, the matching receiver smashed against my own ear was forgotten the moment I caught sight of him. I'd picked it up early to erase the chances of chickening out once he showed up, but his loud voice echoing in my skull was what made me question myself.

Jesse wasn't as surprised as I'd expected him to be. There was a sick hopefulness that he'd recognize me, but it was supposed to have been tinged with surprise and guilt.

What stared at me through dark brown eyes was closer to anger and confusion than any hint of remorse.

But I wanted to know why.

I gripped the receiver hard enough to stop the slight tremble in my fingers. It took me two tries to find my voice.

"I just need to know something."

He waited, and I was grateful that the visiting room was empty except for the two of us and the guards—one of which was standing over Jesse's shoulder and shooting a look at me that made me want to flip him off. No one got to judge me except for me.

The silence became awkward as I stumbled through the thoughts in my head. I'd rehearsed exactly what I wanted to say at least a hundred times, but staring him in the face had made it all seem inconsequential— like suddenly I had something so much more important to ask him than: 'Hey, why the hell did you try to kill me?'

Did I?

Even through the blurred image, I could see him grinding his teeth. His lips thinned with what I could only imagine was an attempt to hold his tongue. Did he want to finish the job? That seemed like a question I should ask.

"Did you write down your real name?" he asked, nodding a head to the door I entered through from the front of the building. When I didn't answer right away, he continued. "On the visitor log. Did you?"

It was my turn to be confused. What the hell kind of question was that? I looked from the door to the man, attempting to find a clue along the way as to where the conversation was heading. Even the thinner guard over Jesse's shoulder had quirked an eyebrow and was trying to catch my attention for me to help him follow the discussion.

You and me both, dude.

"I don't... I don't understand." My voice came out softer than I'd have liked, making me sound weak. I was *not* weak.

"It's a pretty simple question. What name did you give the guards at the entrance?"

He leaned forward a bit, as though we were sharing secrets and had any semblance of privacy to do so. The guard at his back took one small step forward. Jesse didn't notice.

I cleared my throat to finally find my nerve.

"Mine, of course. Why would I use any other name?"

A hand flashed up so quickly that both armed men rested their own on the guns at their hips, but Jesse's hand only ran through his hair and down his face in what looked to be a bad habit. He fixed his gaze on me with a sudden intensity that stole the air from my lungs. The connection I felt between us that night blazed to life, pushing several thoughts forward in my mind.

"I want to know about that night."

"Read the fucking papers," he snapped back. The knowledge that he'd been harassed endlessly about the event was of no consequence. I didn't relent.

"Trust me, I have. What I want to know isn't in them." I sighed at the situation. Nothing had gone the way I'd seen it happening in my head. The plan had been to ambush him at the jail and get him to spill the dirty little secret he hadn't revealed either in the media or the trial shortly after the incident—why he'd targeted us. I didn't truly think he'd cough up his guts upon seeing my face, but I'd at least hoped for a different reaction; one that I most definitely hadn't received.

At that point, not asking the questions was just a waste of a trip.

"Tell me why you chose that particular building. *That* building, at that time, on that day."

Shifting to lean back against his seat, Jesse scrubbed again at his face. When he'd finished, he closed his eyes and let out a soft laugh, like the kind you'd expect to hear between good friends amidst ribbing one another. The sound made me clench my fist even harder around the plastic phone handle.

"You want to know why I picked you," he accused, opening his eyes again but looking everywhere except at me. "That's pretty vain, you know. There's nothing special about you. You were one of, what, fifteen people in that building? It wasn't personal."

Anger seared me from the inside. He'd struck a nerve and he knew it, if the twist of his mouth was any indicator.

But he didn't know me.

He couldn't possibly know the real reason I'd come to see him; the true questions burning at the tip of my tongue, begging to be thrown at him like weapons.

I stood so abruptly that the guards jolted and moved forward. I paid them absolutely no mind.

Jesse might not have been looking at me, but I was certainly staring a gaping hole into the side of his face.

"Actually, I want to know why you lied." His attention snapped to me once more, and his anger finally matched my own. "You held back a lot of information at the trial, even going as far as to drop your plea of innocence in relation to the bombing. But the funny thing about that is that I don't buy it." I glared my feelings into him, wishing I could form them into anything more useful at torturing out the information I wanted; more useful than words could ever be. "I don't think you did it at all."

He stood too, waited only a moment before he slammed down his receiver and kicked the chair at the visitation seat next to him. It sailed across the room as the two guards took hold of Jesse and escorted him roughly from the room.

A touch on the back of my arm startled me and I shoved blindly at the attached body. Fortunately, the officer that the hand belonged to was expecting it and had a tight enough grip on me that neither of us moved due to the outburst. He guided me briskly from the room, a little too firmly for my liking, and asked me three times if I was okay and whether I needed anything before we found ourselves back at the main entrance.

He thought I was shaken over the experience.

I could admit that Jesse's reaction startled me, but I was not afraid.

However, as I collected my purse and cell phone from the guard so that I could make my exit, I glanced down at my own name scrawled in the visitor log and pursed my lips.

Chapter 2 - Marie

The bus ride home did nothing to soothe my temper.

Though, if I was being entirely honest, my anger wasn't the only emotion poked during the confrontation.

How the hell had he managed to hurt my feelings? The man had been accused of trying to kill me, for fuck's sake.

And I had stood in front of him, babbling and shaking like an idiot.

I rubbed my hands along my face and glared out of the nearest window until my stop approached. If I were him, I wouldn't trust me with the truth either.

But was it the truth? Was an innocent man really taking a bad charge for no apparent reason? Why would he do that?

Warm, dry air slapped me across the face as I stepped onto the sidewalk. My cell phone hung heavy in my pocket, reminding me that I was also guilty of doing stupid things that made absolutely no sense— like confronting the man accused of plotting my murder, and not even bothering to tell my best friend about any of it. Though I couldn't yet admit it to myself, avoiding her questions was the sole reason I hadn't turned my phone back on once I left the jail. What would I even say?

"Hey, Leena. You know that man that almost killed me? Well, I went to see him. Funny thing, even though he really did commit murder that night, he didn't actually kill me or anyone in the building he was attempting to bomb, and I'm pretty sure he's innocent of that crime. What makes me so sure? Well, I feel something really strange around him and it tells me that he's a good guy."

I laughed at myself as I walked, but it wasn't an amused sound. Even I could appreciate that I'd come off as a raving lunatic.

Leena would chew me out every waking minute for an entire month if I told her what I'd done. Or what I was planning to do. Yet, I couldn't avoid her scrutiny forever. I'd have to come up with a plausible reason for going dark for so long without explanation—especially considering I'd dug that hole for myself by practically attaching the two of us at the hip for the past too many years of my life. I loved Leena, and that love made me cling to her like she was my lifeline more often than I cared to admit. So why hadn't I just told her about the meeting?

Entering the parking garage, I powered on my phone, thankful that the structure all but nuked cell signal until you reached the door to the main building. It gave me a chance to collect my thoughts and develop a small hope that I could come up with something good enough to avert her suspicion.

As I pushed through the heavy exterior door and beelined for the elevator, the telltale vibrating began, warming my thigh where it pressed against the thin layer of polyester through my pocket. By the time the doors pinged open at the third floor, it finally fell calm and silent.

Thankfully, when I stepped out and scanned the hallway, Carmen was nowhere in sight and neither were her kids. She was a fine neighbor, but she liked to chat and I wasn't in any mood for it after my day. Truthfully, I was never really in a mood for chatting, but I made an exception for Carmen… one that she took full advantage of. I wasn't avoiding her, per say, as I really did like the woman. Most times our schedules nestled opposite one another anyway. Sometimes her kids played in the hallways while she worked—though none of us residents on the floor ever complained—which could have led to a slightly less awkward encounter since they always regurgitated the questions Carmen would ask so that they could update her later. It was quite the network she had going.

It seemed to be a sign that things were looking up for me that all was quiet and empty, so I fished out my phone as I unlocked my door and let myself in, punching in the speed dial for Leena. It took less than thirty seconds for the call to be picked up.

"Oh my god, I thought you were dead," she shrieked into the empty space of my apartment, bolstered by speakerphone although we both knew she didn't need it. Too bad, because I thought better when there wasn't a device pressed against my face that demanded attention.

"Leena, that was *one time*!"

There was a brief pause while Leena decided whether or not she wanted to take my comment as the joke it was intended to be, or go full mother-hen mode on me once again.

"It only takes one time," she pouted over the line. "Ever since that night… I don't know."

"You feel responsible. I know. But like I've told you a million times, I'm glad that you weren't there."

Her elongated sigh meant that I'd won that round. I tried not to celebrate.

"I just wish I'd have let you back out when I did. That's all."

"Listen, I don't believe in your woo-woo any more than I believe in Bigfoot. You may have told me that you had a feeling it would be good for me to go without you but, really, it had no bearing on my decision. I needed a night away, so I took it."

Leena had been my best friend for years. We knew each other well enough that I could picture her on the other end, nodding solemnly because she knew I was right. She pulled in a loud breath before launching back to the point.

"So where were you?"

Internally, I groaned. Externally, I sucked my teeth to buy time. Of all the people I'd ever met in my life, Leena was the most kind and caring by a long shot. She took on a motherly role with nearly everyone she stumbled across, though being her best friend meant that I received the brunt of it. Sometimes, though thankfully not so often, that turned into a situation where Leena felt overly protective almost to the point of smothering. It was a delicate dance to untangle myself from her cocoon without hurting her feelings.

"I was with someone."

The words rolled from my tongue before I could fully process them, though they left the sweet residue of the truth in my mouth, which was followed shortly by relief. No lie there.

"Oh my god," she breathed. I braced for an assault of admonishment. "Oh my god!" Her tone lifted, excitement and scandal tingeing the edges of her words. "You were with *Luke*? I knew it! Are you two back together?"

Crap. The internal groans became external ones. Could I let her think that I was entertaining Luke's groveling and pathetic attempts to rekindle our relationship? Yes. But should I? Probably not. Until Hell swallowed me whole and began its not-so-subtle game of torture, Luke Therion would never be in my life again.

I opened my mouth to say as much, but never got the opportunity. Leena, in her own fantasy world, had begun a long-winded lecture about how she knew we'd always end up back together and what a wonderful thing it was, but not a thing that I needed to keep from her. No secrets between best friends, after all.

Her distraction afforded me the opportunity to digest the day's events; something I'd studiously avoided doing on the ride back home. All in all, I felt like the journey had been rewarding. Once I had sat back to consider it, the comment about using my own name to visit Jesse seemed more ominous than it did strange. Again, the connection I'd felt to him prickled at the back of my mind.

An idea formed quickly, taking me by surprise. I rolled it around in my head for only a moment before I decided that it couldn't hurt to try.

"Leena, I need to run," I cut her off, hoping she wouldn't mind too much. "There are some errands I have to take care of."

Her tone turned sly, her words slower than just seconds before. "Ohhhh," she all but purred into the phone. "Go, go. Enjoy your 'errands', my love."

Appropriately, I laughed just enough to make it convincing, though I didn't feel it much at all. She'd assume it was Luke-related, and I wouldn't correct her.

As soon as the line clicked dead, I shoved my phone back into my pocket, grabbed my wallet from the kitchen counter where I'd tossed it just minutes ago, and headed out the door, keys still in hand.

I also promised myself a movie night with Leena to make up for it.

Chapter 3 - Marie

Two years later.

Soft noise echoed through the mostly empty room as my feet met the cold vinyl floor with the sticky slap that only bare skin could achieve. Living in California meant scorching summer months, so as a compromise to renting a glorified shoe box with barely any furniture to my name, I spared no expense when it came to air conditioning. Everything my fingers met was chilly, borderline frosted. Air all but puffed from my mouth in a cloud of dollar signs. It was as close to bliss as I'd get any time soon.

Besides combating the raging heat outside, the living snow globe in my home did wonders to fully wake me as I stumbled through the hallway and into the living room that also served as my kitchen and dining area. Coffee was my first priority, though I did snatch up the remote to rouse the small TV across the room while I waited. Having a tiny TV never bothered me much except during those times when my bleary vision hadn't cleared fast enough during my wait for a caffeine fix. Good coffee took time and was always worth waiting for, small TV or otherwise. I clicked past the children's cartoons to find a channel that was less likely to annoy me—though, seeing as basic cable was my only option, the task was more difficult than it should have been. I stopped at the image of a local news anchor on screen, curious as to what nonsense was being shoved down the throats of the masses this time. The title at the bottom stated that the segment was meant to educate about the effects of sunscreen on an individual's health. My finger hovered over the buttons of the remote as I read the scrolling text. Would it beat out the clash of animation and falsetto in driving me to insanity? I watched for several minutes, more disgusted than entertained, but still unable to look away. Yep, it would do.

The aroma of fresh coffee permeated the apartment. Inhaling deeply, as though my life hung on that one last breath, the scent filled my soul to the very brim. Along with the physical reaction of my body anticipating the pick-me-up, my memories swam with images of Leena and I working in tandem behind the counter of a coffee bar not so long ago, her hair an impressive sweep of teal that I always admired.

While I didn't have many memories to speak of, those were the happiest that I *could* recall in all of my life. I might not have been able to remember my childhood dreams or my elementary school friends, and I certainly couldn't admit to which celebrities made up my first fantasies, but I didn't need to. It had been a long time since I'd let my amnesia bother me. What I did remember was Leena, my best friend for all of the years that I recalled, and coffee.

They both kept me sane on many different levels.

I watched it brew with familiarity and excitement, dark drops falling slowly into the glass underneath. If I were to ever believe in hypnotism, the only way I'd get sucked under was with the teasing drips of a good, fresh brew. In fact, it felt as though time both slowed and moved at warp speed as I lost myself in the rhythm. Over the top of the pot, the TV screen flashed red, ripping through my concentration and alerting me to the breaking news report that had taken over the regular programming. Giving the volume a few bumps with the remote, I leaned back against the counter to listen.

The reporter was captivating, dark-skinned with high cheekbones and perfect posture, and she contrasted beautifully against the cream background as text scrolled past, both in front of and behind her. Her eyes shone like Lapis Lazuli. She was so mesmerizing, in fact, that I realized with a jolt that I'd missed the actual news she was reporting on. I bumped the volume one more time for good measure.

My mind drifted briefly to the thought that Leena would blush a million shades of red at the idea of me admiring another female in that way. She was a bit traditional in that sense, whereas my preferences tended toward good personalities and eye candy, without much limitation on anything else. There was no harm in admiring, after all. I pushed away the notion and gave the report my full attention.

The reporter's face was serious—solemn, even—as she informed the cameras that yet another body was found.

"Although there is no official confirmation of such, this incident is believed to be connected to the other bodies discovered in many states along the Eastern coast and the Mid-West region in recent days. At this time, law enforcement does not believe that there is any threat to public safety. The current avenue of investigation has led officers to chemical analysis, where they are anticipating that food contamination will reveal itself as the culprit. We will provide updates as soon as they are received."

Sheesh. All those linked deaths, and that wasn't even including the dozens of others reported recently that were equally suspicious, though ruled as isolated incidents. On top of that, crime in general seemed to be on the rise lately, with an increased reporting presence on burglary and crazies of all flavors. I only knew about it because Leena watched the news religiously and insisted on regurgitating the knowledge to me at every opportunity, explaining that it was best to be informed when we worked in the public and lived alone. I couldn't say that I disagreed with her logic, but I also couldn't see the benefit in subjecting myself to the depressing reality of the outside world on a daily basis. Whatever the reason behind it, it was not a good time for humanity in general.

Guess I'd be cooking at home for a good while, just in case. My face pinched together of its own accord. A great cook, I was not.

Leena probably would have been happier if the world events frightened me into being more cautious, but the reality was that I worked a dead-end job for just enough money to keep me showing up every day, and I had no real family or friends to speak of—besides Leena. Truth be told, if someone wanted to murder me there wouldn't be much in it for them. There wouldn't be much loss, overall. I wasn't likely to be anyone's ideal target.

The coffee pot sputtered, informing me that the last of the water inside had been sucked up and redistributed. I fixed myself a cup with a bit more sugar than I would normally take and a hint of milk, opting for a to-go cup instead of the stay-home mug I'd originally intended to fill. With the start of my work day looming around the corner, it made sense to head for the mall early and make myself a nuisance to the patrons instead of sitting at home and only managing to annoy myself. Wasn't there something to be said for sharing the wealth?

The sun was much too bright when I stepped outside, nearly convincing me that it was a better idea to skip work and retreat into the dim, cavernous depths of the parking garage to play another game of 'Are those my own steps echoing or is someone else here too?', but I held steady on my path. The bills had to get paid somehow. Honestly, the coffee helped my decision a lot more than it should have.

Well, that and the *long* lecture Leena had given me the last time I skipped out on work.

"You can't just eat toast and cheese for the rest of your life, Marie. You have to be able to afford groceries," she'd said, hand on hip in a motion that was supposed to have conveyed annoyance and concern, but mostly managed toddler-throwing-a-temper-tantrum. "You're too impulsive. Think things through instead of going with your first emotion all the time. It'll serve you better in the long run."

She'd been right, of course, and I most certainly *had* survived that week on toast and cheese. The instant regret as a spice to that first bite of cold bread was something I'd take with me to the grave. I may have been impulsive but I was also prideful and there was no way in hell I'd admit to Leena that I sometimes regretted my explosively reactive ways.

The memory had me chuckling to myself on my walk, right up until the reality of being outside in the California summer hit me.

Admittedly, at a temperature quickly approaching the low eighties, a hot beverage had not been the most intelligent choice to bring along for my wait at the outdoor bus stop. The saving grace was that when I arrived at the small plexiglass hut along the road, no one else was anywhere to be seen. It was just me, my hot bean water, and the muted hiss of tires against pavement as vehicles passed slowly by. When the city bus finally loomed down the road in my direction, I heard it long before I ever saw it.

"Hi, girl!"

Aw, hell.

I tipped up the corners of my mouth as far as I could manage without it looking like the grimace I was trying so desperately to hide. The three steps up to the main walkway of the bus felt every bit as intimidating as climbing a mountain in high heels. That perhaps had something to do with the fact that Carmen was grinning much too enthusiastically at me from the driver's seat. I hesitated, contemplating how realistic it would be to pretend that I'd forgotten something at home and rushed off before the awkwardness of the situation caught up to us.

It was too late. Carmen waved a hand in my direction, motioning for me to hurry and board. It took more self-restraint than I'd ever admit not to loudly point out to her that there was no one else waiting to board and, therefore, no reason to rush. And also, that I'd rather she just run me over than have to trap myself inside the bus with her this morning.

I kept the commentary to myself. Barely.

Carmen patted the very first row opposite her as I made my way up the steps and dropped my payment into the plastic slot for dollar bills. Thankfully, she didn't notice the immense sigh that I didn't quite manage to stop from sneaking out as I claimed the seat. The singular silver lining to the front row and having to put up with chit-chat was the blissful gust of wind that skimmed along my already sweat-soaked face and neck from Carmen's personal dash fan.

"How you been? Haven't seen you in a few days. The boys were asking if you were okay cuz we don't see you, but I told them you were probably just busy. You work a lot."

My eyes narrowed of their own volition. I widened them again before catching Carmen's gaze in the mirror above her head. Was she clocking my schedule?

"Gotta pay the bills." I shrugged, knowing full well where the conversation was heading. Though I tried, I couldn't find a way to derail it before it got there.

"That man of yours not helping you out? He should be paying some of the bills. He has money. I see the car he drives."

Carmen's eyes narrowed, and I was sure it was entirely intentional. The dark brown waves of her hair swayed against the breeze from her fan, tossing the scent of something sweet and fruity in my direction. If she wasn't such a good neighbor by sending out her three young boys to hold doors and carry bags for me whenever possible, I'd have snuck the two doors down the hall into her home long ago and poured Durian fruit into her shampoo bottle. Well, it was partially that and partially the fact that I'd heard rumors about her children's father not being in the picture because she'd set his car on fire.

Didn't know the context of that, and didn't want to.

While she was a nice enough person, and her kids were fantastic, she just never seemed to take the hint that I wasn't a social person—and, no, I wouldn't like to be invited to dinner, thank you. Not even when I said as much. Directly to her face. Multiple times.

"It's just me now, and I can pay my bills by myself."

Probably.

Hopefully.

With a click of her tongue, and a sharp jerk on the wheel that sent me careening into the window and sloshing some of my hot coffee onto my arm, Carmen slowed the bus to a stop and muttered something in rapid Spanish under her breath. A quick glance around showed no sign of a bus stop, but did reveal a small line of cars in front of us that seemed to be halted in the road. I was pretty sure I heard the words 'car accident' in Carmen's clipped accent, but my Spanish was no good and mostly consisted of Googling the things I'd heard her yell through the apartment hall over the years. If I was being honest, I pretty much only learned the curse words that way.

How I wished I could turn back time to the brief period when I didn't need to rely on public transportation. It felt like an eternity ago.

Leena lived on the opposite side of Redding, and while she'd offered numerous times to pick me up for our shifts together, I declined—mostly because I knew the real reason she was extending the invitation. When I first started working at The Capital with her, it was shortly after my doomed relationship with Luke had begun. There was a short period where I took city transportation back then as well, though it wasn't long before I'd begun riding in style, cruising to work regularly in the lush comfort of Luke's swanky SUV.

Since my parting with him, Leena had also been relentless about her offers to bring me dinner when she'd "made too much", which we both knew was a thinly veiled warning that she didn't feel I'd been taking good enough care of myself. Between the nudges to accept her transportation, and the ones to give Luke another chance, sat looks of admonishment or pity, varying in degree but always applicable to the most recent suggestion she'd made, of which I'd automatically and promptly declined. We'd been in a tenuous game of unwanted mother and ungrateful daughter for quite a while.

In a loving way, of course.

Between idle chit-chat with Carmen, and Leena's worry, I'd rather just have been kidnapped as I risked it all hoofing it to work on foot. As a close second, Carmen won out.

The bus lurched backward an inch or so as Carmen threw levers and pushed buttons at the helm, eventually swinging all five-foot-nothing of herself out of the driver's seat and down the stairs. I glanced behind me to find that I was the only patron on the bus, and therefore no one else would be taking one for the team by checking on her instead of me. Great. Sliding myself out of the seat to follow, I took a large gulp of coffee. What were the chances that the caffeine could instantly grant me the energy to walk the rest of the way to work?

Several drivers and passengers of the vehicles in front of us also began to emerge and shift forward to the front of the line. The top of Carmen's dark head disappeared into a small crowd that had begun to gather in the way that rubberneckers do. My stomach dropped, instinct raising the hairs on my arms in a clear warning that I wouldn't like what I was about to see. A chorus of hushed voices enveloped us as we tucked ourselves into the fold of people, pushing forward to see what the commotion was.

As she was smaller, and had probably elbowed a few people out of the way, Carmen reached the center before I did. I should have known it was bad before I, too, pushed my way to the front, because if I'd learned anything about her in the past several years as neighbors, it was that there was hardly a thing in the world that could stop Carmen from talking incessantly.

And apparently, we'd stumbled across one.

Chapter 4 - Marie

The woman, pleasantly plump and red enough in the face that she might have been part tomato, raised her hand several times to slam it down on the counter in front of her, emphasizing the words that we'd long since been ignoring. We stood a safe enough distance away, behind the opposite end of the counter, that neither of us truly felt threatened by the pointer finger she thrust forward as though it were a spear and she was aiming for our hearts. Regardless, neither of us were amused by the outburst, either.

"I'm so sorry," Leena said in her all-too-familiar low and slow pitch, which was mostly reserved for talking down the crazies. "I understand your situation. I would love to help you; however, I do have to abide by the policies set in place. Unfortunately, your item…" Leena gestured to the balled-up grocery bag in the woman's hands. Inside, a soiled, foul-smelling dress that had clearly been worn a few too many times, and washed a few too little, sat crumpled with the tags still attached as if they were a badge of honor. We'd banished it back to the sack the moment she'd pulled it out to show us, fearing for our sense of smell. "It's ineligible for return at this time. If it didn't meet your expectations, I can walk you through the process for submitting product feedback, and instead assist you with finding an item that might better suit your needs."

Blotches of purplish hue dotted along the woman's face and neck, but she drew in a deep breath and leaned back, away from the pair of us. I let out a sigh of relief. She hadn't moved away from the register, but she also hadn't continued her verbal assault, which I'd bet twenty bucks she wanted to be more than just verbal. So long as she was finished spitting venom at me, I no longer had to bite back my own. My job was safe for another day.

Leena cruised around the counter, stepping dangerously close to the woman in order to lead her further into the store, murmuring quietly about the latest styles.

Turquoise would look great on a raving lunatic.

Why she'd even bothered with the nasty woman was beyond me. I was more than content to let her scream herself into submission, pass out on the floor, and be carted away by security. Leena, however, had a gentler soul and, for what it was worth, I found her to be quite peculiar as a whole—not just in the ways she handled customers.

It wasn't the current pink bubblegum of her hair, styled in ways that confused me the more I analyzed them, nor was it the ever-present, knowing smile quirked on her thin lips that made her strange; neither was it the odd choice of clothing, constant layering of neon-colored garments that always made it seem like she'd been too cold for whatever climate she was currently in, and thus had resorted to throwing on anything and everything laying around for warmth.

No, what made Leena truly odd was the quiet peacefulness and kindness in her. The way she not only calmed and soothed every person in her vicinity, but in the fact that she *liked* to do it. It was fulfilling to her, and extremely unnerving to me. Yet, in moments such as the tomato woman incident, when we were the only two manning the store together, I was glad to have her strange skills around. She could take the nut jobs and I could, well, *not*.

There were only so many tight-lipped smiles I could give out in a day before the customers began to realize that I wasn't the slightest bit moved by their shouting. They tended to not appreciate that so much, which was all the same because the feeling was mutual.

With the store deserted, minus Leena and the sort-of only slightly pink woman at the far corner of the shop, the quiet cocooned me. Sure, there was some noise from beyond the open double doors from the crowds strolling through the rest of the mall, but the mass amounts of fluffy, squishy fabric surrounding my bubble of space dampened it all to a soft rumble. I'd been employed with The Capital for nearly four years, and while a clothing store certainly wasn't my dream job, it afforded me the things that I needed in life. It also rewarded me with moments of tranquility when I needed them most.

The rent was paid every month for the box where I lived that proclaimed itself an apartment, there were moments when blissful silence stole away any nagging worries or stress, and then there was Leena, my best friend for all four of those years plus a bit more. It was pure luck that when she left the world of coffee and transitioned to clothing retail, she did so at a Store Manager level where she was given the reigns to staff as she saw fit—which resulted in one much-needed hiring of me, and some never-needed firing. I wasn't entirely sure that Leena was capable of firing anyone anyway, so it all worked out.

The two women made their way back toward me, the finally remarkably calm customer cradling a new dress in her arms, the old one smashed into her giant purse and quickly forgotten. She laid the pristine garment on the counter with reverence and as I reached forward and scanned the tag, her face pinched at the price that flashed across the register screen. Opening her mouth to undoubtedly remark on the 'ridiculous' price, she paused at Leena's small fingers darting in front of me to push in a discount code, dropping the price only a fraction. Apparently, this was enough to satisfy the tomato lady. She paid without further incident, though she did snatch the dress away and shove it into her purse before I could offer her a bag.

I was not at all sorry to see her sashay herself out the door.

"So," Leena turned to me, her deeply hooded eyes sparking with concern. "As I was saying before we were interrupted—"

Groaning, I threw my hands up into the air. A minuscule part of me had been grateful for the fruit-faced woman's interjection, cutting short an exchange that made my insides clench to think about.

Pushing her glasses up the bridge of her nose, I watched the black tint of her lips rub together in thought. "Why did you even bother coming in today? I wouldn't have expected you to, I mean…"

Another groan escaped me, and this one was intentionally loud and accompanied by the most exaggerated eye roll that I could muster. "What do you want me to do, Leena? Stay home and never come out again? People die. It happens." Folding my arms under my chest, I shrugged the upper half of my body. "Things are weird out there right now, but I still have to live my life just like everyone else."

It had been a mistake to tell Leena about the body we'd stumbled across at the traffic stop earlier in the day, but I'd had to explain why I was late for my shift. I wasn't lying—people *did* die all the time, and unless they personally impacted my life in some way, there was no point in pretending to be bothered by it. But what I didn't tell Leena was the condition of the body; perfectly matching the descriptions of the dozens of other deaths reported through the news daily. I'd hoped that the madness would be over before any of it reached us, but that clearly wasn't the case.

The choice had been made to omit the information for the sake of both of our sanity. She'd worry, and then she'd get frown lines *and* annoy the hell out of me all at once.

No thanks.

Leena's eyebrows rose high on her forehead. Her lightly tanned skin was perfectly flawless, always free from blemishes or wrinkles, but not free of my immense jealously, which I hurled relentlessly in the form of entirely sincere comments that only turned sour in my stomach when I didn't spew them. At nearly twenty-five years old, she was often mistaken for being younger than she was—though that never lasted long. A few moments alone with her tsunami of maturity smacking against anyone would teach them that she was wise beyond her years, of which there were enough to be jaded and choose not to. That's how Leena was. The Yin to my Yang. The calm adult to my emotional-teenager mentality.

"This isn't good," she suddenly croaked, sounding much more haggard than I'd ever heard before. She intentionally missed the glare I stabbed her with. "I'm serious. You need to go home and stay safe. Are you not watching the news?"

My face pinched tight. If the tomato woman had still been coasting from rack to rack, surely she'd have fled immediately at the wave of nonsense that was about to launch itself from my best friend's lips. Once upon a time, the rants had caught me off guard. My body would tense, reacting to the distress welling up from within her to cast a waterfall of emotion over me. I was no longer that malleable girl. Instead, I braced myself in another way; with a deep breath that filled me to the brim, to ensure that there were no weaknesses where the second-hand paranoia could leak through. A sigh started to slip out in a rush of air from my nose, but I cut it off before Leena could see just how ridiculous I thought her antics were. She was sensitive, and I was damn near emotionally inept on a good day.

Thank you, Luke, for the constant reminders that while your flaws were skyscrapers compared to mine, I still apparently needed your coddling to get through the most basic of levels in the relationship.

"Yes, I saw the news," I advised, tone carefully controlled. "Crime rates are increasing, and a good number of people have died due to mysterious causes in other parts of the country. They think it's food contamination. Why should that stop me from working?"

"It's only going to get worse." Her gentle voice was tight with stress—over what, god only knew. It barely took a singular raincloud in the sky to set her off on a tirade of conspiracy theories about the world ending; the recent events were the equivalent of her literal sky falling. While I absolutely adored her, the moments where her madness peeked out were emotionally exhausting. I did my best to console her instead; to return us to some sort of normal standard of a friendship, despite knowing that nothing about our friendship was normal.

"There's nothing to worry about. *We* have nothing to worry about."

She shook her head, ethereal pink strands of hair bobbing back and forth. For several minutes we stood in silent opposition, both of us watching for the other to crack. The low hum of C-list tunes invaded our space as if seeking to fill the void stretching between us.

"I know you're concerned about me, but you don't have to be. Things like this just happen sometimes. It's not going to reach us. Just be careful about what you buy at the grocery store."

The key to breaking the cycle of Leena's conspiratorial thoughts was found in distraction. I'd learned from years of practice. Hefting a bag of hangers from under the front counter, and placing them none-too-gently onto the back counter between us, I split a pile of crumpled clothing into two equal sections and slid one in front of her. Leading by example, we set to work restocking the racks from the returned and tried-on piles. Though the worry held fast in the tightness of her shoulders and the pressure between her tightly locked lips, she changed the topic and I—incorrectly—assumed that I was finally home free.

I prepared myself for another rant, sure that the worst of it was behind us. Until I realized what she'd chosen to lecture me on instead.

"You know, I don't see why you couldn't just talk to him about it."

Christ.

A headache roared to the front of my forehead. Three deep breaths later, my teeth unclenched themselves and I banished all thoughts of violence to the very back of my mind. If anyone deserved violence, it was *him*. Not Leena.

"I *did* talk to him about it. I talked to him about it fifteen times. It's no use." I popped a hip against the counter and leveled a hard stare at the side of her face. "Just like I've talked to you fifteen times about how it's over and you should let it go."

"It's just that you two were basically perfect together. The way you looked at him, the way he looked at you. And you said he was *fantastic* in bed," she swooned, hands clasped against her cheek. "I'm serious. You should have married him. There aren't many men like Luke out there."

"Thank god for that," I hissed under my breath. More loudly, I said, "Too many secrets, Leena. I just can't trust him."

A look passed over her face, fleeting, gone too quickly for me to tell what it had been. For a split second I was sure her eyes had flashed something akin to anger. Spinning a circle, sure to find someone else nearby who'd have garnered that kind of reaction, I had to face the fact that at the end of my turn, we were the only two people around and I'd done nothing that would earn ire like that. When I looked back at her again, though, she had busied herself folding clothing, every trace of the unfamiliar emotion gone as though it never existed.

Yes, Leena was strange, indeed.

But she was *my* strange best friend, and I loved her for it.

The remainder of the night was spent in relative silence, Leena flitting from area to area, tidying, taking inventory, and humming to herself. Staying behind the counter, my gaze flicked over the bodies of strangers as they passed the wall of glass at the front of the store. Men and women alike buzzed past, some alone, some together, but each of them on a mission of their own, seeking food or apparel or perhaps even just socialization.

A couple sauntered by, hand in hand, clearly content with each other's company. My lips pressed together hard without my command, goosebumps raising along my body as I imagined the feel of Luke's hand in mine, my head resting comfortably against his shoulder as we casually loped about, wanting nothing more than to be in each other's company.

Such times had long passed.

Leena might have acted like our split was hot gossip, but it had been nearly a year since I'd broken things off. The bitter knowledge that I missed him had done nothing to dull the infinite anger that had spurred my decision to walk away in the first place; a decision I had not yet come to regret, and was sure I never would. Why Leena had cared so much, and for so long, was a damn mystery, and one that I didn't dare look at too closely. I loved Luke, well and truly, but he hadn't loved me enough to trust me with *everything*. That was all there was to be said about it.

Rustling beside me jarred me back to reality, popping my bubble of daydreams and memories so abruptly that I gasped. A waft of bubblegum-scented shampoo slid across the air, appropriately matching the candy pink locks that flipped to and fro. The pink suited her more than the teal had. As I turned to offer her assistance organizing and cleaning the under-counter area, Leena held out a halting hand and informed me that she could handle the rest of the night alone. Protesting did no good. She insisted, claiming that the sad puppy look on my face had, apparently, been killing her mood. Though it was news to me, there was likely no word of a lie. Poker was definitely not my game. She'd said it with a smile, with no room for further discussion, so I punched out for the night and headed for the city bus stop, wondering along the way about the abrupt change in Leena's mood over the same conversation that the two of us must have had a dozen times too many. But there had been more to the conversation this time than angst. Perhaps, though unlikely, Leena also had a secret of her own.

I could tell when the news had reached the sanctum of my workplace; my walk down the length of the mall strip had proven that there was more to it than simply a slow night. Though the store itself was nestled directly in the middle of the facility, my eyes trailed the railings of the floor above as I traipsed through the building, met with empty air along the way. Silence melted into the irritating blare of radio-reject music, not even marred by the shuffle of footsteps or a wailing baby as it usually was. I glanced at an enormous clock against the wall to confirm that it was only four in the afternoon. A bus would be arriving in fifteen minutes, and I could make it if I hurried.

The deserted archways and quiet halls made the space between my shoulders itch. I recalled the body from this morning—how utterly still it was and how odd that seemed until my mind registered the missing parts. It was as if I'd still expected the person to turn and flip us the finger before revving off, despite the fact that their entire face was caved in and their left arm was all but ripped from the socket. I considered the people I'd seen earlier, wandering the stores as I headed in to work.

Food contamination, my ass. I'd just said that to appease Leena.

Yeah, if I was them, I'd probably head home and lock myself away, too.

It was unlucky that I had something to prove to everyone who thought I should be just as afraid. When I approached the bus stop just as the bus that would take me home pulled up, I waved Carmen off and waited for a second bus.

One that would take me out of town.

Chapter 5 - Marie

Like a tiger in a cage, I was drawn to his dangerous beauty. I found myself imagining what it would be like to stick my hand through the bars and pet the beast, to feel it purr beneath my fingers while my heart hammered at the possibility that it could just as easily bite them off.

Dark, furrowed eyebrows sat above a look that was *all* hungry tiger.

"What are you doing here?"

"The same thing—"

Jesse held up a hand to stop my words. I shifted my attention to the guard behind him, then back, following his gaze as he soaked in the new haircut and color, the blue contacts against my eyes. He didn't say it, but I could feel his approval. I could see it in the way his pupils expanded as he lingered over the changes.

"*Sarah*," he chastised, leaning toward me just slightly. The anger hadn't fully faded yet, deepening his tone just a shade. "What is it that you want, exactly?"

I blew out a breath. That was the tricky part. The fake ID and the southern accent fooled the guards initially, but if I wasn't careful, they'd remember me from before my makeover, and the warning that Jesse had been sending me—of which I still wasn't entirely following—would have been wasted.

It took only a moment of contemplation before I loaded myself for battle and made the first strike. "I wanted you to know that I'm going to go to the press." I hadn't come for idle chit-chat, no matter how intriguing I found him to be. "*I'm* going to the press," I clarified, prodding myself in the chest where he could see it. Marie, not Sarah. "They have the power to find out what you aren't telling me. What I suspect really happened."

It would mean that it was my last trip to the jail; my last attempt at uncovering the secrets on my own before I threw a steel wall between Jesse and I.

"You can't do that!" He all but snarled, gnashing his teeth together. Muscles jumped in his neck, likely a product of the restraint he was showing when it was obvious he wanted nothing more than to reach across the room and strangle me.

I wasn't afraid.

"You're not leaving me much of a choice. I'm here, now, and you're not willing to talk to me."

Silence ate up the space in the room. Even the guard at the door nearest me could feel it, sucking in a long, slow breath, as though it was one of his last. Jesse didn't know who he'd been dancing with, and if he thought I was bluffing, he was about to find out otherwise. He might have been a tiger in a cage but there were plenty of reasons I'd been called *heartless* and *a bitch* in my life. My right knee began to bob under the table with the effort to keep myself from leaping up and storming out.

"Alright," he grated out, then dropped his voice to a whisper. "Alright. You win." His free hand scrubbed his face in his telltale mark of stress.

Just like that?

"You're right. I didn't plant the bomb."

Oh my god.

"Then how did you know—" Realization dawned, pulling a strangled sound from my throat. "Holy shit, you're the one who called in the tip about it. You tried to stop it."

He said nothing, only looked at me with eyes so stormy with emotion that I felt I'd drown at any second.

"And the—"

"You can't absolve me of every crime. There's blood on my hands, and I put it there. Leave it alone now."

He hadn't tried to kill me, he'd *saved* me.

"Damnit, don't shut down on me now. Tell me about the cops."

Pushing to my feet, I placed a hand against the glass, fingers splayed. If it looked like I was begging, I was. I'd been right all along and it wasn't likely that anyone would believe me except for him.

"Tell me!" One quick slap of my palm against the glass had the guard behind me moving forward, but I turned and pointed at him. "Everything's fine. Don't you dare interrupt this." He looked briefly startled, then settled a disapproving glare on me. I was pushing the limits and he knew it.

Sarah didn't care.

Slowly, with leaden legs, I sank back into my seat. "Please, tell me what happened."

The long locks I'd watched in the moonlight so many years ago danced around in my vision as Jesse sighed and shook his head. He pulled the receiver away from his face just long enough to drop his forehead to the table in front of him for a moment, and then he was eviscerating me with his gaze once more.

"I killed them."

"But why?"

His lips twitched in a way that made me wonder how often Jesse smiled. I imagined there wasn't much opportunity for it in prison, but the gesture and its awkwardness made me think that perhaps he hadn't had many opportunities for it even prior to the murders.

"I'm going to do something I haven't done in a very, very long time, and I'm going to trust you, but you're not allowed to ask me why. Are we clear on that?"

Anger bubbled in my gut. No, we weren't clear on that. But what choice did I have if I wanted the answers I'd fought so hard to get? In return, I gave a tight nod.

"The officers were rogue. They weren't following the protocols for bomb handling, and you're lucky I was there to stop them before they accidentally set the thing off. They're *not* so lucky because they wouldn't listen. That's all there is to it."

Squirming in the discomfort of the seat, scenarios whirled through my head.

"How did you do it?"

Surprise flickered across Jesse's face. The guard over Jesse's shoulder snapped his head up at me. Alright, too much attention. "Why haven't you told the truth? Why stay here, on death row, for a crime you didn't commit?"

"Easy. Because of the ones I *did*."

I opened my mouth to argue and then closed it again. He had a point. Would the sentence really have been any different without the bomb charge?

"But why let the person who really did it get away with it?"

The air in the room suddenly felt thick, suffocating. Before my eyes, Jesse's presence seemed to triple, soaking up all of the oxygen around us both. Where he'd been scary and dangerous before, he was lethal and merciless now. My instincts screamed at me to get the hell out.

When he opened his mouth next, I did.

"Who says they got away with it?"

I was chased out by his voice, with a stern warning not to return.

I found myself panting just outside the door to the visitation room, having asked the guard for a moment to catch my breath. Jesse couldn't see me any longer, but I heard the chains rattling that signaled him being led back out of the door on the other side of the facility. My pulse thundered in my ears.

"You okay?" The guard's hand hovered near my shoulders, afraid to touch.

Afraid of me? Probably a good chance.

But *was* I okay?

Straightening, I ran a hand down my front, smoothing the fabric in a bid to buy time. Electricity crackled along my skin where my fingers roamed over clothes.

A soft, genuine laugh spilled from my lips, unbidden.

Yes, I was pretty sure I was more than fine.

I was pretending that the whole encounter hadn't contributed to the slickness between my thighs.

But was it Marie or Sarah who loved the danger?

Chapter 6 - Luke

It took longer than it should have for the news to reach me. Most nights I sat for at least thirty minutes in front of the television, absorbing anything and everything of interest. Some would call it indulgent, and others depressing. Personally, I found it essential; however, I'd been neglecting my daily updates in recent weeks, too complacent with the past several years being entirely uneventful. That was why the images that flashed across my vision filled me with equal amounts of guilt, surprise, and horror. That was why I was weeks behind the rest of the world in finding out about what was happening in my own backyard.

In less than thirty seconds, my cell phone was pressed firmly between my hands and a panicked text message had been sent. She'd ignore it, I knew, but I had to try. There was no turning back once it had begun. I debated calling as well, if for nothing more than to be comforted by the sound of her voice, but knew better and banished the idea as quickly as it formed. She hated talking on the phone probably as much as she hated me at the moment, and the ice was already paper-thin under my feet. Any single misstep would leave me wholly alone to drown, and with her life dependent on me being there when I was needed, it was a risk not worth taking.

Yet, there was so much that I needed to tell her. There were things that I kept locked away, things that would turn her against me in even the best of outcomes, and her livelihood could pivot on those very same secrets. With the chaos closing in on our small city, there was nowhere left to run from my past, or from hers—the one she'd forgotten. If I was running anywhere, it should be *to* her. To save her.

Again.

With a much too forceful hammering of the buttons on the remote, the room fell silent. Beside me, my work laptop lay open, angrily flashing unfinished home plans in my face as I gave attention to exactly everything except it. The client the plans belonged to was a nasty one— one I'd almost fired several times for her unprofessionalism—but I'd kept her on because the project had been one I was interested in, and it had filled my time. Suddenly the thought of building the ultra-modern home made my head hurt.

The bubble of contentment that had settled around my life was thoroughly popped, catching me with my pants down, so to speak. I squeezed my eyes closed, summoning a cleansing breath, and then opened them again. Unsurprisingly, nothing had fixed itself in the thirty seconds that my mind had been utterly blank. It was still up to me to plug the holes in our sinking boat. There were a million possible paths to take, to mitigate damage, to hide what could still remain hidden, but they all met at the same, particular dead-end that I couldn't bear to acknowledge.

She'd left me once. I was sure that this time she'd simply kill me instead. Honestly, it would be the least painful outcome of them all.

Maybe I should let her.

I lifted the laptop and sent a quick email to my clients to inform them that I'd be taking an unexpected vacation. I was sure to have a response from Kelly within the hour, with all caps and multiple exclamation points included, to demand an itinerary for my vacation so that she could follow up with her 'urgent' changes immediately upon my return. In fact, I was sure she'd file another complaint with my boss just as she'd done when I took more than two days to respond to her life-threatening crisis involving the size and shape of her closet doors. Building wasn't even scheduled to begin on her project for another year. Truth be told, even the difficult clients were welcomed at the end of the day, because I enjoyed the work so much.

Just maybe not that day.

Architecture was my life, outside of Marie. I lived and breathed it. I reveled in the ability to create functional masterpieces that impacted the lives of my clients in a positive way. Sure, some of it was also pride— being able to look at a finished home and say: "I created that." The swell of feeling useful that accompanied a finished, functional project was intoxicating, drawing me into a rabbit hole of project after project and endless weeks of daydreaming about them until they came alive.

But none of that mattered anymore. It was the beginning of the end, and nothing could matter to me after what I'd learned.

I closed my laptop, stowing it away underneath the coffee table where it would sink to the back of my mind. With any luck, I'd wash my thoughts quickly of the matter at hand and return to business as usual in just a few short days. I'd even welcome the scathing emails from Kelly when I returned, because it would mean that I *had* returned; that I was successful and life could return to some form of normal.

Until then...

Turning my cell phone over in my hands for several seconds, just as I turned over thoughts in my mind, I finally pressed one of the speed dial options and held it to my ear. I was not impulsive like Marie was, but there *were* times where acting on your gut could save a life. Whether it was my life or hers that I was needing to save, I wasn't sure quite yet.

Perhaps it was time to live like the other half.

One ring, and I was still working to convince myself that the call was a good idea.

Two rings, and the doubt began to gnaw at the base of my confidence.

Three rings, and I was sure it had been a mistake.

Four rings, and I pulled the phone from my face with the intent to hang up and pretend like it had never happened. That was when the man's voice erupted from the other end of the line so unexpectedly that I visibly flinched.

"Well, I see you're finally caught up on the world's events. I can only imagine how terrified you must be."

The amusement rolling through his tone grated against my insides. It felt as though I'd swallowed an angry eel that was fighting for its life in my belly. It took nearly all of my effort to force words from between my own lips in a reply that wasn't as prickly as his was light. His rich, deep timbre always stirred the red devil of anger within me. His entire being commanded authority, left no room for question or doubt. He knew everything—and I did mean absolutely everything—but his information came at a steep price, and sometimes that price was not a reasonable one. Our history afforded me the courage to pull on our connection, to test my boundaries when I knew I was well overstepping them. He hadn't yet come to collect on my debt, which I was sure would be paid with my life. I had a theory that, in the meantime, he'd been watching me like a bug caught under a glass jar. Waiting, observing. Learning.

"Why is this happening?"

"I told you that it would. You seemed to think you had the power to stop it."

"Is it your doing? To punish us?"

A belly laugh rose against my ear, loud enough that I had to jerk the receiver away and squint against the echo in my head that threatened hearing loss if I wasn't careful. I pictured him sitting in his home as we spoke, the greasy smile splitting a face so otherwise devoid of emotion that I wasn't entirely convinced he knew how emotions worked to begin with.

How *he* had ever...

I shook my head to clear the thought before it finished forming.

"Tell me this, then. Man to man." Saliva flooded my mouth, nearly strangling the words. The ironic laugh that tried to spring forward at the implication that the person at the other end of the phone was in any way a *man* died in my throat. "Is this it?"

A long pause. Silence stretched until I was suitably uncomfortable, all but wriggling in my seat. It occurred to me then, as it had nearly every time I communicated with this vile being, that I still wasn't afraid of him. I certainly should have been. Anyone in their right mind would be. Yet, somewhere deep inside, a boatload of undeserved respect lay buried, resurfacing at the most inconvenient of times; times such as those where a phone call that I never should have made begged answers that I denied knowing all along.

"Yes, I believe it is." His chuckle slithered down my spine, coating me the same way it coated his words as he spoke them. I suddenly felt filthy. My breath hissed out between my teeth and my lungs seized, refusing to draw in any more oxygen. "Luke, if you ever contact me again, I *will* settle up on your debt. This was your last free meal at my table."

He didn't hear me swallow so hard that I coughed, because the line was already dead.

I wasn't sure whether to laugh or cry; a problem that often presented itself after interactions with him.

I deposited the phone back into my pocket, thinking while pacing long trails through the living room, into the dining room and kitchen, and back. I'd designed my home, of course—what else was an architect to do—and the immense amount of gorgeous bare wood in accompaniment with the cathedral ceiling was intended to remind me of the towering trees in the forest. It was supposed to have been calming. The mind-numbing circuit that my feet insisted on traveling through my main living floor was anything but calming. Calloused fingers sifted through the dark chestnut of my hair, artfully arranged earlier in the day, though hard to picture since it'd been tousled so violently by bad habits.

Photos mocked me from their homes on the walls as I passed. Dozens of photos of Marie, or of Marie and I, teased me with their haunting memories. Smiling. Happy. She'd be furious if she knew I still kept them displayed, but they reminded me of what I had to lose—they reminded me that the pain was worth it. I almost smiled at the thought that she'd turn an absolute shade of beet-red if she knew I still kept a drawer of her clothes laundered in my dresser on the off chance she'd find her way back to me.

A good boy scout was always prepared.

But it didn't matter that I had spare clothes and photos of her, because people were dying and I was probably the only person in the world that knew the real reason behind it all and had any inclination to try and stop it.

The situation weighed on me, pressing any hope of another smile into a grimace as my options swirled around in my head.

Instead of continuing the aimless path through the house, I veered off of the living room and entered the master bedroom. There was one thing that absolutely had to be done before Marie could be allowed to learn the truth.

A small box sitting innocently on my dresser, covered in dust, caught my eye. I hadn't gathered the strength to move it since I'd placed it there, though the surface it sat on was spotless. A memory of my parents surfaced, the three of us sitting together at the tiny dining table of their home, which was not so far from my own that I visited often.

Between us sat a small box, open, so that the two of them could glimpse the diamond ring nestled inside. My mother's usually hard gaze had softened, a hand raised into the air halfway to covering her mouth before she'd stopped it. My father's eyes had filled with tears.

"When?" Mother asked finally. The silence had swallowed us whole several minutes before when I'd placed the ring on the table to announce my intent.

I'd shrugged, a dopey smile plastered on my face. A man drunk in love. "Tonight, I think."

Without warning, my father launched himself out of the wooden chair, which protested the movement with a series of creaks, and wrapped me in a hug that nearly squeezed out my insides. He'd probably done it so that I couldn't see the tears fall, but he hadn't been able to hide the tremble of his body against mine.

I knew what they were thinking; that they never thought I'd find someone. That, after all the years I spent hating myself, I'd not been capable of love.

My mother's smile shone so suddenly, so brightly, that I wasn't surprised when she also stood and moved forward to plant a kiss on my cheek. I couldn't remember the last time I'd seen either of them so happy.

The memory faded and was replaced by another, several months after the first had taken place.

"You cannot go through with this," my mother hissed at me. She was furious, her whole body rigid with controlled rage. "I don't care how much you love her."

Thankfully, my father had chosen to stay inside, hiding far from the anger that sizzled between my mother and I on the back lawn of their home. Through the sliding glass door, I glimpsed the dining table we'd crowded around when I first announced my intent to propose. That night had been one of love and happiness. Where had that gone so quickly?

"Are you saying that you're not going to support my marriage?"

"Not to her, I won't. Not now that I know." She raised her chin into the air, reminding me that she was in charge. No matter how old you grew, mothers always wanted the last say in your life. "If you do this, she's going to ruin you. I'm not going to sit back and watch that happen." The words were all but dripping with contempt.

"She's never going to find out. I'll make sure of that." I urged my voice to carry every bit of the confidence I felt. I shoved it at her in a desperate attempt to make her understand. This was love; the kind that you only ever found once in your life. "I want a life with her. I need it."

Her response came quickly, like the knife you didn't feel until it was nestled in your back. "Yes, but at what cost?"

I sighed, pulling myself from the memories. They clung, much like the gooey insides of a good brownie, tempting me to give in. A headache began to thump angrily against my temples.

The decision was made.

Hastily, I stuffed a duffel bag from the closet full of clothes and haphazardly slung it over a shoulder. Anything necessary for a quick getaway was tossed inside the closest open pocket. My mother had been right, and yet I hadn't regretted the decision to propose to Marie, nor any of the decisions that I'd made afterward to keep her close to me.

On the way to my vehicle, I dialed one last number on my cell phone, informing the person on the other end that I'd be arriving shortly and would be planning a brief stay while we sorted out the details of how I'd likely be dooming the world, or possibly just myself, to save the woman I loved. It didn't matter that I hadn't greeted him hello; we weren't on greeting terms. I needed his help and he'd give it to me only because it would cause me an immeasurable amount of pain in return.

A curse bubbled to my lips as I settled into the driver's seat, but I didn't let it loose; an old habit of mine, biting back the inappropriate words.

There was one thing I'd forgotten to do before I could leave.

I dashed back inside after depositing the duffle into the trunk of my SUV. At the far back of the house, through the kitchen, sat a cage that housed three baby rabbits, not yet old enough to be let loose into the wild. Their button eyes watched me as I approached, still too young to understand danger. I'd saved them—or tried to—once I'd discovered them in my yard, hiding among the bodies of what must have been their mother and siblings. I assumed the scene had been the aftermath of an interrupted animal attack. I suspected a neighborhood cat or stray fox, but it didn't really matter who the culprit was. What mattered was saving the helpless creatures. Like any man with something to prove, I'd taken them into my home and worked desperately to save their lives.

Did I know anything at all about rabbits? No.

Did that cause me to hesitate at all in bringing them into my home? Absolutely not.

Marie had scolded me so many times in the past for similar actions.

"Focus that energy inward instead. You can't save everyone, and eventually you're going to do more harm than good by trying."

She'd been talking about us, about our relationship at the time. I'd argued with her, as I'd always done, and she'd let it go if only for that moment.

Looking into the innocent eyes of the rabbits, I knew she had been more right than she'd wanted to be. She'd have been giving that arrogant smirk of hers if she'd known what I was about to do. Lifting the cage from the table, I slid open the back door, dropped the metal housing just outside it, and opened the tiny door that protected the frail, fluffy bodies from the outside world. I simply couldn't risk anyone coming into my home to care for them, nor could I guess how long I'd have to be away. Their lives weren't worth giving up my secrets.

The odds of them being able to fend for themselves were greater than the odds that I'd survive and return to care for them before they starved to death. Their only chance for survival was on their own.

I didn't wait to see if they escaped. I simply closed the sliding door, pulled the blinds, and returned to my vehicle. I wanted to feel guilty or angry, but all that greeted me when I contemplated the status of things was fear. I'd spent the last decade lulling myself into a false sense of comfort, thinking that the big bad demon of my past would never return. How naive I'd been.

Without another wasted moment—there were no longer moments left to be wasted—I revved the engine, backed out of my driveway in a squeal of tires that was sure to be heard by the entirety of my neighborhood, and flew toward my destination like a bat out of hell.

Chapter 7 - Marie

I found myself outside of the gate just as the sun rose overhead to trap me like a spotlight catching a thief in action. I certainly felt as though I was doing something wrong. Birds chirped behind me somewhere in a line of large maple trees. Impossibly warm, even the clouds had been chased away by the blistering heat all around. The ride over had been suffocating, the bus filled with stale air that all but singed my lungs as I inhaled. Or maybe I was just feeling bitter.

Shifting from foot to foot, the soles of my sneakers began to feel sticky against the surface of the pavement. Under the shadow of a high ponytail, the hair at the back of my neck began to dampen. With no desire to remain outside and contemplate my own motives, I slipped through the door of the guard house and moaned into the welcomed slap of air conditioning that greeted me. A head whipped up to glare at me from the back of the small room. I shrugged at the man, who instantly returned his gaze to the book in his hands. Apparently, he was busy.

It was all I could do to bite my tongue against the sarcastic comment that fought valiantly to escape. See, I *was* working on my impulsiveness.

Flapping my shirt over myself with pinched fingers to circulate the cool air against my skin, I made my way further into the room and studiously ignored the guard directly in front of me who looked as though it would more than make his day to kick me out. Considering the ruckus I'd caused before, I couldn't say I'd blame him.

Instead, I smiled my most disarming smile—which I had to admit was a bit rusty—and lifted the logbook to sign it. I wasn't the praying type, but I said a few words for luck that no one recognized me and immediately removed me from the premises.

A frown creased well into the man's face when I replaced the book and he read the name printed next to mine in very sloppy print.

"*Who* are you here to see?" The disbelief dripped from him, permeating the room so thickly that the man at the far desk put down his book and moved closer to view the interaction. My finger twitched with the urge to point at the name that I knew he'd already seen, and ask him if he could read. Instead, I cleared my throat, thankful at least that they didn't seem to recognize me from a previous visit, and stood a bit straighter.

"Jesse."

The men looked at one another, then back to me.

"Jesse…?"

It was growing more difficult by the moment to keep hold of my patience. They knew exactly who I was referring to—both of them. I wasn't sure what game they were playing, but I wasn't interested in taking part.

"Jesse Rowe. The inmate?" I waved my arms a bit in frustration, my tone biting. "Death row? That one. Physical visit, please."

The second man leaned back a bit, sized me up. The sunglasses hanging from his shirt pocket reflected my own annoyance back at me. An ugly brown name badge on his shirt read 'Atley', curled around the edges from too many washes.

"You'll have to turn over your purse for security check and undergo a pat down. I'll hold your cell phone here." The way the muscles in his cheeks jerked at the end of his words made me wonder if he was hoping that would scare me away. I lifted both arms, showing that I wasn't carrying a purse, and also that they were welcome to approach for the pat down. 'Welcome' was a relative word, but desperate times and all.

"I'm familiar with the process."

Atley considered me for a moment, then nodded. Apparently, he'd decided I was worth being taken seriously. When we were finished and he was satisfied that I wasn't carrying a weapon or tool for escape on my person, he led me through the facility to the visitation room, though I didn't need him to.

The route was ingrained in me, nearly a ritual of summoning peace from somewhere within. By the time we reached the smattering of tables at the far corner of the visitation room, I was cooled, calm, and as clear-headed as I could remember being in many weeks. Though I hadn't visited recently—partially due to embarrassment—I'd spent a decent amount of time there over the years.

It took only a few additional minutes for Jesse to be brought out to me. His hair was longer than I ever remembered it being. It was stringy and unwashed, falling in a curtain to cover most of his face, but I'd know him anywhere. Jesse had only been in my life for a few short years, but he was one of the few people I'd give my life for. And he was innocent.

Jesse's piercing green eyes met mine, widening in surprise.

Green? Yet when he looked away and back again, they were as muddy as they'd always been.

I pressed my lips together in vain hope that it would keep me from losing what was left of my mind. Don't let the crazy show, Marie.

"Hi," I said, reaching for his hand. He stopped just short of my reach. "Why?"

I sighed and took my seat at the table, motioning for him to do the same. This was an old dance for Jesse and I, but one that Atley must not have seen before. He watched us with barely hidden interest and what I would only assume to be confusion. I flicked him the finger as I turned away from his intensity, fully aware that the cameras would catch the gesture.

"I just needed to see you."

Jesse's expression was unreadable, the planes of his face the only thing that had softened in the time since his incarceration. "*Sarah*, the more often you come here, the more likely someone is to find out."

It was a well-tread conversation. I held back the groan of annoyance that bubbled up. Why did everyone insist on rehashing fights we'd had a million times?

Change the topic, Marie. Stay on track.

"Have you been able to keep up with the news?"

He took the seat beside me and leaned back against it, the blonde in his hair picking up the fluorescent lighting above to highlight the greyish hue of filth that clung to it. A sigh escaped him. "Is that really worth the risk? Coming here to ask me about the news?"

Worth it?

Punching him right in the jaw would have been.

I curled a fist on the table, which he covered with one of his hands. Atley shifted behind me, clearly uncomfortable with the contact despite it still being Jesse's right. The urge to turn and spit California law at him burned on my tongue. Death row or not, Jesse had every right to see me and I had every right to hold his hand. If Atley kept on grating my nerves, I might just try for a big 'ole kiss at the end. Jesse wouldn't mind. In fact, he'd probably know exactly why I did it.

I put my other hand on top of Jesse's, trapping it.

"Truly, I came to try to change your mind again. I could really use you out there. It's getting..." I dropped my voice to a whisper as I changed my mind about the conversation topic. No need to get him worked up about life outside. "Your execution date is coming up, and you know I'm not going to let it happen." A tense moment stretched between us. That time it was *me* resurrecting an old conversation from the grave. I sighed and tried again. "I know you don't deserve to be here. Not on death row, and not in jail. I don't care how you feel about it; what you did was—"

His mouth curved, but I couldn't tell in which direction. "I do deserve to be here. I killed them."

"I'm not disputing that." I tapped his hand once with my fingers, hard. "But I'm not going to let you die for it. They made the wrong call. If you hadn't stopped them, they'd have stormed into the building and set off that bomb... and all of those people would have died, myself included. You did the *right* thing," I pleaded at him with my eyes— something I rarely did for anyone. "I still don't understand exactly how you did it, and I'm not going to press you for details, but one day you will need to explain it to me."

"They were *cops*." The sigh that escaped him seemed to carry his entire soul. At the end of it, he looked like nothing more than a pile of tired bones, heaped into a chair like a Halloween decoration used to frighten anyone who dared look closely enough. I waited for him to speak, but he didn't. We sat in silence until Atley stepped forward and advised that our visit was over. I didn't truly believe that we'd had the entirety of our visitation time, but I wasn't in the mood to cause yet another scene over being cut short.

I squeezed Jesse's hand, still between mine, and hissed into his ear as I bent forward to stand. "I'm getting you out of here, whether you like it or not. I suggest you get on board."

He stood as well, though he didn't look at me as he retracted his limb from my possessively curled ones. He didn't bother to hide his parting remark as he leaned in to place a kiss on my forehead. "Let me die in peace, love. Please don't come back here again. It's better for both of us."

Fat chance of that.

When I retrieved my cell phone from the guard house, having sidestepped the curious glances that were thrown my way the entire walk back, I made a fast retreat from the jail to the bus stop.

Aside from being physically worse for wear, he was the same Jesse that I'd known before the incident. The same, innocent Jesse, who refused to forgive himself and only looked out for others. But in one aspect, he was right; if anyone knew that he and I were close, or that I was visiting him more regularly than he'd like me to, there would be scrutiny of my own life and the issues of my amnesia would be hard to hide.

I hadn't wanted answers since the day that Leena and I spent hours Googling symptoms and declared ourselves doctors, deciding that it was probably a PTSD reaction and was best left unprodded. I certainly didn't need anyone digging into my past to surface what I'd obviously locked away for a reason.

I took a seat on the bus bench and waited.

My cell phone jumped in my pocket, a bright glow pressing through the fabric of my pants. Green outline meant it was a text message. Groaning internally, already certain enough that it was Leena to bet my next paycheck on it, I shoved a hand into my pocket and withdrew the phone nestled there. Encased in a vibrant violet case, which advertised itself to be able to withstand drops from eight feet high—though I'd never dared take the chance just for the sake of finding out—it was my lifeline. The case had been a gift many years ago, but I couldn't quite remember who'd bought it for me. At any rate, they'd known me well because the shade was as spot-on as you could get to my favorite color.

The corners of my mouth dropped instantly as I skimmed the screen.

Luke.

"We need to talk," it said. "Soon." Nothing more, though I'd wished it said a whole lot less. Less, as in *nothing*.

I cleared the message but didn't bother to respond. The thudding in my chest could be heard even over the roaring of blood rushing in my ears. Time slowed to a crawl, then raced forward again while the blood shifted from my ears to my face.

How dare he contact me.

We most certainly had nothing at all to talk about.

Tiny pink shoes crossed my vision, dragging toes against the dirt in an alternating rhythm. A book clutched under each arm, she crouched into my eyesight and tipped her head as far to the side as possible for such a flexible little body. Big green eyes locked onto mine, startling me with their ferocity. As she spoke, the drawl of still-forming pronunciation made her already painfully high pitch seem even loftier somehow.

"You okay?"

I pushed myself upright, realizing that I'd been holding my head in my hands, phone safely tucked back into my pants pocket. My fingers untangled themselves from the hair at the sides of my head.

The girl's head tilted to the opposite side, painfully far, and she repeated herself.

"You okay?"

She inched forward in a crouch much like a penguin waddle, a shifting of bulk rather than precise movement. Her wide eyes blinked, waiting for acknowledgment.

"Yes, I'm okay."

Fully lifting my head, straightening my back, my gaze caught the girl's mother, standing just a few steps away with a look on her face that said I may have fooled her daughter, but I certainly wasn't fooling her. My chin tipped up of its own accord.

Chubby pink fingers swam into view. I recoiled instantly, shuddering back a few inches, but the quick hands—likely experts at picking toys off of store shelves and tossing them into shopping carts unnoticed—clasped each side of my face firmly. With a gentle pull that was mostly conscious leaning on my part, the girl leveled our faces and searched mine as if she was cataloging my very soul. After a moment, she released me, opting instead to briefly pet the left side of my head and then lean in for one of those kid hugs that's nothing more than a lightning-fast cheek press into whatever body part was closest at the time.

"Shh, it's okay," she said, petting me one last time before prancing back to her mother's outstretched hand.

The woman's kind face held apology. I shook my head at her and wondered what they were doing outside the jail. Who inside it belonged to the child with the large eyes that approached strangers in distress?

But then they were gone, as fast as they'd arrived. I watched their taillights fade over the hill in the road, wondering whether I'd hallucinated the entire exchange.

Deciding it was entirely too hot to wait outside for the bus, and wanting to run from the oddity of what had just happened, I scuttled my way across the rows of bushes that lined the parking lot and walked the path around a small man-made pond. Sunlight reflected from the surface of the water to momentarily blind me several times. Combined with the thick air, the sweaty clothes that clung to my body, and the stifling temperatures, it was a wonder I survived the long walk to the opposite end of the water.

Ducking under a storefront awning, and covertly scoping out the expanse of concrete and glass before me, I selected my target. The strip mall housed two clothing stores, a café, a smoothie shop, a tiny pawn shop, and a sunglass store. Without needing much convincing, my feet immediately began the fast trek to the smoothie shop, imagining the sweet relief of cold drinks and air-conditioned seating. Halfway across the walkway, however, a group of rambunctious preteens unloaded from a minivan in a rush and herded themselves toward the wall of windows.

There were five, six, eight—jesus, were they multiplying in there?—ten of them, all talking loudly to one another as they gathered on the sidewalk. One squealed, shaking fists in the air out of what I could only assume was excitement. She sprinted for the smoothie shop, the remaining girls following like a pack of ducklings after the mother. They crammed themselves into the open door, spreading like a disease through the seating inside, giggles and "oh my god"s punctuated by the scraping of chairs against hard floor.

I veered left just before I reached my destination, wanting nothing more than to avoid the guaranteed headache that awaited me in the land of fruit and barely-contained estrogen. The café that I chose instead was quiet—empty, in fact—with a familiar buzz that greeted me as I stepped into the lukewarm air perfumed with coffee. Four years ago, that very building had been my home away from home. The staff had since changed over, so it wasn't quite as uncomfortable being inside as it had been when I'd recognized the faces of the workers, but I still tended to avoid it whenever I could.

Truthfully, I'd have braved it over the gossip squad next door any day. Plus, the café had excellent seating—the kind meant for curling up in with hot coffee and a good book.

Approaching to order, I startled the cashier who'd been leaning against the counter with his back to me, clearly expecting a day filled with emptiness. I remembered those days. He gave me a sheepish smile, guilt crinkling the corners of his eyes as he did. I ordered an iced coffee, paid, and moved to the pickup window. Apparently anticipating exactly zero customers, there didn't seem to be another staff member currently scheduled. The man shifted with me, positioning himself behind the coffee bar to prepare my drink. I tried not to grimace at the awkwardness of it all.

After a few moments, he slid forward to the window and quietly announced that the shop was out of the toffee syrup for my drink. Disappointment drooped my shoulders. It was shaping up to be a crummy day. He offered several substitutions, none of which came anywhere near sounding appealing when compared to what I'd ordered. With a deep sigh, clearly frustrated that I'd interrupted his day of gazing lovingly at a drink-splattered back wall, he proposed refunding my order.

Annoyed, I pressed on. Another cycle through the options and a thought crossed my mind.

"Did you check the top shelf above the computer in the back?"

Confusion and slight offense rippled across his face. Gone was the innocent, helpful facade he'd first presented.

"I used to work here. We always kept an extra container up there during the months that it was really popular."

We both looked around the empty shop, neither of us explicitly pointing out that *nothing* was very popular right about then. After a long look, the worker finally retreated to the back to check. He emerged a few moments later with the bottle of syrup in hand, no less annoyed than before.

Maybe it wouldn't be such a bad day after all.

When my drink was made, and I'd just curled into the comfiest of the chairs, the bell chimed to announce a new customer. I recognized the old woman from my apartment building, but couldn't guess her name correctly even with a gun to my head. Though I couldn't imagine she'd have traveled too far from home just for a FastGrind fix, I didn't want to consider the other option that offered itself up in my mind—that she'd also been visiting the jail.

Why else would she have made such a long trek? She smiled at me and I nodded so that I could turn it into a surreptitious sip from the straw in my cup.

She didn't get the hint. Approximately thirty seconds later, with a steaming cup of black coffee in hand—seriously, how did old people move so fast?—she lowered herself into the seat beside me. The way the chairs angled toward one another suggested expected company and close relationships, neither of which I shared with the woman whose name I couldn't recall. Yet, she shot me an expectant look once she was settled.

"How are you, dear?"

I tried not to cringe at the endearment. "I'm alright. You?"

Her response was a tight smile and a polite sip of coffee that I was sure had burned her tongue. Apparently, she didn't intend to share any more pleasantries. "I've been wondering where that young man of yours went off to. He used to help me up and down the stairs when the elevator was acting up."

My teeth gnashed against one another. Perhaps I had been lucky to have survived almost an entire year so far without these conversations. What did it say about me that they noticed his absence more than the absolute heartbreak I'd experienced after the breakup? The thought made my drink taste sour as it hit my stomach.

"We split. I wouldn't expect to see him around anymore."

"Oh, dear," she said, clearly more sorry for herself than for me. "With everything happening these days, I felt a lot safer with him around. He was a pretty big fella, you know? Bet he scared off any trouble before it even thought about looking his way."

I made an appropriate 'mm' noise and buried my face in my drink. Though she was nice enough about it, she was nosy, and my patience was thin. I did have a life outside of Luke, even if no one else noticed it.

She shifted to look out the window. When she spoke again, it was less to me than it was aloud. "I've lived in that apartment for forty years. I thought about moving out when Merv died a few years back, but it just seemed too much trouble." An awkward pause had me scrambling to find a response that wasn't outright rude. She continued without one. "I don't feel very safe anymore, by myself and without any big, strong men around. I've been thinking that I might need to move out and go live with my granddaughter in Colorado."

The easy response was to point out that women could do everything that men could do, and in some cases *more*, but the old bat was contemplating moving and if it got me out of this conversation, I didn't plan to stop her. If it meant never having the conversation again, even better.

She rattled on for a while about the community in Colorado where her daughter lived—how it was a group-living situation that would be hard for her to adjust to, but that she wanted to try. It's possible that I inadvertently encouraged her move; and truly, it was inadvertent. For a large section of the conversation, I found my thoughts drifting to matters plaguing my own mind instead. Appropriate listening noises were given at acceptable times, but my mind was not present with the old woman who was soon-to-be *not* from my apartment.

It was on whether or not moving away was also in the cards for me.

Chapter 8 - Marie

The bus ride to work was more packed than I'd ever seen it. Groups of people hunched together in the seats, whispering fervently to one another. They exited in clumps, replaced nearly instantly with another secretive group who also huddled together. The air was buzzing with hushed conversation. None of it interested me. In fact, it annoyed me more than anything. With the vehicle at close to capacity, my ride had resulted in being jostled several times, elongated travel times due to actually pausing at every stop for once, and having my toes stepped on by an elderly man whose companion was more concerned with keeping panicked sight of everyone else around them.

I'd rolled my eyes at most of it, but had to swallow down some very nasty words on the last one. On top of it all, Sue was driving the bus. She was a nice elderly woman who always gave polite greetings and casual banter, but she drove cautiously, which was most certainly unhelpful when I wanted nothing more than to zip to my destination at light speed and escape any further contact with humanity.

When my stop finally arrived, I rushed ahead and 'accidentally' elbowed the woman trying to exit before me. No way was I getting trapped in a line of bodies waiting for the amateur bus riders to slowly descend the stairs and consider the gap between the platform and the road before making a leap that I likely would have pushed them over anyway. Besides, Sue might try to start a conversation I'd have to entertain for at least a polite minute and I was far from in the mood for that. Perturbed, I stalked the entire way to The Capital, already in a foul mood and wondering how much worse my shift would make it. The mall was, once again, mostly deserted, making me wonder where all the people on the bus had been rushing to.

Leena greeted me with wide eyes as I pushed through the double doors. Opening my mouth to explain the frustration evident on my face, which I knew would sound petty no matter how it was phrased, only a grunt of frustration tumbled out from between my lips. Funny how exposure to the general public always made me grouchy. I was pretty sure I was allergic to people.

"Marie, go home."

It was my turn to give wide eyes.

"I'm serious. Go home and stay there."

I looked suspiciously around the sales floor, searching for any shred of evidence as to why my best friend had been acting so strangely the past few days. No one gathered around the clothing racks as I'd expected, grouped and full of whispers. Truthfully, this was the emptiest the store had been in a good while. Leena could surely handle any customers on her own, but the question was why she'd want to.

"You want to explain why?"

It wasn't my birthday or work anniversary, so hiding a surprise party or gift was out of the question. There wasn't much else coming to mind that would justify Leena breaking the tradition of working together and accompanying me to the bus on the way home. In fact, there wasn't a single other time I could remember where we hadn't joyously and completely shared our work rituals on shifts together. Well, if you didn't count the days I woke up tired of it all and immediately called out of work, and the strange way she'd sent me home alone the other day.

She approached, grabbed my hand, and dragged me behind the counter, pink locks bouncing harshly enough that one of them came loose from a pin at her skull and hung limply at the back of her head. The elastic and barrettes holding it up were clearly visible, shedding light on the mystery of Leena's complex hairstyles but shrouding her behavior and carelessness in even more mystery. She'd be so embarrassed if she knew, I mused. Her gorgeous trusses were one of the few things she held sacred. My suspicion of the situation rocketed up to alarm.

"You need to start watching the news. People are *dying*, Marie."

Christ. This again. I hadn't turned on the news since I'd stumbled upon the body with Carmen days ago. I didn't want to know, but clearly, she did.

Leena, ever the doomsayer.

"We've been through this before," I hissed, yanking my hand—which she'd continued to hold, and quite firmly, at that—from her grasp. "It's not that big of a deal."

"This isn't normal. Hundreds of bodies were found in the past two days." She rubbed small circles over her temples with her fingertips. "Hundreds."

That did give me pause. Surely that was an exaggeration. There had only been a hundred bodies found up to then, in total. What would that mean if *hundreds* had actually died in the past handful of days? Was whatever it was getting worse somehow?

"Did they say what the cause was? Some sort of poison or something? That's a lot of bodies to stumble across. It almost reeks of cult…"

She shook her head, slowly. "There's no explanation. But, Marie," she dropped her voice to a whisper as she said my name. Her eyes darted around and then back me. "Everyone's talking about it. Dozens of those bodies were found near White City. You can't say that it isn't going to reach us anymore. It's already here."

I stilled, thinking. That *was* a bit too close to home. No known cause, coupled with the sheer number of bodies, left plenty of room for unsavory theories. Leaning back, away from her, I pursed my lips and crossed my arms against my chest.

"Why do I have to go home but you get to stay here? Aren't you in just as much danger?"

Leena straightened her own spine, pursed her own lips in response. "Because I said so."

Had she been any less gentle than a sleeping kitten, she'd have made a convincing argument. As it was, her tiny frame and the mounds of clothing draped across it seemed to shrink back against my determination. No one had ever accused me of being easygoing.

Sensing the tension building between us, a couple passing by outside halted their conversation and turned curious faces in our direction. One of them had inched forward, blocking the view of the other so they could get a better angle on whatever it was we were doing.

What *were* we doing?

"Listen, I can take care of myself. You don't need to worry about me."

"I care about you. Of course I need to worry. Plus, you don't seem to take anything seriously and you really ought to. This is life and death."

Still annoyed from the journey into work, anger began to seep through the wall I'd tried to erect deep inside me.

"I don't need you to mother me," I spat, suddenly seething. All of the frustration washed over me at once—her insistence that I forgive Luke, her refusal to support my decisions, and the recent nagging feeling that she, too, had been keeping secrets from me. Knowing that it was what took Luke from me—someone I very deeply loved—made it all the more unacceptable that she was doing it as well. It wasn't going to fly anymore.

"Someone has to," she bit back. Gone was the meek shell of Leena that I'd known.

I recoiled, taking the blow as she'd meant to land it—hard. Being my best friend, which also made her my confidant, Leena knew things that had the power to shred me from the inside out. She knew them because I'd trusted her to never use them against me. My trust, it seemed, had been misplaced. First Luke, then Leena; it seemed as though I was learning the hard way that you never really knew someone, no matter how long they'd been in your life and how close you thought you'd become.

Most of my childhood was what could be considered normal. I grew up with everything that I needed, went to decent schools, and worked for what I wanted—because that was how the world worked—and when I turned eighteen, I started a life on my own. What could be considered *abnormal* is that I had absolutely no recollection of my parents; not what they looked like or sounded like, nor any true memories including them. Names or locations were always fuzzy—schools, towns, people. Nothing concrete ever swam to the surface for me, even after all the years had passed. At best, any hint of parental presence in my mind left only blurred shapes as sad replacements.

Without any idea of where to look, or any true inclination to do so, I accepted it and resolved not to unlock what my mind had worked so hard to protect me from. However, the loss was hard to take sometimes. Leena knew that, guarded the information, and commiserated with me even though she couldn't relate; or, at least I thought she had.

"Fine. I'm going, but you don't have to be such a bitch about it."

Bristling, she sucked in a breath. I turned on my heel and stomped back toward the exit. In a few days, it would blow over and things would settle into a semblance of normality. Leena would be immensely apologetic, as she always was when her tendency as a worrywart was proven unfounded. Typically I'd forgive her, and we'd laugh and move on.

But things were different. Leena had crossed a line that I wasn't sure could be redrawn. It was no wonder she wanted me to forgive Luke for his transgressions. She was just as untrustworthy as he had proven to be. Birds of a feather.

"And, Marie," she called at my back, her voice rising. The sound I'd only ever recognized as being slow, patient, and soothing was bitterly tinged with rage and—very likely—also *fear*, as it echoed against the walls. It was the only time I'd ever heard Leena shout.

"You're fired!"

I sulked all the way back home, not even capable of finding scathing remarks to spit when the still-full bus forced me into the only open seat next to a man talking animatedly on his cell phone. Dodging flailing limbs the entirety of the ride, I contemplated whether anyone would notice if just one more thin, pink-haired body was found. The thought bulldozed its way through my skull, melting my active anger down into a sharp headache that promised a rousing game of pain-induced insomnia for the night.

A hand flew at my face, missing my cheek by inches and retreating instantly to rest in the lap of the oblivious man that it belonged to as he carried on his conversation.

Perhaps two bodies.

Chapter 9 - Luke

The entire house—if you could call the run-down, converted shed a house—was coated in brick-red dust. Had it been a more consistent pattern, or a slightly more even coating, it could have passed for being intentional, even trendy. But the dusty film was not intentional, and was not even expected when it blew into the country from far across the sea. The air was thick with it, tinting the world something a bit more depressing than what could be considered rose-colored. Anomalies were becoming more comfortable rearing their heads once the floodgate had been blown wide open in the chaos of the world.

A long-winded creak greeted me as the door swung inward, beckoning me inside the dark interior of the shack. Unsurprisingly, it lacked electricity, climate control, and plumbing. I could make out a small cot in one corner, a thin blanket and lumpy pillow included, as well as a large abstract painting hanging on the wall opposite the entrance. At first, I thought the frame was spotted in blood, the dark patches all but glowing ominously in the fading natural light that peeked over my shoulder from the open door. Dust invaded my nostrils, refusing to allow in any scents. Using the flashlight on my phone to better inspect, a sigh of relief crept out at the realization that the abstract was, indeed, created in reds, purples, and blues. Harmless as it may have been, the longer I stared, the more intimidating it became.

Was this the yellow wallpaper of their kind?

A shudder ripped through me. The duffel slid from my shoulder and landed with a thunk on the floor, kicking up a dust cloud to inform me—as though I hadn't already known—that the entirety of the interior was *also* sporting a nice coat of filth. I rolled my eyes. I hadn't truly expected a warm welcome, given our history, but leaving me in the equivalent of a human doghouse was beyond insulting.

A floorboard groaned behind me, alarming at another presence besides my own. The man smiled at me as I whirled on him, and the smile was everything but pleasant.

"You should know better than to sneak up on me like that. I could have killed you, and then where would we be?"

He tipped his head to the side, as though contemplating my question for the sake of politeness and not because he actually needed to consider it. "Bold of you to assume you'd win a fight between us."

He chuckled, but I didn't see any humor in it. My entire being vibrated with restrained energy. It didn't matter that I'd called him, that I'd asked for his help; he was the enemy and my instinct was to eliminate him on sight. Adrenaline thrummed through my skull, ricocheting horrible thoughts that took more effort than I'd dare admit to keep from turning to action. The man before me smiled, that time very much considering my reaction, and finding himself very much amused by it.

"You really do think you'd win. Shall we find out?"

"That's not what I'm here for."

A hand waved nonchalantly through the air between us, a ring glittering on his finger in the failing sunlight. Or was that just my imagination?

His large step forward closed the distance between us, our chests nearly brushing. I dared not give any ground, holding my spine straight against the implication that backing down meant admitting inferiority. I would do no such thing. I had anticipated a great deal of ribbing, the entirety of our presence in each other's lives drawing up all kinds of hostility, but I hadn't prepared for the amount of dominance games. It was a dangerous dance he was leading, and yet I had asked for his hand when the song had begun to play.

Was it a mistake?

No. No matter what the cost, it was not a mistake.

I raised my hands slowly, settling them on the shoulders of the man mere inches from me. There was no thrill of satisfaction at the fact that he rested several inches shorter than I did. He didn't shrink back under my touch, not even when I gave a gentle squeeze. I allowed the desperation I'd been drowning in to fill my eyes, hardening them into glassy orbs. The words I didn't say hung in the air, not needing to be spoken aloud to convey.

An eerie silence settled heavily, like a wet blanket, emotions running through his own eyes, though muted behind anger and whatever thoughts he didn't wish me to see. It had been many, many years since I dared rest my gaze on him—and for good reason, as neither of us was quite capable of reigning in our violent outbursts around the other—and his face looked no older than it had back then. I tried to imagine my own face, the changes he'd see in the slight darkening under my eyes, the creases lining the edges of my mouth when I spoke. In fact, thinking of the subtle differences he'd be able to find in my own features made me all the more unnerved that there were none at all in his.

It wasn't that I'd anticipated him looking older or anything—okay, perhaps I did a bit—because I knew exactly what he was and what came with the territory. I was maybe a bit jealous that his face still resembled so closely the memories I held of him from a time when he was happy and carefree; a time before the world had turned him ugly and evil.

What a thought. He had become what I used to be, and it was my fault, just as it would be my fault if anything happened to Marie. Frankly, I deserved to have to make a sacrifice of epic proportions. It was karma that put me exactly in that position.

Fast as lightning, though truthfully still slowly enough that I could have deflected or dodged it if I wanted to, his hand flew out and connected with my cheek. I stepped back, cradling the wound that realistically stung my pride more than it had my body.

He straightened, flashed an arrogant smirk, and announced: "Even though you let that happen, I'll take it. Any excuse to pummel you is a good one."

It was a tentative truce, and one I'd greedily accept for the time being.

Outside the ramshackle shed, someone crunched through the dead grass and twigs that littered the ground, kicking up dust with the movement that swirled into the open doorway. A face slipped itself into the threshold, beaming at the two of us as though she'd laid eyes on her two favorite people in the whole world. The deep scarlet of her irises was laughably distracting compared to the full set of her lips or the brightness of her teeth, and they stole the whole of my attention. Fear spiked through me, only briefly. Anger roared forward in its place.

"I'm going to need help with this," the man said, motioning to the woman. "So I've asked Genevieve to lend some assistance."

"I know who you are," I snapped, gaze still locked on the unwelcome addition to the party. Something had gone very wrong. Not only had I not agreed to anyone else knowing about the situation, but *that* particular woman was notoriously bad for business where secrets were involved. Sure, she commanded the exact concoction of power and connections that were needed for my plan to end in success, but there was a reason I hadn't made the introduction myself and asked her for help instead of lowering myself to begging for it from *him*.

Genevieve stepped into the room, long legs gliding her across the uneven floor as if she'd instead set foot in the grandest of ballrooms, ready to sway and twirl herself to her goal. Bright as embers and every bit as striking, her hair cascaded nearly to her waist, unruffled by the accumulating dust. She extended a hand toward me.

"I don't believe we've met, so please allow me to formally introduce myself. I'm Genevieve. You must be Luke."

My name was a question on her tongue—a question of whether she could convince me to trust her; a question of whether she was going to be able to weasel out whatever it was she wanted from us. She knew exactly who I was. I did not reach for her hand, nor did I provide a response.

"Listen," the man barked between us, directing his impatience at me. "I don't have the manpower to do what you're asking. Not for any true length of time, and we don't know how long it will take for this all to blow over. I don't have the status that she does in her community. So, you can either accept Genevieve's help, or you can do this alone. I'd be happy to throw you on your ass."

Every fiber of my being screamed to retreat. Her presence oozed greed, destruction, and danger. But did I have another choice? The real answer, the one I didn't want to admit, was no. I didn't.
Genevieve's eyes glittered, amused. A small laugh trickled from between her dark-painted lips. "Gentlemen, you have my attention. What exactly is it that you're getting me into?

Chapter 10 - Marie

The next several days were spent in a wash of sadness and anger. Hopping between the library, coffee shop, and my thrift store couch, days and nights rushed together, toppling over one another until there was no sense of time left at all. I'd turned my cell phone off, opting to leave it at home even when I left the house. Truth be told, I wasn't seeing more than my slate-grey walls all that often anymore.

I was pretty relieved the first day I'd killed the power to my phone; I didn't want to read Leena's apologetic texts or have to dodge her frantic calls. Even better, an added bonus was not having to pretend like I hadn't read Luke's cryptic texts anymore either.

The news channels continued to filter negative energy into my life, but I found them to be the only consistent shows airing on the television anymore. It was better than nothing. Because I was alone all of the time, the droning filled the empty space in my mind *and* in my apartment. It didn't matter what was being said, even if it *was* a warning about my own safety.

Without any idea of a pattern or target or cause for what was happening in the world, I continued to live my life in a depressed version of what it was prior to the insanity. The additional time spent in my home was less due to fear of harm and more due to fear of people—in a general sense. Trips outside became necessity-driven; grocery outings when food became sparse, a small walk around the block when the stale indoor air became hard to breathe. For the time being, the bubble of dwindling funds but ever-increasing waistline was plenty fulfilling for me. What else did I have to do with myself?

As such, it was quite an unwanted surprise when a knock sounded on the front door in the middle of the godforsaken day.

Alarmed, I tumbled from my position on the couch, landing with enough force that my downstairs neighbors would surely be banging on the ceiling for revenge while I slept. The joke was on them—I'd been snoozing during the day, having screwed my sleep schedule way beyond repair. My elbow stung, so I rubbed it in an attempt to soothe the pain as I extracted myself from the tangle of blanket on the floor. Through the peephole, a face swam into view. My body stiffened with unpleasant recognition, my arms crossing over themselves as I curled my fingers into fists at my chest.

I counted to ten, not daring to make a sound. The knock came again, then again a moment later. The insistent raps were not gentle, nor were they characteristic of the body unleashing them. Wondering how long I could feasibly stand inches from the hallway without being caught, I kept my eye pressed against the metal ring of the hole. My visitor shuffled, shifting foot to foot, glancing each way down the hallway every few seconds. Another knock, followed by: "Please be home. I need your help."

The scared, desperate way they moved tickled at my spider sense for danger. My body tightened at the thought, pulse picking up at the anticipation and concern. I caved at the worry that also bubbled up inside me—or at least that's what I told myself—and cracked the door. Leena's distraught face loosened, her body sagged in relief. She stepped forward as though she intended to make her way inside, but when I didn't open the door any wider to invite her in, she stalled.

"I'm sorry. I really am sorry."

"I'm sure." The clipped tone was harsher than I'd intended it to be, but I didn't take it back. "What do you need?"

"It's—" She glanced around the hallway again surreptitiously. Her voice was barely a whisper when she spoke again. "I didn't know what else to do. They broke into my house."

We both stood in silence, absorbing the information separately. I finally noticed that Leena had a backpack slung over a shoulder, likely packed for a sleepover, like old times. Weighing the options, considering heavily that it could be a ploy to weasel back into my good graces enough for a more influential apology, I stared her down. Hollow green eyes met frightened black ones.

A month ago, I'd have flung the door open at her first knock, welcoming her in to make herself at home. A month ago, I'd have known she was coming because I'd have been reading her texts and answering her calls.

A month ago, she hadn't betrayed me in the worst way possible.

"What are you expecting from me?"

Recoiling slightly, her head swayed from side to side in a gesture that could have been disbelief. Her bubblegum hair, usually so artfully arranged, hung stringy and flat against her scalp in oiled clumps. Truly, that said more about her situation than any amount of words could ever hope for. I used to admire the care she gave to her appearance; the new, flashy color she'd dye her hair on a whim, the expensive-looking layers she'd don that always managed to be highly fashionable, the way her makeup was always perfectly applied and never seemed to run or smudge.

Standing on my doorstep, looking shifty as hell, I could only stare at her and wonder if the hair and clothes and makeup had been her way of hiding all along. Constantly shifting, changing.

Never the same.

"Can I just stay with you for a few days while I figure out somewhere else to go?"

When I didn't say anything for several moments, she added: "I know you don't want to see me. We don't have to talk about it. We don't have to talk at all. I'll be out before you know it."

Reluctantly, the door swung open. My arms had apparently made the decision while I considered.

Cautiously at first, and then hastily before I could change my mind, she stepped over the threshold to her new, temporary life. Leena was familiar with my home, which meant that she had to steel her face against what I could only imagine to be a look that would betray her surprise at the current state of the place. Dirty dishes nestled themselves on most available surfaces, the sink having overflown with them long ago. Crumbs were scattered throughout the hard flooring and crunched underfoot on the carpet. Looking down to take in my own appearance, I let the grimace show.

Gesturing to the couch first for approval, Leena dropped her backpack and began to tidy up. Vaguely, I wondered if the blanket was still warm from the previous hours I'd spent cocooned in it, and whether she'd be able to tell how long I'd been living in there. Then, I wondered if I actually cared.

Dragging my tired bones toward the hallway to avoid actual contact with Leena, a hot shower called to me instead. At the very least, I could clean myself up and use the time to think about how to get out of the situation I'd just created. Maybe it was a blessing that Leena showed up to force me into a bit of self-care, even though I'd nearly rather it have been Luke to walk through that door. At least with him staying over, I'd get decent orgasms out of the deal. Damn, things really were bad. Cranking it to full heat, steam rose as clothing dropped to the floor. I stole a glance at myself in the mirror over the sink as I stepped into the water.

Yep, a good cleaning was definitely needed.

Feeling slightly more refreshed once I'd cleansed and redressed in fresh clothes, I ventured back out into the living room. The disadvantages of living in a shoe box were numerous, and of those, topping the list was having nowhere to relax outside of your own bedroom when an unwanted guest was crashing in the living area. Fearing confrontation, and not feeling anywhere near capable of handling it yet, the only option left was to evacuate. I was not ready to forgive her.

Leaving a spare key on the counter where it would be seen, grabbing my phone for once, and tiptoeing past Leena's sleeping form on the couch, I made my way for the door. Along the wall where I fashioned a small writing desk and some bookshelves, I noted that Leena's bright pink backpack—to match her hair, perhaps?—sat propped on top of the furthest shelf. Next to it, a mid-sized plant sat, proudly displaying its giant, bushy leaves. Well, that was new; my black thumb certainly didn't bring it into the house. I cut my eyes to the couch. It seemed odd that, while fleeing her own home under apparently unsafe conditions, she'd have stopped to collect a *plant*. Leena was most definitely of a different breed.

Unbidden, a wash of warmth flooded through me, carrying with it memories of the good times that we'd had together. A tsunami of ghost touches rose along my skin where Leena had wrapped herself around in me hugs of excitement, or comfort, or simply friendship. The whispers of her words of encouragement from every time I doubted myself bounced between my ears.

"You're capable of so much more than you know."

"You are an amazing woman, Marie. Just believe in yourself."

The smile on her face every time I'd done something absolutely ridiculous that she'd love me for anyway, nearly brought a smile to my own.

I didn't let it.

The entire situation reeked of things unsaid. I was angry at her—unforgivably angry—but I'd spent so many years loving her, and with my lapse of memory, she'd been my entire world. My brain fought for the silver lining and any possible way to reconcile, while my heart wanted to shove her out of the third-story window.

I shut the door quietly behind myself, locking both bolts in place. Hesitating, I rested my forehead against the door. Leena said her house had been burglarized; would that happen to my home too? Should I stay home and keep watch?

My new best friend, the stress headache that had kept me company for many of the recent weeks of my life, roared to life. Funny how that one had managed to hurt me less than my previous best friend had.

"Oh, you're here!"

Shit.

Carmen's smiling face greeted me from her doorway, her arms waving to flag me down. "I wanted to check on you, you know. You've been all alone and I don't see you leaving much anymore."

The urge to roll my eyes nearly won out over my sense of civility. "I'm actually on my way out now."

She didn't take the hint. "You been eatin' okay? You look like you could use a good meal." There was no pause for me to respond. "You know what, I'm gonna send over a nice meal for you later on. It's no problem."

I nodded appropriately while she rattled on for several more minutes about how she was worried about me and wanted to make sure I was doing alright. I gave affirmative responses in all the right places, even thanking her for her offer and her concern. Eventually, she was called back inside by one of the boys seeking her help with something and I was free to go.

Finally!

Fishing my cell phone out of the makeshift purse I'd slung across my body, I powered it on. It buzzed incessantly, alerting me to dozens of calls and text messages that I'd received while it was turned off. I didn't care. I deleted them all without checking either the messages or the senders. If my home was broken into, at least Leena would be there to inform me. And I knew she would.

Unsure quite where to go, I took the first bus that screeched to a halt at my stop, immediately thankful that it was Randy behind the wheel and not one of the less regular faces instead. As I boarded and chose a seat near the front, my eyes scanned the rows of empty seats behind me. Not a single other passenger was aboard. The clock on the front dash advised that it was just before noon, making it peculiar that businessmen and businesswomen weren't roaming for a lunch break from work, or that parents weren't fetching groceries or otherwise running errands before the children arrived home for the day to eat away their time.

I sifted through what I knew of the routes, double-checking with the LED board across the top that I'd hopped onto the Grey line. This particular bus was popular with tourists and would take me through most of the shopping districts in the area. While certainly not my first choice for escape, it did afford me the opportunity to lose myself in a crowd or perhaps people-watch for a time. Not ideal, but sufficient. I'd needed a distraction, hadn't I?

I pressed my forehead against the window to watch the city as we lumbered past. The buildings were not all that tall, nearly all remaining squat but firm. Most of the city had a small-town vibe that was slowly losing its charm thanks to the rehabilitation efforts of the city council. Plenty of crumbling buildings had been "restored", which was a thinly veiled bait-and-switch used to turn a historical building into an ultra-modern one while using funds from the historic budget.

The city center, with its new shopping plazas and dining establishments, boasted no hint of the times past. It was all shiny metals, sharp angles, greys and tans and whites. "Greige", as the trendy customers called it. Always clean, always neat.

At least, that's what I'd expected to see when we started the mind-numbing journey.

We passed through the outskirts of several residential neighborhoods first, though there were no eager passengers awaiting us at any of the stops. It was highly unusual, and highly unnerving. There were nearly always passengers waiting along the route; stay-at-home moms or teenagers skipping school to finish some last-minute shopping before having to run back home. Out-of-town visitors were brought here by local family members to see the only real 'tour' that Redding could boast. It was never empty, never quiet on that bus or those streets.

The reason slapped me in the face as soon as we breezed past the third city bench at barely a rolling stop. Far back, nearly obscured by the tops of maple trees, the charred remains of a home loomed. Its blackened exterior cried uselessly for help, the fires long since gone and having taken most everything with them. The missing glass from the two highest windows stared back, reminding me of a face with sad, empty eyes. I shuddered.

The next stop we slowed in front of was much the same. This area didn't seem affected by any fires, but instead displayed several homes with angry red and blue lettering scrawled across their faces and driveways. One home even had a vehicle tagged in neon green along the side: "You don't belong". Upon closer inspection of one of the vandalized homes that we crawled past, two large windows on the bottom floor were covered with plastic and tape.

I bristled, remembering again that Leena had just been a victim to such things. The destruction was a lot closer to home than I'd realized.

We rounded the last corner that opened to a stretch of road with shopping plazas hugging each side. Expecting to see crowds gathered to celebrate the slightly less-than-scorching temperatures, we were instead met with desolation. Silence, emptiness, and fear poured from the space outside the safety of the bus. A tumbleweed floating across the street wouldn't have surprised me at that moment. Randy slowed at the stop, making eye contact with me in an unvoiced question: You getting off here?

Straightening in my seat, I took a long look through the windows all around me, waiting to see a glimmer of hope. 'Open' signs glowed in many of the store windows, beckoning for patronage from the empty streets. Was it even safe out there?

Concern welled up within me—not necessarily for my own self, but certainly for Leena's sake. She'd been touched by that madness.

"Do you mind if I just ride for a while?"

Randy smiled, shook his head silently, and revved the engine. He didn't slow at any more of the stops.

Chapter 11 - Marie

The sky was a beautiful gradient of cobalt to navy to midnight blue as it neared full dark. I'd just stepped into the mouth of the parking garage, ducking under the arm utilized by most of the other residents at my complex, when a noise rose in the air that stood my hair on end. Somewhere between a howl of triumph and a yelp of surprise that never seemed to end, the noise reverberated against the concrete walls, seeming to come from everywhere and nowhere at once. I scrambled across the uneven floor toward relative safety, losing my footing only once. I crashed shoulder-first into the hall door, swearing when it didn't magically read my mind and get the hell out of the way. Three tries later and my clumsy hands finally managed to swipe the access card to unbolt the lock and allow me passage.

Safely inside, with the door re-bolted behind me, I sagged against the wall and clutched my chest. I tried desperately to listen for any hint that the noise was closing in, but it was hopeless around the thundering of my pulse.

Jesus, what the hell was that?

Struggling to catch my breath, I ignored the voice in my head that was all but strangled in the pressure undulating in my skull. Yes, yes, *flee*. My heart rate thundered louder than it ever had back in my prime track and field years. Adrenaline raged up, trying to convince me that I could have run the length of the parking garage another fifteen times before I felt any of the effects. At least until after it wore off, anyway.

Taking only a moment to catch my breath, I pushed the elevator button for the third floor and shook out my limbs one by one while it descended to scoop me up. The building was as quiet as the streets had been earlier, nearly eerily so, which only made me all the more nervous.

It was no wonder most citizens were tucked safely inside their homes after what had been going on. Truthfully, I should have been, too. It wasn't smart for me to have ventured out like that.

Impulsiveness: 1; Marie: 0.

My mind briefly shifted to Jesse. Had the destruction reached him? I suddenly felt guilty for not having visited recently enough, which would be impossible to do with Leena hawk-eying me from my own home. I'd come up with something.

Old and barely functional, as was most everything else in the building, it took much longer than expected for the first ring of the bell to alert that the elevator was on its way. The door to the stairwell caught my gaze momentarily, but three solid thumps of my heart trilled in warning that it just might have been safer to brave whatever was outside than it was to launch myself up the stairs under so much physical exertion already. With long, steadying breaths, and my hands locked above my head, I willed myself calm. Embarrassment and soreness were all that remained of my adventure by the time the metal doors finally dragged open with a teeth-rattling squeal.

Sulking, I dragged myself into an elevator car that stunk of old cigarettes and bodily fluids that were better left unidentified. It wasn't unusual to catch a young couple exploring boundaries in the elevators, though my disgust with it was likely due to the fact that I had recently been one of them. The memories of Luke's hands between my thighs, his mouth claiming mine in a hungry connection that sizzled on my skin— those were banished as quickly as they surfaced. With gentle ascent, and a whole lot of time, I finally reached the third floor. Proud of itself, the elevator marked its success with a light ping that barely managed to rip my mind from the assault of unwanted mental images.

Crossing the hallway slowly, my muscles angry and seeking revenge since they'd begun to cool, I unlocked the door labeled '314'. With a flurry of sounds that startled me more than they actually scared me, and a body pressed solidly against my own the moment I pushed open the thin door, my fight response resurfaced with a vengeance. As the adrenaline hadn't fully tapered off, it was purely instinct that raised an elbow and shoved off the mass with enough force to tumble them backward onto the floor in a painful-sounding impact; an instinct that was immediately admonished when realization dawned on me in the form of an overly feminine squeal. Leena.

Shit, I'd forgotten about her.

Eyes more wounded than her body would be, Leena speared me with a look from her seat on the floor.

"Sorry," I told her with a single-shoulder shrug. "Forgot you were here." I didn't sound very sorry; that was perhaps because I *wasn't* very sorry. She'd damn near assaulted me for walking into my own home.

"I was worried about you," she said, the pout in the words quickly replaced by a careful lilt as she spoke again. It was the sort of tone reserved for someone teetering on the edge of sanity. "Did you go out?"

At the accusation in her tone, my shoulders slung back and my spine straightened. It was my house and my life, and no one would be telling me what I could and couldn't do with either of them. "I did." Finality coated the words, as intended.

Confusion and a bit of offense creased her features, making her look—for the first time that I could ever recall—older than she was. The flash of satisfaction that ran through me in response was trailed briefly by guilt, but not much of it. Brushing past her emotional turmoil, both mentally and physically, I made my way into the kitchen and poured a glass of juice from the fridge. What the hell was her problem? She fired me. How did she expect me to survive if I didn't leave the house?

I sipped my beverage slowly, glancing at Leena's face over the rim. Truth be told, once I'd calmed down, I began to notice that she'd done a decent job of cleaning while I'd been out. There wasn't a single dirty dish to be seen—not even in the sink—or a crumb left anywhere around the house. In fact, the counters had even been wiped down, and I'd bet money that she'd dusted the entire place from top to bottom as well. I should have thanked her, said something to show her that I was grateful for the work she'd done, but the lasting sting of her hateful words kept my kind ones shuttered.

Though my heart did ache over the rift between us. Before her betrayal, we could have hugged it out and made up watching movies together on the couch; her staying over would have been the equivalent of a teenage sleepover, not a marriage on the rocks. Yet, she'd done this to us, and I hadn't. Secrets that had been given in confidence were no longer so much of a secret. There was no going back. The fact that she was even allowed into my home was proof of how deeply I had cared for her once upon a time, but it did not mean that we were still friends. The realization of it hit Leena as she watched me; I could see it in the fall of her face, which had been waiting with guarded hopefulness. Not anymore.

Finally, painfully slowly, Leena extricated herself from the floor and moved toward me. A hand was pressed against her chest in a sign of self-soothing. Typically, Leena stripped the layers of various clothing in the safety of my home, allowing me to see the rows upon rows of tribal tattoos lining her arms—the very ones she kept hidden from everyone else. While it never made sense to me, because it was a shame to be embarrassed of something that cost so much money and time, the simple act always showed me how comfortable she felt. How safe. As if to punctuate the canyon in our relationship, Leena's bright colors remained layered, covering both her tattoos and her regret.

"I need to tell you something."

I couldn't stop the snarky remark from tumbling free, though I winced as the words fell from my lips. "Is it about why the hell you stopped to grab a plant when you were supposed to have been running in fear for your life?"

Both of our gazes flicked to the aforementioned plant, sitting innocently in its pot of sunshine yellow across the room. Leena's hands wrung together, still clutched over her chest. Tension turned her softly tanned knuckles white, though from anger or worry, I'd never know.

"There's a lot that I want to tell you. I'll start with this." She drew in a deep breath, let it out slowly. Then another. I itched to grab her by the shoulders and shake the words free. Patient, I was not. "The attack on my house was not random. I've been targeted."

"Who'd you piss off?"

"I didn't!" Her voice rose, defiant, strangely absent of the hint of whine she normally adopted in the face of confrontation. Apparently, I'd touched a nerve.

Silence tumbled down around us, uncomfortable and punctuated by Leena's ragged, angry breathing. A wail of sirens bled through the thin walls. I wondered vaguely whether there'd been another fire, and how close the trouble was this time. Then, I wondered if it had anything to do with the noise I'd heard outside. My body shuddered involuntarily at the echo of the sound inside my memories. It was nothing I ever wanted to hear again in my life.

Polishing off the last of the juice and tossing the cup into the sink— which gave me slight pause, as it meant marring the perfectly clean kitchen—I pushed past Leena to head into my bedroom. I was startled to see that the mountain of laundry, which had all but sneered at me from the foot of the bed that morning, was missing. The act felt both invasive and kind in equal measure. Had I really been gone long enough for her to have done all of that?

Her presence practically a dig against my already foul mood, Leena hovered in the open doorway, trailing me like a pouting toddler. I exhaled, tried to wrestle my emotions into something that wouldn't make the situation any worse.

"Where's the rest of your stuff?"

"I quit The Capital yesterday. I sold what I couldn't carry or didn't explicitly need." She paused, hesitated, as though unsure how much to say. "You know that pawn shop next to the cafe where we used to work?"

Grunting in the affirmative, I sank into my bed, speaking to her from the flat of my back. There didn't seem to be any more point in beating around the bush, so I changed tactic and voiced the question I most wanted an answer to: "Did you bring your trouble to me?"

Silence. Slowly, I closed my eyes, cursing internally at my kindness, my curiosity. She should have never been let into the house to begin with. Aside from what I'd intentionally sought out, the danger had steered clear of me until Leena showed up, and suddenly it was all but at my door. The urge to snap at her to pack her shit and leave must have translated into our uncomfortable tension.

"Maybe another day or two, so that I can find somewhere to go. That's all I need. Please."

Rolling, I gave her my back.

Damnit.

Yet, I couldn't deny that a small part of me wanted to see what was coming.

After a moment, she retreated, closing the door behind her and ushering in a silence that finally wasn't full of unspoken words. Exhausted, it took me only moments to fall into a fitful slumber, though I woke shortly thereafter to a parched throat and screaming muscles. Taking the opportunity to kick off my shoes and change into clothes comfortable enough to sleep in was enough to release the tension that was bunching inside me.

Perhaps Yoga was in my future.

A headache raged to life the moment I tried to curl back into bed. The clock on the bedside table blinked angrily back at the scowl I shot it, all but mocking me for waking in pain and thirst at two in the morning.

Quietly exiting the bedroom, cloaked in the darkness of night, I tiptoed into the hallway, expecting Leena to have also crashed hours ago. Instead, the vague outlines of her back greeted me as she shuffled around in the shadow of the room. I stood silently for several minutes, following the shape of her as she leaned over the bookshelves. At first, I assumed she was searching for a book, huddled closely in the dark to better read the titles. Why she hadn't just turned on the lamp to see was beyond me. Another two steps closer to her, however, and I realized that I was wrong.

Her body was bent awkwardly, not over the bookshelf, but over the *plant* on top of the bookshelf. As my eyes began to adjust to the dim natural light filtering in from the living room windows, the thin cord of an earphone materialized, swinging underneath Leena's lifted arms. With the knowledge that she couldn't hear me, and likely couldn't see me either, I braved a few steps toward her, intrigued by any possible reason for her to be tending a plant in the absolute dark at two in the god damned morning.

Another few seconds passed, and I could decipher just a little more of the scene unfolding before me. In one hand, she held something unfamiliar. It was difficult to make out with only the glow from the partially-curtained window for help, but it appeared to be metal of some sort, shaped vaguely like a horseshoe, and definitely not smooth. The light, though minimal, warped and twisted as it reflected over the metal ridges of Leena's object. I squinted, bent forward at the waist, and still could not find any more clues about it.

What in the ever-loving hell was it?

Another step forward. I was inching closer, but walking at her back and losing my vision of what was happening directly in front of her. Just about to close the distance and end the mystery of it all by asking her directly, her voice picked up in a whisper. I froze, frightened for a moment that she'd seen or heard me and was admonishing me for spying. Straining my ears, daring not to breathe, I waited for a full minute while the sound continued before I felt confident that *whatever* was being said was not specifically directed at me.

In fact, the words never made it to my ears at all; they didn't need to. As her voice hit stride, a rhythm emerging in the sounds, the tattoos all along her body—which were finally laid bare to the air around us— thrummed and pulsed in a glow of neon green. Startled by the flash of brightness and nearly blinded, I stumbled backward, bumping against the wall and slapping a hand against my mouth to stifle the grunt of pain.

The hand gripping the mysterious metal disappeared in front of Leena's body, to what I could only imagine to be directly above the leaves of the plant, before I could use the light to get any clearer of an image of it. Only growing in intensity as the seconds marched on, brightness assaulted my eyes, forcing me to cover them or risk permanent damage. Throwing up an arm to tuck my face into, I recoiled and turned my back against whatever insanity was happening in my living room. Christ, I had to be dreaming.

Suddenly, as though it had never been there to begin with, the glow faded, the whispering stopped, and Leena stood, turned, and caught my eyes in the dark as I fought to do the same amidst my rapidly fading vision. The dangling cords fell from her ears, clattered together with the sound only thin, cheap plastic can make. The lamp resting on the bookshelf blared to life. Behind her, there remained no trace of the metal object she'd been holding. Instead, the leaves of her darling plant had sprung up as if by magic, growing by at least six inches in height and half that in depth from what I'd seen of it yesterday.

Yesterday? Had it really already been an entire day?

Words scraped out of my throat without first passing through the filter in my brain, though I wasn't sure that I'd have phrased it any better if I had allowed myself time to ponder it first.

"What the fuck are you?"

Chapter 12 - Marie

Leena packed abruptly. Having been caught doing whatever it was that she was doing, she felt it best to not spend any more time in my home. Not a word to her own defense was uttered as she hurriedly shoved her belongings into her powder pink backpack, though I tried several times to ask her to explain herself. Thousands of theories, millions of previous conversations between us rushed through my skull as though I'd blown down a dam inside my mind. Or perhaps she had, with whatever magic I'd just seen. It didn't matter; what truly stung was that she hadn't shared this secret with me, not once. She knew all of the intimate details of my relationship with Luke, as well as the past that I shared with virtually no one, and all the while she held in something bigger than all of it combined.

No secrets between best friends, my ass.

With the backpack slung over a shoulder just as it had been when she'd arrived, she carried the bright yellow pot in her hands as she headed for the door.

"Where are you going to go?" I demanded as she stepped out over the threshold. Sure, I was angry, but I was also concerned. If she was somehow mixed up in what was happening across the country, I could help. I would do anything I could, regardless of how angry I was with her. She just needed to be honest with me about it first.

A sad smile stretched across her face, but she didn't bother to respond—not to *anything* I asked or demanded or pleaded for. As quickly as she had come, she was gone, leaving only stray strands of bubblegum pink hair behind as proof that she'd ever even been there to begin with.

At least, that's what I thought at first. Tucked into the cushions of the couch was a teal blue, puffy hair tie, which most certainly didn't belong to me. It felt wrong. Out of place.

I tugged it out and set it on the table to stare at it in disbelief before I shoved my hand back in between the cushions to root out any more hidden treasure. My fingers skimmed something soft and sharp enough to cut me, and I yelped and retracted my hand. I tried again, more gingerly, this time lifting out a crumpled newspaper. I frowned at it, knowing that it, like the hair tie, was most definitely not mine. I couldn't recall the last time I'd looked at a physical newspaper.

Turning it over in my hands, a pale yellow sticky note grabbed my attention. It was folded over onto itself, covered in dirt and crumbs, and once unfurled, I realized that it was not written in handwriting that I recognized.

Hope ur ok. We r here if u need n e thing. - Carmen & boys

Confused, I unfolded the paper. It was dated recently and seemed pretty standard—mostly filled with articles that matched what had run through the TV outlets over the past few weeks. Then I turned the page and my breathing stopped. The entirety of the inner pages consisted of names, ages, locations, and a brief synopsis of the autopsy reports of the initial hundred victims. It was the same information that the news outlets had guarded *so* closely that we'd been left to fend for ourselves with conspiracy theories and fear.

I scanned the list, feeling more sick every time I encountered the phrases: 'no blood left', 'bite marks', 'crushed limbs', and 'unknown weapon'.

The revelation should have frightened me. It should have made me want to run screaming from the room. What it did was make me angry. If they were sharing information with us, it meant that the law was in over its head and they were turning to the public for answers.

Rage lurked beneath my thoughts, reminding me that I'd been out for most of the day, and that Leena had been in my home to receive the gift from Carmen. She'd not said a thing to me about it, choosing to shove it down somewhere that I'd likely never see it.

Why?

Was she involved?

The silence that I had reveled in just days prior suddenly felt suffocating. The emptiness of my tin can of an apartment served as a reminder of how alone I truly was. Spotless and unfamiliar, the rooms no longer felt comforting, no longer inviting or warm. It was not the home I once knew.

Perhaps I'd hit my head, imagined everything that transpired last night, and Leena had truly gone because of the fight we'd had just before I'd fallen asleep. Knowing how easily offended she was when it came to the two of us, it certainly wasn't beyond the realm of possibility.

I felt around my skull gingerly, anticipating my fingers stumbling upon a knot or tender area that never existed, but would justify the weirdness of the past few days. Nothing. The strangeness was, apparently, just my life.

Leena lied to me.

She'd been targeted, though. She'd said that; it couldn't be explained away as misheard or misspoken. It was clear as day. Was the glowing green woo-woo what she'd been targeted for? Or maybe the metal she'd somehow hidden away *in her plant*?

Shit, was that why she didn't let anyone else see her tattoos?

The all-too-familiar headache railed against my temples, thrashing inside my skull in the hopes of breaking me enough to leak out into freedom. At least, that's what it felt like. Spots of black ate at my vision. Snatching up my cell phone, I glanced at the screen. The calendar flashed into view and I grimaced. Rent would be due soon. I'd pulled everything out of my bank account a few days ago and there definitely wasn't enough money left between the four crisp $20 bills sitting in my wallet to cover it, since I hadn't been to work in weeks. Or was it months?

Thumbing through the contacts stored inside, I hit the call button when Sandra's name came up. Five rings in, it clicked to voice mail.

"Hi, Sandra. It's Marie. Listen, Leena and I got into a bit of a fight and she fired me. I was just hoping that you might consider hiring me back, since it's your store and all? I really need the money and you know I can do the job. Please call me back."

My stomach lurched at the pleading tone that edged my voice. Had I really just begged for work? At a clothing store? Anger, spurred on by embarrassment, washed over me. My life had certainly changed in the past few weeks. Who'd have known I'd fall from being contented with a decent job, the love of my life, and the support of my best friend, to being utterly alone, broke, and restless in my own skin? Oh, and not to forget, also clinically insane.

That was it—I was just crazy. It was easy to believe that the stress of my messy life had knocked a few screws loose. After all, who didn't have a complete and utter mental breakdown every so often? With the condition of the world outside the walls of the crumbling apartment building, mental instability didn't even rank on the list of weird.

That was believable, right?

Right?

68

Convinced that I'd hallucinated both Leena's incident and the noise outside the parking garage alike, I did feel much better. Explaining the strange occurrences as figments of my imagination allowed me to move forward, and required only a small amount of self-chastising about taking better care of myself. Really, I *had* just mourned lost love—in both senses of the word. A little crack-up was to be expected under such circumstances.

Deciding to indulge in some obviously needed self-care, I popped a frozen dinner into the microwave, grabbed a slightly-less-than-divinely-fuzzy blanket and turned on the television to flick through the channels. I settled on a re-run of something that promised to be humorous, and not just because it was the only channel that wasn't news, grateful for the opportunity to laugh again. Though the humor came slowly, smiles reluctant to surface after the trauma of the past few weeks, comfort eventually swept me up and cradled me in its warmth. It wasn't long afterward before I succumbed to missing sleep, and it wasn't long after that when I was woken again to the buzzing of a call on my cell phone and the bright, intruding sunlight streaming through the living room windows.

"Hello?" I croaked into the phone, scrubbing crust from between my eyelashes.

"Marie, hi."

"Sandra? Hi. How are you?"

There was a slight pause from the other end, Sandra's breath carrying over the line for several seconds before she spoke again. "I guess you haven't heard."

"Heard what?"

She took the confusion in my voice as her cue to lay on the drama, ever a diva when sympathy could be tossed at her feet. "It's awful," she wailed. "The store. It's gone. Burnt to the ground!"

I sat up, fully awake. "What? When did this happen?"

"Four days ago. Both my unit and the one above, totally destroyed. There was some damage to the neighboring units as well, but they'll survive. Of course they will," she muttered the last under her breath. "That damned Gina is going to run her smelly cooking school next door until she dies." A brief pause, a deep sigh. "But The Capital is gone. Isn't it awful?"

I didn't respond—couldn't—as the information raced desperately through my mind to find a spot to click into place. Sandra continued, entirely unaware that I was struggling to process her words; that, or she hadn't the smallest fuck to give about it.

"No one's sure yet whether it was my store or the floor above that the fire was intended for, since there was plenty of damage to the neighboring stores on the upper floor as well. We'll have to wait for the investigation results. They're a little backed up right now, though... you know, with all the other fires in the city."

I didn't need to wait for an investigation because I was pretty sure I already knew which unit was targeted. Well, I did if I was back to subscribing to the theory that I wasn't a nut job after all. "I'm sorry to hear that, Sandra."

"Yes, well, until the insurance comes through, we can't rebuild. I'm sorry to say, you'd be out of a job anyway. I'll make contact when things are up and running again, if you'd like. We'll show Gina that you can't take down The Capital!"

Mumbling a thanks and disconnecting the call, I sat, stunned. It was all too close to home for comfort. How many times had I reassured Leena, telling her that the craziness of the world that had frightened her so much would never reach us? What an idiot I was.

Did Leena's break-in have anything to do with the store's fire? Logic told me no, that it wasn't possible, but something deep within me was screaming and flailing mercilessly at the red flags piling up. Without a second to convince myself otherwise, my fingers flew over the buttons and the phone was ringing against my ear. Silently, I pleaded to hear Leena's voice on the other end.

Her voicemail picked up.

I hung up, instead sending a text message with a request to call me. After another moment, I followed up with a second one, stating that it was urgent. Something was going on and I would certainly be getting to the bottom of it. It was time that someone started giving me the damn truth.

Both Luke's and Jesse's faces flashed through my mind, summoning a sigh of frustration. It seemed everyone liked to lie to me, after all.

A shower later, feeling no better than when I first stepped into the steam, I resigned myself to achy muscles and pounding headaches for the foreseeable future. At least until I could figure out what the hell was going on. A quick peek at my phone revealed that I hadn't received either a return message or phone call from Leena. Judging by the clock, she'd left roughly four hours ago. Where would she even have gone?

Attempting to pull memories from the long-forgotten parts of my brain only resulted in a deeper throbbing against my temples, and I wasn't entirely sure that I could survive—mentally or physically—if I didn't get some relief in that department soon. Swapping to what I hoped were easier questions to answer, I settled back onto the couch and stared into the silence while I skimmed along the surface of the informational well inside me.

What did I know about Leena's parents? Not local, not even local to the country, if I recalled correctly. They lived in... what was it, Tibet? That's where Leena was from, I was pretty sure. Not much chance that she'd have gone there, though I wasn't putting anything past anyone those days. Come to think of it, I wasn't sure Tibet was in any better shape than the States were anyway. There'd be no sense in bringing the danger to her family, assuming it would follow her that far.

Would it?

It had followed her to my doorstep...

Definitely something to consider, but the train of thought didn't feel like it was leading me toward the answers I needed. She'd come to me instead of hopping on the first international plane she could find, and she hadn't sounded like she was waiting around for ticket prices to tank. She was looking for somewhere to stay. Locally.

Was there anyone else who would know more about Leena's whereabouts? I scoured years of memories of our previous conversations for mentions of a boyfriend or other close friends, coming up with several first names but no accompanying last names or methods of contact. Damn. Since when did Leena play things so close to the chest? And how had I not noticed that I'd been fed partial facts and redacted stories all of our years of so-called friendship?

Focus, Marie. Be pissed off later, but find her first.

Regardless of emotional betrayals, and in light of more recent events, Leena was still my best friend and she was scared. And also, apparently, in danger. What would I do to protect myself in the same situation? Honestly, probably exactly what she did.

I scrubbed a hand over my face, trying hard not to sidebar with myself for some brief chastising. If I'd just calmed down for two entire seconds and looked at the oddities of her behavior, I'd have seen that something was wrong. I'd have been able to talk this through with her.

It was all my fault.

Thrusting my cell phone into my pocket and snatching my keys from beside the door, I made my way to the bus stop, horrific recent experiences forgotten entirely in the wash of determination—or perhaps, more accurately, desperation. While we may not have been the best of friends at present, there wasn't anyone else that Leena had wanted to turn to in her time of need. That counted for something.

I waited only a few impatient minutes before a bus began lumbering its way toward me at the stop. I noted the sign on the front that specified its next destination. That particular route would take me past the scenic areas of town, near the rural edges where our city brushed against those surrounding ones. It was possible that Leena had decided to find a park shelter to curl up in, or was still making her way in whichever direction it was she'd decided was best. It was a fifty-fifty shot that the direction the vehicle would carry me was the right one.

I got on.

Carmen was driving, which seemed unusual enough that it gave me pause. Didn't she know it was dangerous out? She was the one who'd passed the newspaper to me, so it wasn't like she had no idea about the deaths.

Strangely, she didn't start a conversation right away, instead assessing me first.

Taking the very first row and turning to press my face firmly against the window, my eyes locked on every shadow that we passed, hoping to see a beautiful face framed in soft pink peering back. The jittery ride, which slammed my forehead and nose into the glass painfully on more than one occasion, was not nearly enough of a deterrent to prevent my hawk-eyed investigation. If she was out there, I wouldn't miss it to save myself from a bloody nose or a bruised forehead.

Carmen's eyes scanned me several times from her large rear-view mirror; I felt them as surely as if she'd waved her arms and pointed at me instead. I met them for just a moment, which was apparently enough contact for her to break into a nervous version of her usual chatty routine.

"Not many passengers lately, hmm?"

"Nope," I said curtly. Then I reconsidered my tone. Carmen had nothing to do with the fact that the world was upside down. What would turning my anger on her do for either of us? Plus, it was smart not to anger the woman driving me to destinations I'd rather not have to walk to on my own. Less aggressively, I said: "What are you even doing still driving this thing around? I saw the newspaper you left for me. There's a whole mess of crazy out there. Best to keep far away from it if you can."

Her face twisted in the mirror's reflection, lips scrunched together in worry. "Got kids to feed, you know. Can't let them go hungry on a 'maybe'. Someone wants to take me out? Fine. It was meant to be. 'Til then, I'm not letting those babies starve." She paused for a moment, then more quietly said: "Ain't no one else willing to run the routes anyway, 'cept for Randy, so it's good money right now."

"Randy's still driving too?"

"Sure is. Said it's his duty as an American and if he could do it all those years ago with bullets flying everywhere, he could sure do it now." She rolled her eyes in a teasing manner that spoke volumes of her admiration for the man. "Them old folks, you know. Just built different."

I wanted to warn her to be careful, but she knew that already, and I wasn't her mother. I had no business telling her what to do. Carmen wasn't what I'd have considered a friend, but I had a healthy amount of respect for her, even if she couldn't take the hint about my lack of affection for social interactions. Occasionally we'd bump into one another as we crossed paths, often with a friendly hello—mostly from her end and less so from mine—and a brief one-sided conversation. Recently, it was less frequent that she'd stopped me—"Let Oscar help you with your grocery bags. He's thirteen and he can help out as the man of the house."—"Knock any time if you need anything at all. None of my kids would turn away a woman in need."—and I imagined that had a lot to do with both the extra shifts she'd been working as well as my significantly decreased outings over the past several weeks. As a single working mother, she was perhaps the strongest ally I had at the moment.

I held my phone out to her across the aisle, a photo of Leena and I displayed on the screen. "Have you seen her today?"

Carmen glanced at it and shook her head, forehead creased. "She in trouble?"

"I'm not sure."

She seemed to understand what hadn't been said, and we shifted into a comfortable silence. Ages passed—or at least what felt like it—before we reached the first major landmark that had any promise as a refuge. A long stretch of open field welcomed me, cloaked in darkness from the night pressing in. There were no benches or tents, or truly any good place for sleeping, but there was a small overhang to the center-right that covered a set of public water fountains and might have made a final-resort sleeping pad. A small wooded area clung to the far side of the field, but I doubted that Leena would be caught dead sleeping on dirt or concrete if there were other options, so I stayed seated and we forged ahead. The next promising stop was the Sundial Bridge, a towering structure that was every bit as large as it was impressive. The bus idled briefly at the mouth of the bridge opposite it. At night and during the early hours of morning, the structure was lit with an array of bright colors; it was exactly the type of place that would draw someone like Leena. I surged forward, forcing Carmen to brake where she hadn't intended to. She gripped the wheel with two hands and braced herself with her forearms, shooting daggers at me despite the fact that I'd stumbled forward and banged my knee even without her inflicting any intentional pain on me.

"I'd just like to take a quick look. Would you mind waiting for me? I swear I'll be *right* back."

She sighed, glanced into the long mirror above her head once more, assessed the empty space behind us where no other passengers waited, and shrugged.

"Do what you gotta do."

Two homeless men huddled under the bridge, far enough from one another that you wouldn't mistake them for being friendly. The stench of unwashed bodies and what was likely a bottle or nearby hole where someone had been relieving themselves rammed itself up my nostrils, from which I recoiled. Leena wasn't there. No way. Yet... I'd never have assumed her to be harboring secrets and possible *magic*, either.

More than ready to hustle back to my ride and escape the smell, I paused, crouched under the shield that the structure provided, and spoke directly to the two men in a loud enough voice that I didn't have to approach them any more closely. Neither of them had seen her; that, or both of them had very accurately assumed that I had nothing to offer in exchange for information and therefore had no intent to provide any. Resigned, I boarded the bus again and thanked Carmen for her patience.

The final two stops were alongside a vast, gorgeous lake which provided absolutely no coverage for anyone to hunker down unseen—so the area was easy enough to check off the list—and a small historic stretch of road where buildings had been boarded tightly when they dared to show their age. I wrinkled my nose against the implication that the historic homes were an 'eyesore', as our Mayor had stated several times during re-election campaigns. Couldn't have that in this pristine town, didn't you know? Aging was so *uncouth*.

Though I scrutinized every nail and two-by-four in sight for signs of breaking and entering, I eventually had to admit to myself that there was no sign of Leena and withdraw my strained eyes from the smudged window.

We traveled back to my home in silence, the same as we'd journeyed most of the way from it, but it felt heavy suddenly, like Carmen had figured out what really happened between Leena and me and sympathized with my misery at not locating her. Trying one more desperate time to reach Leena's phone, I hung up on the voicemail message.

Chapter 13 - Leena

What had I done?

It was a stupid thing to do, bringing that danger to Marie's doorstep, and I was an even bigger idiot for entangling her in the life I'd kept hidden for so long. She'd have questions, and she'd ask them—that was Marie's way.

The problem would be whether she'd ever get answers.

My heart constricted at the thought that I'd have to come clean to her in order to even attempt to soothe the rift between us, and that was just the start. Marie could reject me for everything I confided in her, including the fact that I kept it a secret for so long.

God, especially since I'd been preaching over and over that best friends shouldn't keep secrets.

I was a hypocrite.

I was a *double* hypocrite.

Would answering her questions about myself lead to me revealing the secrets I held for others? Marie would *hate* me.

At first, I headed directly for the bus stop, intending to jump on the first bus that showed up and ride to anywhere. But when the metal monster approached, it was Carmen that I saw behind the wheel and I couldn't bear to explain to her why I was so upset. I couldn't handle the sympathy that would swim in her eyes as I spilled the whole of what I'd done to Marie.

Instead, I turned on my heel and marched in the opposite direction, cradling my plant in my arms. My apartment was no longer safe, nor was Marie's. I could call on Luke and he'd surely let me stay for a while, but then I'd have to explain my relationship to him when Marie discovered where I'd been. That led me right back to the big, bad, whopper of a secret I wasn't ready to admit to yet.

Crap.

After the darkness of night retreated, an orange glow began to bleed into the sky, lighting bits of my path as I traveled. My cell phone sat somewhere among the mess of things I'd shoved into my backpack, so I didn't dare stop to shuffle through to check the time. It would be somewhere near six in the morning, if I had to guess. Plenty of establishments would be opening their doors shortly, and I could take refuge in them. I didn't *look* homeless yet, though that was only a matter of time if I didn't formulate some sort of plan.

I needed help, but the only help I could reach out to would raise more questions.

In fact, there was little doubt in my mind what exactly the threat could be that shadowed me. There still remained plenty of questions as to how they knew where to look and what, exactly, they were looking for. But that was not the problem at hand.

I'd hidden the necklace as best I could and if I could find somewhere to stash it, to separate it from me to keep it safe, that would be best. Honestly, I should have left it at the pawn shop, but something about that plan felt off when I considered it.

As the sun rose to greet me and chase away the coldness of the night, my spirits lifted. A pristine brick sign loomed into view high above the tops of the buildings nearby, advertising a small business park. Though still early enough that the employees would, at most, just be rousing from their beds to start their days, I turned at the next street block and headed in that direction. An ache had begun in my calves, warning that I'd have a hell of a time starting again once I stopped walking. It didn't matter.

Around the back of the long, conjoined suites, I settled on a packing crate near the dumpster and rifled through my bag. The urge to text Marie welled up the second my fingers brushed against the hard plastic of my phone case, but I shoved it back down. I'd not involve her any further in my mess until it was over. I did, however, lift the phone and type a quick, concise message to Luke to explain the situation, both my current one and the one with Marie.

His response was immediate and imploring, seeking a way he could assist me. Of course it was. Luke was a bona fide boy scout in a man's body and would do whatever he could to help, no matter the cost to himself.

I responded once more with finality—that I was okay, that he should check on Marie, and that I'd regroup with them both when I had more information and was sure that I was out of the woods.

The decision to leave my phone on wasn't an easy one. It was inevitable that Marie would call at some point, and I couldn't answer when she did, but turning it off would mean that she'd worry instantly, and I didn't want her to worry. Plus, if I really needed to reach out for help again, I could do so faster.

The fruit and nut bar squished nearly to a pancake at the bottom of my bag was almost stale enough that it was tough to chew in places. Food was my absolute next priority. And water.

Though I didn't entirely recognize the area, it was a mixture of business and residential, which meant at the very least there should be a gas station or convenience store nearby.

My legs screamed as I stood and tapped the toes of my shoes on the ground. A few stretches later, they still weren't happy, but they had no say in the matter. Rounding the back end of the building the same way I approached it, I froze at the sight of a vehicle in the parking lot. The silver SUV would have been inconspicuous to just about anyone else, but their positioning at the direct center of the lot and the idling engine together knotted worry into my stomach. The vehicle shifted into gear and eased out of the parking space, gliding in my direction at a speed that wouldn't raise alarm.

Except that every fiber of my being snapped to alert. Fear pulsed through me, feeding off of the waves of aggression that threatened to swallow me whole.

Ignoring the complaint from my body, I turned and ran. The small patch of forestry at the edge of the back lot welcomed me as I dove inside and crouched, listening for the sounds of tires or car doors. When the faintest crunch of a rock hit my ears from the left, my body instantly carried me right. Bursting through the end of the woodsy plot and onto an open road, the flat park three blocks ahead beckoned. Even from the distance, and despite the early hour, a jogger with a dog stood out against the green emptiness of the land.

My pursuers would hesitate around people.

With every ounce of my strength, I commanded my legs to race forward, fumbling to pull my backpack around to the front where I could reach it as I ran. If I could just get to my phone and send a message...

But there was no use.

I barely made half the journey to my destination before a looming presence pressed against me from behind and I turned, though I knew I shouldn't, to see a figure reach forward and take hold of my arm.

The moment our bodies made contact, it was over.

Chapter 14 - Marie

The next several weeks were filled with worry, anger, and endless news reports. With each unreturned call, dread knotted my stomach. With every bleak story that aired, tension built around me. Even the bodies in the units nearby took to bunkering themselves indoors, mostly surviving on fear alone, it seemed. It was almost a tangible beast, merging from one person to another, growing like a snowball as it avalanched to bury us all. There had been no response to any attempts to reach Leena via phone, not even as much as a one-word text message. Desperate, I'd placed another call to Sandra, praying that she'd heard from Leena herself and that she was just *really* upset with me.

Nothing.

As a last resort for information, the news blared constantly from my television, even into the wee hours of the night. Amidst what had been days of monotonous updates, totaling the new bodies found and displaying cycles of crime scenes and destruction, a new sound blaring from the TV screen startled me. Hope bloomed, then died again the moment I recognized it as an emergency broadcast. My tiny apartment filled with the sound of alarm, echoing against the barren walls. I hurried from the bathroom, toothpaste smeared across my lips, toothbrush trailing milky-colored water across the floor. Expression torn between horror and shock, under a loose mask that was supposed to have suppressed both but failed miserably, the on-air reporter gave a breathy reading from the teleprompter opposite her.

"We've just received word of a tragedy that has occurred. According to our sources on the ground in Washington, D.C., the White House came under attack earlier this afternoon. Investigation regarding the culprit is still underway and I have no further information regarding the perpetrators at this time."

As she spoke, the woman's thin lips trembled. She paused just long enough to suck in a breath that didn't appear to have done her any good. Frozen to my spot, the toothbrush fell from my hand at her next words.

"At the time of the attack, all of the members of The Cabinet, the head of the Government, and the President of the United States were reported to have been convened at the White House, conducting a closed-door meeting regarding the ongoing situation in the country. At present, we have no evidence to suggest that there are any survivors. The bodies recovered from the scene mimic injuries consistent with those of the other unexplained deaths across the nation, and match exactly the number of attendees. Coroners have been asked to identify the fallen as their top priority, however, the bodies are in such a condition that—"

Everything said after that was merely noise, sifting into one ear and immediately exiting through the other. The *Government* had been taken down. All of it. What did that mean for everyone else?

No one was going to save us from it. It would never stop. The realization hit like a physical blow, knocking the wind out of me just as surely as it had snatched the forgotten plastic from my grasp moments earlier. Where fear should have reigned, anger roiled. Any sensible person would have abandoned hope, joined the masses of zombified citizens who'd surely, more than ever, sit helplessly in their homes and wait to be slaughtered. What other choice was there?

There seemed no reasoning behind the attacks, making the difficult job of stopping them even harder by sheer lack of suspects. Where would someone even start?

With Leena, of course. How she'd known that she was a target, as opposed to being a randomly-selected victim, was still unclear. What wasn't unclear at all was that she was running and seemed to be doing so with an idea of what was chasing her.

That was as good of a start as any.

Using the Internet on my cell phone to run a Google search, and scrolling only momentarily, I dialed the phone number it produced. The ringing line sprouted hope, quickly dashed after four whole minutes passed without an answer or a voicemail box to accept a message on the business's behalf.

Stuffing the phone back into my pocket marked my decision of how to proceed. I exited the apartment with the TV still loudly droning and the fuzzy toothbrush still drying on the carpet.

The ride was short, mostly bumpy, and pleasant enough since it was entirely empty besides myself and the familiar face of Randy as he greeted me. He nodded at me when I stepped on, and waved me away when I attempted to pay. Apparently, you got a pretty steep discount when life as you knew it was ending.

After the second stop at which no one waited to board, he turned to me and asked politely where it was that I wanted to go. I told him. We retained the original route but deviated in that the empty benches were simply bypassed, without any semblance of a pause, until we reached my destination. Though the streets remained uncharacteristically empty aside from the odd piece of litter, nearly a third of the structures—residential and business alike—sported some form of scar from the state of things. From broken windows, to vandalism, to scorch marks, not a single block was untouched. I hadn't truly expected to see people milling about in their Sunday best, yet the vision of our world looking as broken and vacant as we felt was jarring nonetheless.

As I suspected, when we finally halted to signal that we'd reached my stop, the scene was grim. The smoothie shop and coffee shop stood in pristine condition, though they both remained dark inside despite it being midday; the pawn shop and the clothing store that neighbored it on the left were entirely blackened and slumped into a depressed pile of rubble. Broken bits of metal and wood jutted out at odd angles, daring anyone brave enough to make it out with their life.

I stepped out into the muggy night but paused when Randy waved for my attention.

"I'm about twelve minutes ahead of my schedule right now. If you're done by then, I'll take you to your next stop. Otherwise I'll have to swing the route again."

Nodding, acknowledging his kind offer despite the tightening of my throat that halted my words, my feet dragged me purposefully toward the destruction. Clearly, I *was* brave enough to trek through the devastation.

Carefully stepping only where there was enough solid-seeming purchase, and ignoring the neon yellow caution tape decorating what was once the building's exterior walls, I found myself excitedly scouring the ash for anything at all. It wasn't likely that anything of Leena's would have survived what had happened, let alone anything that could point me in the direction of finding her, but with nothing else to go on, and more time than I knew what to do with, I pressed on.

Two large filing cabinets stood toward the back of the building's footprint, boasting their toughness with their misshapen bodies still standing tall amidst the debris. Picking my way toward them revealed oodles of silverware and tools strewn about underfoot. They clanged off the toes of my shoes as I navigated, playing a solemn final song. A section of pots and pans sat nearly untouched in a heap along the right side. Though covered in dirt and soot, they'd done their job. The image made me laugh out loud. It was certainly a sight to see—a crazed woman wading through the remains of a fire and laughing as she did.

If I cared what anyone thought of me, I might have been worried.

Though I'd braved my way across the wreckage, and managed to do so without any serious injuries, the cabinets did not reward me for my courage. Both sets of drawers were locked, doubly sealed with warped identical corners as though something large and heavy had fallen on them both. Cursing under my breath, I kicked them. It wasn't like I could do any more damage; however, the effort nearly landed me on my ass when I slid from the effort in the sifted ash.

Christ, couldn't *something* go my way once in a while? Maybe a forgotten diamond ring would pop up that I could hock for grocery money or a fireproof cash drawer could magically pop open as I approached—full of money, of course.

Cursing, angry that nothing had come of my venture, save for the confirmation that Leena was right and she *had* been targeted, I sulked back to the bus and boarded it. The filth covering my shoes left dark footprints on the floor of the vehicle, though neither of us commented on it. Surely, I'd leave a soot ass print on the seat as well. A whispered thanks was sent up that the seats were leather and easy enough to wipe down. I told Randy that I'd like to go home, though I asked if he could take a small detour for me and drive me past the newest renovated section of the city. As it was only a small distance off-route, and he still had a little extra time, he obliged, and in just moments a gleaming white expanse of building loomed into view.

Several years ago, in an effort to connect the far reaches of the country—and, of course, during one of the city's "renovation" projects—an entire group of city blocks were torn down overnight. Under the guise of re-invigorating the older parts of the city, a replica White House was erected in the newly vacated area. It was supposed to serve as a sort of 'summer house' for the Government; like a bad divorce, the idea was that they'd split their time between their section of the country and ours, showing what was supposed to have been equal support to both coasts of the United States.

In theory, though no one was falling for it, it did sound like a genuine attempt at inclusion—after all, it's hard to police an area that you never physically make contact with. The idea was initially met with eye-rolling and indifference, which slowly grew as time passed without the grace of Governmental presence. Mostly, the building sat empty, occasionally allowing a wedding or two on the front lawn for the uber-wealthy who could bribe hard enough to make it happen.

We drove past the gargantuan building slowly. My eyes darted left and right, up and down, searching for any sign that it, too, had been targeted. It appeared as it always had—pristine and useless.

The day had been a total bust. Well, mostly.

We returned home.

Thanking Randy, the day's earlier anger ebbing away into exhaustion, I dragged my tired bones through the parking garage with my metaphorical tail tucked between my legs.

Chapter 15 - Luke

In the morning, with the dense humidity all but strangling me, I managed two more text messages to Marie. There had been nothing but radio silence since the last round of messages, which had begun to gnaw at me. Beads of sweat trailed down my back, pulling my t-shirt tight against my spine where the rivulets had previously dried to a gritty sort of glue.

Genevieve had agreed to help me by offering her community's protection to Marie, as long as I delivered her quietly to them; though I still wasn't entirely sure what she would be getting out of the deal. She actually hadn't asked for a single thing in return, which seemed off. I suspected that to be because I'd held back the entirety of the truth from her and she was hoping that our deal would eventually lead me to revealing it. If she thought that our proximity would unveil my deepest secrets, or Marie's for that matter, she was in for a disappointing ride. I'd be damned if I let that happen. It was also possible that she was simply accepting an IOU, though the idea of owing her a favor with no barriers attached was nearly as terrifying as what I was running from to begin with. It took knowing only the bare minimum about the woman to foster a healthy distrust for her—perhaps even fear.

But I knew more than the bare minimum about Genevieve.

Strategically, it made sense that she was called into play. With just myself and my begrudging enemy-turned-temporary-ally, the chance for me to turn on him was high; though he didn't want to admit it, I was sure I could win against him if he ever made a play for me. With Genevieve backing him, there was both zero chance that I could double-cross him, and a significantly higher chance that the two of them could eliminate me without breaking a sweat, taking my bounty for their own. The only saving grace was that I was more valuable to him alive—and in excruciating mental pain—than I was dead. I hoped that was enough for him to convince Genevieve to restrain herself.

Hence my plan to keep my secrets close to the chest. It was strictly a need-to-know operation, and neither of them needed to know everything in order to play their parts. Hopefully, they never would.

Genevieve had given me a phone number before disappearing into the night, apparently finally satisfied after weeks of negotiations, and the action decided upon up to that point.

"Call this number when you're ready," she'd said. "Neutral fourth party."

A long, manicured nail had tapped at a wrinkled scrap of paper held out between us.

The shock must have been neon painted on my face because she'd laughed her horribly arousing, full-bodied laugh, then reminded me that our plan couldn't be accomplished overnight, and winked before she was just suddenly *gone*. Poof. The relief that blanketed me at her absence was overwhelming, though it turned quickly into an exhaustion that I suspected had more to do with her presence than my own emotional turmoil. Nonetheless, I'd calendared the date and made a special notation in my phone before stowing away the slip of paper.

My reliance on technology used to amuse me, once upon a time. Having been reared in an era where it was not commonplace, there had been quite a learning curve in getting myself up to speed. In fact, the age gap between us used to make Marie blush when anyone pointed it out. But I'd been determined to assimilate, both to lessen the divide between us and also because I liked to learn. Truth be told, a lot of that had been with Marie at my side, guiding me through the more difficult electronics and ensuring that I kept up-to-date through her sheer willpower alone. Once she'd no longer been part of my daily life, keeping abreast of new technology had been more to remember those times with her than it had been for any other reason. Despite the motivation behind it, I was thankful for the mostly-unconscious use of technology.

But thinking of her was always a double-edged sword. Thousands of memories of Marie tried to shoot forward in my mind, angry that I wouldn't let them surface.

An ache in my heart nearly brought me to my knees as I shoved dirty clothes into my duffel with much more force than was necessary. God, I missed her. The long strap ripped free from its connection to my bag, releasing a groan of frustration from me along with it. It was so hard to control my strength through the emotion; I'd never been good at it, and the millions of gaping scars in my past should have been lesson enough for me to get a handle on myself. Yet, without Marie's gentle presence to tamp down the rising fear and rage, I remained the fool I'd always been. Frankly, when I was on my own it was difficult enough to keep bodies from dropping when my emotions ran hot, let alone soothing them to less than temper tantrums.

Flashes of her face swam through my vision, first smiling and happy but then disappointed, pained from the ocean of secrets I refused to reveal to her. My darling, hard-headed Marie, too curious for her own good. It was cruel that fate would give a man with so many horrible skeletons in his closet such a devastating amount of love for a woman with a penchant for sticking her nose too far into everything she found even remotely interesting.

Yet, I wouldn't dare change a thing about her.

That was a lie.

There was one thing that I *had* changed about her, and she had no idea.

A wave of regret slapped me hard enough that I rocked back into reality, to my current mission. The plan was set into place; I just had to follow it and never risk contacting either of my two co-conspirators ever again. I stepped out into the bleak sunlight, constricted in walls of air that had no business being so dense. *He* leaned against the driver's side door of my vehicle, an amused smile playing at his lips as though he'd sensed the pain within me and very much enjoyed it.

He probably did, on both accounts.

Insects hummed nearby, somehow reveling in the nearly unbreathable climate. An ocean of greenery enveloped us, appearing to strand the hut on an island of reprieve from the tall trees and lush overgrowth. The singular trail, barely large enough for my SUV—which was strange because a standard vehicle would labor immensely trying to navigate the forest terrain—nestled covertly underneath the branches of a gum tree that even I would struggle to uproot, if I'd needed to. I was no small man.

I called out to him, egging him on though I knew it was no good for either of us. "Three full weeks of heated negotiation in that tiny space didn't give you your fill of me?"

His head tilted to slide a look in my direction, but he only stared. Apparently, he intended to neither take the bait, nor answer the question. Instead, he asked one of his own.

"Do you know why I'm doing this for you, despite what you've done to me?"

Nodding gently, I stepped toward him. "Because it's going to devastate me. Because she will never want anything to do with me again when it's all over. It's fair. An eye for an eye; Marie in exchange for—"

Harshly, more of a bark of anger than real words, he cut me off. "Don't!" His chest heaved, suppressed violence pushing to the surface. "Don't you dare say her name, you fucking monster. I don't know how you can even live with yourself after what you've done. I know that I can barely stand to look at you."

He was right. That didn't mean I had to like it, but he was.

We stood in silence, the broken strap of my bag dragging along the ground behind me as I swayed, trying desperately to shove down my knee-jerk reaction to the threat in his tone. The already thick air was charged with the potential for violence, nearly electric. One tiny misstep would send my plan tumbling into the abyss. Though I'd never dare admit it out loud, there was no one else who could do what he was capable of; without him, the fallout would be catastrophic. In that moment, I needed him nearly as much as I needed Marie.

His form vaulted from my car door, but instead of moving toward me, he turned his back and headed for the tree line. Like a giant magnet, the energy trailed him, leaving me shivering both from the sudden chill that had nothing to do with the temperature, and the desire to chase down my enemy. The instincts would never fade, no matter how long or hard I fought them down. I held my place until he vanished entirely, barely daring to breathe through the loose chains of restraint I'd metaphorically draped over myself. It was not a time to take any amount of risk. There were already more people involved than there ever should have been, and it made me itchy. I released the tension in my muscles one by one, working my way down my body until I felt that I could drive without the threat of ripping the steering wheel from its home and forcing myself to find another way to travel back across the country. If I had to ask one more damn favor from either of the two bastards I'd just contractually bedded, it *would* be the death of me.

With a sigh, I carefully placed myself in the driver's seat and set off in the direction of home. My cell phone remained silent on the way, the only communication received being several hundred emails from clients and contractors who'd inquired about my sudden 'vacation'. No word from Marie. I did, however, pause to read an email flagged with the 'high importance' tag from a media contact I'd bribed for a heads-up on specific information before it was released. Seems he'd paid off on more than one account. Scanning the article, my stomach rolled with a sickness that hinted at permanency.

If ever there was a time to use a forbidden curse word.

Punching buttons quickly, I ended the GPS navigation and re-routed myself, pushing the gas pedal harder than any law-abiding citizen ever should.

God was surely peeing on me, I mused, as fat drops sailed into my windshield for the remainder of my drive. It didn't manage to stop me from making the trip in record time.

The badge in my hand was, *technically*, not mine. Waving it against the pad at the entrance of the parking garage, the arm blocking the path lifted, welcoming me into the mouth of the structure. An honest man would have returned it ages ago, and, truly, I'd had no intention of using it except in the case of an emergency. Not even so much as a peep in the form of communication for weeks did constitute an emergency in my book.

Navigating to the first of two spots for apartment 314, the engine died and a calming silence flooded in. A few deep breaths later and I headed for the elevator, which dumped me just outside my destination's front door. I knocked first like a civil person would, but after several moments and two more unanswered attempts, my patience melted away. From my pocket—nicked from my glove box, where I tended to keep a spare set at all times, *for emergencies*—the lock pick set emerged and made quick work of the basic key lock that the complex manager was much too cheap to upgrade or replace, and much too stubborn to allow a generous donor to take care of on their behalf. It was a fight I'd brought, and lost, many times in my years with Marie.

Swinging the door wide, I stepped carefully inside and shut it behind me. Utter silence greeted me, aside from the TV which screamed out replays of news reports from days prior. A toothbrush lay absently on the floor. Marie had to be home; there was nowhere else for her to be. Try as she might, she would not be avoiding me any longer. I had a plan for her.

Chapter 16 - Marie

It was nowhere near dawn when I was jolted awake by a sound in my apartment. Eyes bleary, sitting upright in a pool of blankets and covered in the thinnest of soft clothing, there was no hope at all in defending against an attacker. It was more likely that I could seduce a stranger than it was that I could battle it out with them, especially in my current situation.

Still, I rolled silently out of bed and tiptoed across the room. There was absolutely nothing within reach to use as a weapon, and I cursed myself for not being more prepared.

Of course someone would check here. I knew that just as surely as I'd known that the pawn shop would be destroyed before I even checked; if someone was looking for Leena, her trail would lead them right to my rickety front door—which, frankly, was about as burglar-proof as a cardboard box could get.

I visualized the intruder entering my room in my head as I hid behind the door and tried my hardest to plan my attack. If they were looking for Leena, is it possible that they'd let me live?

Thinking back to the rubble of the pawn shop and the fire at the store, I decided that it wasn't likely. I'd have to fight for my life.

Footfalls on the cheap laminate flooring echoed slightly, the heaviness hinting that it was more likely to be a man slinking around than a woman. I crouched down, pressed my ear against the wall to try to judge the distance and direction. To my utter disappointment, the door flung open and crashed against me, pinning me to the wall and cracking so forcefully against my knees that they refused to react for several seconds. Stunned, panicked, I pushed to my feet as quickly as I could and shoved the door back at the body on the other side with all my might. It collided against him, throwing him off balance.

A deep brown jacket, which looked nearly black in the dark, wrinkled as the wearer's shoulders hunched together at his neck. He was wearing rumpled trousers and fancy dress shoes, which seemed to be both an unusual and amateur choice for breaking and entering. The thought blossomed the tiniest bit of courage in me. If I was dealing with an amateur, I might just make it out of the encounter alive.

Wasting no more time, I leaped at the man's back, clinging to him like a spider monkey the second I made contact. Both of my legs wrapped tightly around his chest, pinning his arms as best I could under the muscle of my thighs. My hands, empty as they were, pressed against his head, controlling the movement, and against his throat, miming a weapon that wasn't there. The threat had to seem real.

"Marie?"

Familiarity slammed into me, tightening my grip around the body beneath me to a crushing pressure. I recognized the voice, but I didn't like the person it belonged to any more just because I knew them. In fact, their presence in my house at all still made them suspicious, regardless of their relationship to me.

"Christ, I'm glad you're okay."

Was he?

"Are you going to let me go?"

Truthfully, there were about a million ways he could have badly hurt me in that position. I'd taken the risk because I thought my life was in danger, and although I wasn't entirely convinced yet that it wasn't, there was a worm of doubt threading through me. Slowly, he turned and lowered me to the bed so that I could dismount as gently as possible. When he swung around to crouch and look me over, I suddenly felt naked, embarrassed. Then those feelings quickly turned to irritation.

"What are you doing here, Luke?"

There was a pause, a brief moment where his face sobered, nearly held a look of pain, and then it was gone as though it had only ever been alive in my imagination. The scent of his skin so close pushed a shiver through my body, which Luke, thankfully, mistook for a reaction to the cold once the adrenaline had receded. He strode across the room to my dresser, pulled out several items, and tossed them to me. I had no need to ask how he'd been able to get in; Luke was the only reason that I knew how to use lock pick tools, myself.

"Get dressed, we have to leave."

"Why?"

"Marie, don't argue with me. I'm glad that you tried to defend yourself, truly, but you'd have been killed if it hadn't been me in your house today. We need to go. Quickly."

"Is this about Leena going missing?"

He didn't show any amount of surprise over the information, as though he'd already known. Birds of a feather, indeed. Our eyes met for far too long, heat rising up in me for more than one reason. Though he affected me effortlessly, my response was typically not either anger *or* arousal—it was both in equal measure. A challenge hung between us, thickening the air in the room before Luke decided that he'd had enough of it and stalked out through the threshold, swinging the door closed behind him. His steps placed him at the end of the hallway, but he moved no further from there. Apparently, he'd wait.

Confused, still slightly stunned by the whole ordeal, I dressed despite my complaining knees. My mind flashed back to the text message he'd sent weeks ago: 'We need to talk'. I'd ignored it, just as I'd intended to continue doing, but it never occurred to me that the subject could have been something other than my relationship with him. If Luke was involved in whatever was happening, or knew anything about it, he could be the key to finding Leena. That was worth putting up with him for.

The rationalization that Luke's involvement in whatever was happening in the world might also be linked to the secrets he'd been keeping from me, spurred me on. It might very well have been a two-birds-with-one-stone situation that had fallen into my lap.

It was still dark outside, I discovered as I peeked through my bedroom blinds. My cell phone was left abandoned on the kitchen counter last night and I'd never bothered placing a clock anywhere else in the house besides my nightstand. Unfortunately, it appeared to have broken in the scuffle, lying on the ground in three very distinct pieces. The absence of bird chatter outside the window told me that it should be around one in the morning. When was the last time I'd seen one in the morning? Not long enough ago, that was for sure.

Fully dressed, with Luke's alluring aroma still wafting around inside my head, I sat on the bed to think. A million questions wanted to burst from my mouth, including asking Luke whether he was ready to spill the secrets he'd been so intent on keeping. If he did, would that fix the chasm between us? I wanted to say no, but my heart was doing somersaults at the idea.

If I was being honest with myself, with the threat of danger winding down, I couldn't deny the effect that it, in combination with Luke, was having on my body.

"Focus on the present situation," I chastised myself out loud, hoping for the words to stick.

A gentle knock sounded on the bedroom door, followed by it being pushed open without so much as a pause. I glowered, shielding my peaked nipples with a hand.

"It's time to go."

"What if I wasn't dressed yet?"

"That's a chance I was willing to take."

I watched emotion flash across his face and chose, wisely, to ignore it. He held my phone out to me, which I took, and then gestured for me to walk ahead of him to the front door. Two steps in front, I turned and blocked the path, forgetting all about the heat between my legs.

Tired of the state of the world, tired of the constant questions buzzing around inside me, tired of the anger at things kept secret, and more than a little exhausted from it all, I was no longer going to be playing by anyone else's rules. Holding out a hand to halt Luke, his fists clenched in restrained frustration as a response. He'd never dared lift a finger to me before, but the gesture placed the smallest of hesitation in my words.

As I was learning, you never truly knew anyone.

"I'm not going any further until you answer some questions."

"We don't have time for this," he pleaded, a hint of desperation circling the edges of his words.

"We have nothing *but* time," I countered, taking a bold step forward that sent him back one. "Why do I need to leave in such a hurry?"

The most handsome face I'd ever known darkened instantly to something dangerous, a hint of the murkiness that took home inside him. I held my ground. I would not be pushed aside any longer. Whatever evil was living in him needed to face me, once and for all.

"Answer me, Luke."

"You know I could just make you come with me."

My own face matched the intensity of his. "You could try."

"Marie." He was angry, more furious than I'd ever seen him before. Nostrils flaring with the effort to fight his breathing back to normal, I was suddenly aware of a thread of fear growing inside me; but I would not back down. He leaned in toward me. I held steady.

With Luke's face mere inches from mine, his endless brown eyes sucking me into his will, it took enormous effort to keep my wits about me. The heat from his skin radiated warmth into my own, ensuring that every part of me was well aware of exactly how close we were standing. Strings of dark brown hair hung loose in front of his forehead, broadcasting the angle at which he had to lean downward to meet my face with his own.

I may have felt other things, but intimidation was not one of them. I clenched my thighs and steeled my voice.

"You've been keeping secrets from me for years. I let you keep them. Now you're here, telling me that I have to leave my own home at an instant's notice, when my friend is missing and the world has gone to shit. If you know something, you'd better share it before I start taking matters into my own hands."

Silence descended on us, cocooning our fight into a world of its own; the problems of the outside couldn't touch us when it was just Luke and I, in that moment. A small part of me wished that the scenario was under better terms—that I could reach up and crush his mouth against mine, as I'd longed to do so many times since we'd parted ways. My resolve was stronger than that, thanks to the passing of time that I had used to reinforce my will.

If he truly felt the need to remove me from my apartment in any expeditious way, he'd have to answer my questions. It was that simple. It was not a lie that he could physically remove me if he wanted to, but he'd have a hell of a time doing it. Loud, struggling, difficult extraction did not seem to be on the agenda, based on the catlike way he'd entered my home. The ball was in his court; what he did with it would tell me exactly how dire the situation truly was.

Instead of responding, he clicked his tongue, sighed, and brushed past me toward my living room. It was an interesting enough turn of events that I followed, but I did not help him when it became apparent that he was searching for the remote to the TV. Instead, I watched, bemused and slightly satisfied with the reminder that not everything Luke did was graceful and perfect. My lack of assistance did not go unnoticed, and he shot me a look that could have wilted flowers when he finally fished the remote out from between the couch cushions and flicked the TV to a different news channel—one of only three that still seemed to be broadcasting regularly.

A bright white glow instantly lit the room, neon yellows and deep reds flashing across the screen intermittently.

Another emergency broadcasting.

We both watched in silence as the reporter wrapped up the segment and started anew, rehashing the same information over again so that anyone tuning in would have the opportunity to hear the story in full. She seemed tired as she recited the lines—borderline detached, truthfully— though anyone forced to read the same block of text over and over, while remaining entirely serious and professional about it, would likely feel the same. Large, dark bags hung under her eyes, shooting a guilty thrill of commiseration through me at the realization that I was not the only person struggling through what was happening around us all.

Sparing a glance in Luke's direction, who was turned away from the TV and watching only for my expression, I pulled a face. Flawless as usual, the chaos didn't seem to be having any effect on him at all. Lucky bastard.

Flinching under the scrutiny of his gaze, which had not wavered, I returned my attention to the TV just as the image changed and a photo engulfed the screen.

The face of a gorgeous woman with nearly burnt orange hair filled my vision. Her full lips were painted black to match the swish of dark, thick eyeliner, though only one eye could be seen because the left half of her face was covered in a dense curtain of those luxurious orange locks. She did not smile, though her unnaturally deep red eyes held humor. After a moment, the image began to move and I realized that it was a video. Tipping her head to the side, staring directly into the camera, her hair fell away from her face and a smattering of silver earrings could be seen trailing up her ear lobe. She was uniquely attractive—enough so that I wondered if she modeled professionally.

Then she spoke.

As her mouth opened, formed words that poured from the screen, my mind recoiled. Tiny fangs protruded from behind her lips, glistening white against the dark paint across her mouth.

"You may be wondering who is responsible for the turmoil you've experienced lately. It would be easy to say that it is me, but I am only one of many. My name is Genevieve, and I am the second-in-charge of the vampires; quite nearly the biggest of the baddest, you could say. We are searching for something that has been hidden from us and we will not stop until we find it. There's no use running, no use hiding, because we will find what we're looking for. You humans will die at our hands, one by one, until we receive it. There is nothing that you can do to stop it because this is, simply, the natural order of things. It's up to you now."

The video paused on a hideously violent smile, fangs included.

Luke still watched me.

"Is this a joke?"

The weight of his gaze was intense. His head jerked from side to side only once.

"So there are vampires. Out there." I waved a hand in the air to encompass, well, everything.

"Yes."

"And they're after Leena?"

"Yes."

"*Why?*"

Shoulders bouncing lightly in a soft shrug, he moved toward me. "Perhaps they believe she has what they're looking for. All I know is that we need to get you out of here."

"And the natural order she mentioned—vampires killing humans. What in the hell is that?"

"I would guess it's their justification for killing. You know, the hunters and the prey. The natural order."

My face squished in thought. I wanted to be frightened, but it wasn't happening. It felt too make-believe. "Are you scared?"

A brief pause. Then, quietly, "You have no idea."

"You don't show it."

A response wasn't provided, nor was it needed. Luke had always been the strong, silent type. If he thought that showing his fear would help me in any way, he'd do it, but until then it would be shoved down into the same hole I imagined was already bursting at the seams with the half-truths he hoped would also never have to surface.

Thoughts turned over in my mind, piling on top of one another as my brain raced to absorb the new information. Vampires existed. Vampires were targeting Leena.

Wait a minute. If the vampires were still looking for Leena, that means they didn't know for sure if she had what they wanted because they hadn't caught her yet. Leena was probably alive, and likely still on the run. However…

How did Luke know all of that? Damn it all, he was *still* keeping secrets, and not just his own, but about my best friend as well.

Raw steel shaping my words in a giant sign above my head wouldn't have made them any more firm. "I *cannot* do this with you, Luke."

A yell broke from his mouth, half rage and half desperation.

"Listen to me," I said firmly. I waited for the silence to follow. "Leena isn't here. If they're coming here, that means they don't know where she is; since I've had no luck finding her, and they seem to be hot on her trail, they're my best bet to figuring out where she went."

"We can look for her together. I will help you. Just, *please*, we have to go. Now."

I gave him a hard, appraising look. "I'm not going with you until you tell me what the secret is that you've been keeping from me. How do I even know that I can trust you?"

A thought blossomed, taking root and winding itself into my brain. I scrutinized him, head to toe, looking for any signs of proof of the accusation I was making. I saw none, but then again, I didn't exactly know what I was looking for. So I asked.

"Are you a vampire?"

He laughed at that. In fact, he laughed so hard that at the end of it he had no more anger and, apparently, no more words left either. When he was finished, and he was able to breathe again, he left my apartment with no further confrontation and only a disbelieving shake of his head.

Christ, was my life complicated.

Chapter 17 - Jesse

"I need you to do something for me," he demanded, his dark eyes daring me to refuse. I never got the chance, as he continued in a tone that told me clearly who he thought was in charge of the conversation. "I know what you are."

Shock slackened my face into an unreadable mask while I processed the information. I knew Luke Therion by proxy, from the numerous times he'd starred in Marie's stories. I knew all about how he broke her heart. What I didn't know was how he'd learned about me. Truthfully, it wasn't even that he knew *what* I was that had thrown me for a loop; it was how he'd come by the knowledge of my relationship to Marie.

It was possible that he was bluffing anyway.

"What could I possibly do for you?" As if I needed to, I shrugged my shoulders to encompass my current, imprisoned, situation.

Luke was not deterred by that fact. He'd come with a purpose. "Use your magic on Marie. I need to know what she sees." Again, he gave me no chance to interject before throwing another explosive piece of information into the air between us. "You are a siren, aren't you?"

He said it quietly, but not with any inflection. Just a fact. A tidbit of knowledge; no clue as to what he *thought* of the information I'd yet to admit to.

There was only one way he could possibly have that intel, and it wasn't good—not for me, and not for Marie. Luke was one of *them*.

If that was the case, there was no use denying anything. He was already as sure as he needed to be.

"Why would I do that?"

"Because I'm going to save you a hell of a guilt trip in return—and I'll save your life, as well." Something flashed in his eyes. I thought I recognized it. "Marie plans to do something very stupid—something that's either going to ruin her life or get her killed, and she's doing it on your behalf."

I opened my mouth to argue, but he held up a hand. "I know that you don't want her to, but we both know she's going to anyway, so let's just cut to the chase."

The weight of his gaze made me feel like a mouse caught in the sights of a hungry hawk. Marie's stories hadn't given me any warning about how intimidating Luke was.

"I'm going to save her the trouble and do it myself. I'll get you out of here, and then you'll do what I've asked."

No room for question.

Was he saying he'd break me out, like Marie had planned to do?

I'd been resigned to my fate and more than ready for my long life to be over, as repentance for the lives I'd taken in the name of my own twisted version of justice. So what interest would he have in saving my life, unless he'd simply intended to take it himself after the fact?

Was that it? The accolades of killing a bona fide siren?

It had to be.

Luke's expression shifted, softened. What I'd seen before in his eyes resurfaced, and I knew I was right the first time. He was madly, deeply in love with Marie—enough that he'd give his life for hers without question.

I, of anyone, would know what love looked like.

And, truthfully, what he was offering *would* very likely save her life, crazy as her plan was bound to be. It might also end mine, just as I'd planned by staying on death row in the first place.

Win-win.

I reached a hand across the table between us and took no offense when he didn't do the same. "As long as you can promise me that she won't know the truth about me, you have a deal."

He nodded, and was gone. The guards returned as he exited, their stint of willful disobedience of the rules only as lengthy as Luke's presence. Interesting.

I'd made a deal with a powerful enemy; one that I didn't intend to keep.

If Luke was who I thought he was, I needed to stay *alive* and on the outside to protect Marie. To keep her as far away from Luke as possible, before he learned what she was hiding and decided to exact justice on her as well.

The most amicable of the guards lifted me by the underside of my arm and guided me gently back to my cell. I hardly noticed the trek back across the cement floor, hardly processed the jeering from the other inmates as we passed. I was busy thinking, plotting the first move I'd take to betray him when Luke broke me out of death row.

Part Two

Chapter 18 - Marie

It'd been months since the emergence of vampires in my narrow world, and none of the questions that needed answers had received any of them. It was clear to me that, with the reveal of otherworldly beings such as vampires, more was likely lurking around the corner. Lo and behold, two months after the vampires announced their existence, so did witches. If nothing else, my suspicions about Leena had been confirmed; she was something else entirely. The news began, collectively, calling them Obscure.

Police presence increased slightly for a few weeks, patrol cars circling the streets religiously, but they vanished as quickly as they'd appeared, retreating back to whatever depths they'd been hiding in since the beginning of the chaos. My guess would be that they realized quickly enough that they were either outmatched, outmanned, or outsmarted. After all, how did you tell exactly which of the unfamiliar faces was Obscure and which was human? It was no wonder they'd given up the ghost. It was a disappointment, however, because with the fuzz scuttling through the city, hope had returned that news of Leena would surface.

No such luck.

Every call still remained unanswered and unreturned, no one having seen her in months. Luke had attempted at least once more to reach out to me, but it took only one round of deleting notifications for him to take the hint. Whatever danger he thought I was in would be mine to face alone until he decided to come clean about everything.

My life had devolved into cycles of traipsing through the city, notating which new buildings were touched by vandalism or arson, whether there were any hints of Obscure, and copious descriptions of any people spotted out and about. The bus drivers—Randy and Carmen, the only two still operating—had practically become family, acting as my personal chauffeurs and waving me away when I tried to pay fare for the rides. Honestly, though my landlord had never come to collect rent since everything had begun, I was still running dangerously low on funds and silently thanked them when they did it. Temporary utility outages had become a regular occurrence, prompting me to leave the house whenever possible to avoid having to work around them. If I had to guess, the landlord had high-tailed it out of the area at the first sign of danger, leaving the residents to fend for ourselves. Him, and most of the other building residents.

Most often, with the sparse smattering of riders, Carmen and Randy took me directly to my destination, patiently waiting while I jogged street blocks on foot to catalog any changes. I stored all of the information in binders that sat piled onto the bookshelves in my apartment. There was no real purpose to the routine other than to keep me occupied and optimistic that if Leena surfaced, I'd know. There may have perhaps been a small amount of satisfaction gleaned from feeling as though I was being productive despite the rest of the world seemingly giving up.

In a binder separate from the ones where I logged my routes, I dutifully noted all memories of Leena that could point me in the direction of what she truly was. The night at my apartment claimed the top of the first page, with notes in the margins to detail every fleeting inner thought in case I forgot any of them in the passage of time. Behind my notes on Leena sat a page each on vampires and witches, empty as they were besides the information given during their separate grand reveals. The majority of that information was salvaged from the videos they provided to the media, and from any and all news reporting that had mentioned them since. It was defeating to see the large voids where facts should have been, but there were just so many unknowns—too many guesses and not enough answers.

The last page of my secret binder had only one word, followed by a giant question mark down the page: Luke.

It was more than strange to me that Luke had knowledge of the Obscure, but when added to the other secrets he'd had—and kept from me—thus far, his name on the pages of that particular binder felt right. A mountain of memories and snippets of conversation could fill those pages, just as I'd been filling Leena's, but something about the situation with Luke felt *different*. There was no basis for that feeling at all, only a tiny woman in a world of Obscure who was helplessly, and resistantly, in love with a man who had charmed her out of more than one tense conversation on the matter.

There was nothing to do besides gather more intel.

In fact, since Genevieve had come forward in representation of the vampires, speculation had kicked up around why the second-in-charge had done so without mention of who was *actually* in charge. The leader of the vampires was being cloaked, and the only good reason for that was so that their identity could remain concealed as they walked among us humans. I was suspicious of anyone and everyone.

At the first stop of my daily routine, I logged five people milling about. While it wasn't a crowd by any means, it *was* a higher count than I'd seen in recent weeks. During a normal route, I'd also have walked the block on foot to check the status of the buildings. Deciding not to take the risk of mingling with potential Obscure, I instead nodded Randy onward to the next stop. Three more people wandered there, just a small group of two and a singular wary man out for a stroll. I noted them all but continued on within the safety of the vehicle. The pattern continued; more people than I'd seen in months seemed to be casually strolling about without a care in the world. It was as if they intended to simply *ignore* the elephant in the universe, dispatching it by sheer will alone.

It was startling, an unexpected pocket of normality from a life that seemed long gone. The question hung in my mind, dared not spoken aloud, of whether life would ever be 'normal' again. Either Obscure were more confident since they were common knowledge, and felt that they were safe to roam free from the guise of humanly fear, or the humans were no longer willing to live under the thumb of previously-unnamed beings since they'd been identified. I guessed putting a face to the villain was all it took for the world to start getting over it. Was that an uprising, or was it cockiness?

I completed my circuit without moving from the discomfort of the worn cloth seat.

To shift an odd day immediately into an unfortunate one, Luke was propped against my apartment door when I arrived back home. I tried, unsuccessfully, to duck back out through the parking garage door before I'd been spotted. As soon as the hefty door slammed closed, shutting me out into the stifling, stale air of the garage, I sighed in relief—but my short-lived solace crashed down around me as the echo of another closing door chased me out.

Muttering to myself, I jogged out of the parking structure and took a hard left onto the street. Two bodies leaned casually against a building at the top of the small hill there, the soft mumbling of conversation floating between them. With the cover of dark, I felt vulnerable to the things I couldn't see, but grateful still for the cover in which I could hide from Luke.

Despite my quick pace, it took only seconds for Luke's strong hand to wrap around my arm. His darkly bronze skin was a drastic contrast to mine, always the perfect effortlessly golden shade that made me envious. Staring at his fingers, I was struck once more with a jealous, selfish streak that threatened to tip the scales of my carefully controlled composure. Why was it at all fair that he was gorgeous, strong, financially stable, great in bed, and so, so amazing to me besides the well of hidden information that he kept locked away inside? I wanted to both slap him and kiss him at the same time.

"Marie, I swear this is important. It's about Leena."

Jerking out of his gasp, I turned to eye the pair that still loitered up the street, oblivious to mine or Luke's presence. Though I'd only admit it under strict torture, the feeling of safety was radiating through me, coincidentally in time with the feeling of Luke's breath against the back of my neck. Carelessly, I'd have walked past the strangers purely out of pettiness, but with his body next to mine, the lingering feeling of his skin on my own, the peace of mind was unrivaled.

I swung back around and shoved him backward. I continued forward, pushing at him, the two of us making an awkward stride back toward the parking garage. He never once raised a hand to defend himself against what he had to know was only a frustrated version of a slapping contest. The muscles of his chest likely did more damage to my hands than I had done to him, but I reminded myself silently that I was sure I could have done real damage, had I wanted to.

When we were close enough that I could turn and walk into the dimly lit structure of the parking garage again, and once my anger had dissipated from the outburst, I led the way back into my unfortunate apartment. The TV was on, as always, but muted so that only the flashing light interrupted the calm of the room. Flopping onto the couch in the most unladylike of ways, leaving barely enough room for Luke to sit beside me, I pressed the button to stop the images on screen and turned my attention to the man I least wanted to give my attention to at that moment.

"Go on, then. Where is she?"

He stared hard at me, his mouth pressed into a tight line—whether from my attitude or the news he intended to hit me with, I wasn't sure. There wasn't even a hint of sadness in his eyes when he observed me, only the weary ghost of a light that once shone so brightly there. Leaning his bulk against the wall in front of me, attempting an undaunted reaction to my clearly attention-seeking behavior, he spoke.

"She's dead."

I closed my eyes, let my head fall back against the couch. Somewhere deep inside, I'd known already. Even past fights with her had never lasted so long; she'd have called and apologized months ago, spouting news of her life since our brawl and chastising me about the awful way I'd been living my own. She *would* have, had she been alive.

They'd found her, then, and she didn't have what they wanted.

Expecting sadness or anger to rise up and meet the truth, it was disturbing even to myself that only exhaustion surfaced instead. There should have been tears. Where were denial, anger, or bargaining? Gone. Lost in the tide of fear and uncertainty that drowned me long ago, probably.

"Why?"

It was not a question that anticipated an answer. It faded into the air between us, neither wanting to break the spell and tip the other into any particular emotion. I opened my eyes to find Luke statuesque against the wall, hands buried deep in the pockets of his khaki trousers. Perhaps he also found my reaction odd.

"What are you, Luke?" I asked. Then, in a whisper seething with hurt, "Why won't you tell me?"

"I can't—" The words died on his tongue. There was no hint of tension in the air, no urge to bridge the crater between us, knowing that only sadness and desperation lay in wait on either end. Neither of us spoke for several minutes, until he sighed with all his might and started again. "There are people who want this to stop. I'm one of them. Really, I think that's all that matters right now."

He was right. It was all that mattered in that particular moment. There would be no more Leena, no more normal life. There were vampires and witches and god only knew what else, and that was our new world. Mine, and Luke's, and the legion of humans who'd been attempting to smoke out the Obscure on their own; self-proclaimed vigilantes. It seemed that we were all on the same side, after all.

So why did I still feel so alone?

Chapter 19 - Marie

After Luke's harrowing news, I'd asked to be left alone. There was more that he wanted to say—I could tell—though he did hesitantly accept my offer to reconvene again later to finish the conversation. It was a true testament to the weight of the event that he'd left me with less than an entire checkup as a prerequisite. He was nothing if not a bit overprotective, and a gargantuan heap secretive.

In fact, it hadn't occurred to me until after he'd gone that he'd not made another peep about stealing me away from my apartment. For all his bravado that night, it didn't seem that it was really that big of a deal anymore. Funny thing, that.

To mentally prepare for another encounter with him, a distraction was in order. While I hadn't felt the pull of him in the brief time he'd delivered the news about Leena, I attributed that more to the state of my emotional well-being; putting any amount of hope into the idea that I was falling out of love with the asshole was too dangerous. To be sure I would be well prepared for another meeting, I needed to clear my head. Pronto.

I decided I'd try a new tactic. I set out on foot, wrapping around through the parking garage to take the route that had been interrupted the night before. There were no bystanders for the first leg of the journey, no one to cast my suspicions on or reflect my innermost insecurities toward as we crossed paths. It was only me and the general nonsense banging around in my head that had become, startlingly, more familiar than I'd have liked to admit.

Too much had happened in recent months. The events and information all sort of jumbled together into an ugly lump, like badly burnt rice when it became a dark, mushy mess of nothing. My thoughts were overcooked, my brain in semi-liquid hell. I was waiting for a pinch or startle to wake me from the nightmare of what my life had become—what all of our lives had become.

Enveloped in my thoughts, I wandered further from home than I had intended to, nearly bumping distractedly into the first pedestrian I'd encountered amidst the fog of my own churning emotions. The misstep forced me to stop and reassess my own personal safety. There was no time to lose focus. One single forgetful moment could push me into the hands of a vampire, or worse. I slowed to a crawl and glanced around. Bright and lush, I almost didn't recognize the area.

Even the small, circuitous walks I'd been taking while attempting to gather information had made tremendous strides at building my stamina and forcing me back into the physique I'd have had years ago if I didn't love sweets so much. The path around the lake was a significantly greater distance than I'd have attempted for several more weeks; it was exhilarating to find that I was more capable than I'd thought. Take *that*, Luke. I probably actually *could* do some damage, if I wanted to.

The thought made me wonder what else I was capable of.

Well, besides agreeing to a voluntary meeting with Luke. Even I'd surprised myself with that feat of strength.

The day was what would reasonably pass for pleasant. Birds sang from the trees, fleeing when approached a little too closely, and while it was warm out, it wasn't the kind of weather that baked you alive the second you stepped into the open air. The sun was still a bit too bright for it to be called beautiful, but it was close.

Several of the shops had reopened in recent weeks—even those that neighbored businesses that had burnt down not so long ago. The radical humans had taken to committing arson themselves, in an attempt to root out Obscure, causing nearly as much destruction as the Obscure had. Double the trouble. What they intended to do with any Obscure they discovered, I had no earthly idea—and I suspected that they didn't either—but the action itself seemed to make everyone feel more confident, more in control.

It was either that, or a large part of the remaining population had been exhaustedly searching for any tiny reason to pretend that the past several months hadn't happened. Whatever the reason, more people braved the outdoors than ever before. It raised the question as to how many of them were Obscure and how many were human.

I wondered how long it would take for realization to hit the general population that every home or business or so-called Obscure that they accused was another human life that they'd destroyed. For nothing. Who really had the higher body count when you got right down to it—the

Obscure or the humans? And how could you truly discern one monster from another at that point anyway?

Though, on the other hand, anything that allowed for returning to a semblance of our old life was strangely appealing. Not that any of us really *enjoyed* our old lives, but it did seem alluring when compared to the circumstances surrounding us lately. Morale seemed to be at an all-time high since it had all begun, despite the fact that it was nothing more than false security.

I jogged past yet another shop with their 'open' sign proudly displayed in their door window. The hand-painted sign above the entrance caught my eye, making my thoughts churn. An idea weaseled itself in my mind, taking hold like a leech. On a whim, I opened the paint-chipped door and stepped inside. Like fate throwing a wrench into my plans, the power failed just as I slid the door shut behind myself, washing me in dim natural light. The damn electrical rations were getting ridiculous. Two more shops across the road flicked to dark along with the room in which I stood. Within seconds, a rather young, gangly gentleman emerged from a hallway further in the building, grumbling to himself under his breath. He paused when he noticed me standing in the entrance, quickly looking over each shoulder as though it was more likely I'd be here to see anyone else besides him.

Just you and me, buddy.

He took in my casualty, the easy way I approached him, cogs whirling in overtime inside his head. Confidence was a double-edged sword, and I had it in spades. Sensing his unease, I took a step back and held up my hands. "I'm not, um," I started. Sheesh, how long had it been since I'd spoken to a human other than Luke and the bus drivers? "I'm not *one of them.*"

His eyes narrowed behind thick glasses, magnifying his skeptical expression. The blond crop of hair on his head was stuck up in patches and badly in need of a trim. Sleeping at the office would be the culprit—I'd bet on it. I tried again.

"Actually, I'm trying to compile some information on them. I was wondering how difficult it would be to obtain copies of previously run newspapers. Specifically, ones with mentions of them and the bodies that were found before they—you know," I trailed off, unsure how to continue. Saying that they'd 'come out' seemed offensive. I shrugged, hoping he understood. It occurred to me, belatedly, that he could also be an Obscure, himself. His caution could easily be faked, mimicked from any one of the other humans on the planet who dared venture out into the light.

Be careful, I reminded myself.

"Well," he said, taking a careful seat at the desk near the front door. Our eyes met in a struggle of will. He let the word hover in the air for far too long, focusing all of his attention on that one look, searching for any excuse to turn me away.

Nothing about his demeanor screamed that he trusted me, not even a tiny bit. I held my breath as he mulled over my words, angling his head to better fix me with a judgmental stare. The freckles speckling his cheeks made the shape of a star if you were to connect them with a pen. I hoped desperately that the concentration directed his way had been mistaken for earnest, or even flirtation. A come-on was a workable plan if he leaned toward telling me to take a hike.

Finally, mercifully, he spoke again. "You'll have to wait until the power's back up, but I could do it. We're talking about a lot of information, here." A pointed look. "It won't be cheap."

Biting my lip, I shoved a hand in my pocket and fingered the bills secreted away there. My refrigerator was practically empty and the last of my money was supposed to have been exclusively for fending off starvation. "How long would it take?"

"I can't say for sure. It will depend on the reliability of our utilities." He eyed the dark electrical fixtures warily. "Give me a week, I guess."

Scrunching my nose, as if it was an inconvenience to me, I pretended to consider his offer. "Alright, I'll come back then. I can pay when I pick up?" I phrased it less as a question and more as a confirmation. Confidence. In spades.

He sucked in a loud hiss of air, intentionally—not that I could blame him. A lot of us were hard-up for the cash, mostly out of work from the fires, the death, or just the fear in general. He probably needed to eat, too. I couldn't imagine many people flooding his particular brand of business any time soon, but I was certainly no meal ticket.

An eternity and a day later, he slowly nodded. I thanked him, scribbled my phone number on a loose paper at his desk so that he could call me when it was ready, and left quickly before he could change his mind.

Truly, I wasn't sure what good the newspapers would do me. Obviously, there were missed tidbits of information, as none of us were looking in the same directions then that we were more recently, but it was an unexplored avenue that gave me a thrill of excitement. The idea of unearthing just one shred of a clue that would topple me down into a well of answers—even more specific questions were acceptable at that point—was exhilarating.

Perhaps, in another life, I was a detective.

I wondered vaguely what Jesse would think of what I was doing. During our last visit, he'd once more tried to convince me to drop my plans to break him out, or to stop visiting at the very least.

Yeah, he'd definitely not approve.

Imagining the print man hustling out of his shop, realizing what a mistake he'd made to take on my job, a large helping of pep was thrust forcefully into my step. I'd come too far to turn back toward home, the path of unexplored area stretched before me beckoning for my attention. Crunchy leaves scattered across the sidewalk, tap-dancing in the barest of breezes. It felt as though nature was trying to entice me to continue. I did.

Navy skies descended quickly overhead to chase away the light. Breathing became easier, the air thinner on the heels of fading heat. An ache crawled its way into tight thigh muscle, burrowing deep to gnaw at my stamina. The length of one stride dropped into two, then three. Teeth clenched against the pain, I pushed on, sprinting through the agony until a smooth stretch of wall sprung up from around a corner and I felt compelled to stop for a rest. I'd come quite a long way. The journey back home no longer seemed an inconvenience, but a downright chore from as far out as I'd come. My concentration slipped inward, split between quieting the heaving breaths and keeping an eye out for my surroundings. A lone male crossed the narrow street as I pressed my back against the wall, his head glued to his feet as he scurried along.

Another body was a good sign; it meant the area felt safe to someone. That sounded like as good a place as any to catch my breath and soothe the screaming muscles of my legs.

Aside from my ragged inhalations, it was as quiet as could be. Behind me a large, recently empty but relatively old, business building stretched, ominous and dark. The exposed windows were intact, free of the graffiti I'd come accustomed to seeing. Only smudges of dirt and small pockets of moss broke the clean aesthetic of red brick. It was a stark contrast to the small strip of parkland nestled on the opposite side of the road. Rusted playground equipment swayed and creaked in time with my breathing. There likely hadn't been any kids squealing and tumbling on it since long before the Obscure snatched away their livelihood.

Further up the road, another figure stepped into view from one of the many side roads. The only discerning item was the bright pink that flashed on the soles of their shoes when they stepped, which told me nothing about their gender or humanity. Sweat cooling against my skin sent a shiver down my spine; or, at least that's what I told myself. It was quickly becoming too crowded for my liking.

From my peripheral I watched the crossing man finally step onto the sidewalk, uncomfortably close to me considering the state of things. The hair on my arms stood at attention. He turned abruptly on his heel, taking brisk strides past me, giving a wide berth and a withering look—as though I was the sole star of his never-ending nightmares—until he rounded the corner from where I'd emerged. A sigh pushed itself through my lips, slightly unhinging the progress I'd made to regulate my breathing. Above, the skies had darkened nearly to black, and I realized unhappily that it was much later than I'd thought it was. Damn you, summer sunlight.

I stood, stretched briefly, and limped off in the opposite direction to retrace my route back home. As I swung around the street corner, something strong and solid slammed me directly into the wall. My left shoulder cracked against the brick, pain blossoming immediately. Startled, confused, my mind reeled to understand what was happening. Before me stood the man who'd only just passed me by moments ago. His arms were bare, the short sleeves of his shirt having been cut off to show the muscle that could only have been meant to threaten. His jacket lay abandoned at his feet. Apparently, *he* was the nightmare, after all.

My body went limp for just a moment before my head snapped up, locking onto his face. A smile spread slowly, first just lips, then teeth. And then fangs.

Shit.

A single large step would have put us chest to chest, which was exactly the opposite of where I wanted to be. Thoughts flooded my brain, some insisting that it was possible to outrun him, others pleading to crack open his skull and spill the secrets inside. I was, after all, making a very amateur attempt to learn everything that I could about the vampires. Could he tell me about their leader? Perhaps, I thought ironically, that would be a faster way.

Without another soul to be seen on the stretch of street—which was probably intentional—whatever happened between the two of us would remain between the two of us. No witnesses.

One hand crushed into his pocket suddenly, fingers searching. With the knowledge that nothing good would come back out of that hidey-hole, my body acted on its own. I lunged forward, locking one hand around the wrist of his occupied one. With as much force as I could muster, I yanked him forward as my tightened fist made contact with his face—specifically, his cheek. A snarl was all the response I received, his focus entirely fixated on jerking free of my hold to retrieve the secret item from his pocket.

Whatever was in there needed to *stay* in there. Of that, I was absolutely sure.

My knee lifted to his groin just as his free hand shoved me backward. I managed to make contact with him, but not as forcefully as my back and head did with the wall, which successfully stunned me just long enough to be a problem. My hand slipped free of his wrist. The strange vampire finally lifted out a syringe, cloudy with a liquid I dared not try to identify, which he hoisted into the air between us to ensure that I got a good enough look. His arrogance did little to frighten me, as I was sure was the intent. Instead, I used the time to assess my options.

It occurred to me, several moments too late, that with the time he'd taken to retrieve the needle, he could easily have killed me instead; but he hadn't. It seemed more important to him that his needle potion make it into my body. That was possibly more terrifying than the thought that he *had* been trying to kill me.

My shoulder was on fire. His bald head reflected a nearby streetlight as he lunged at me. I tried desperately to regain my wits against the solid wall. No such luck. At the sight of his body flying toward mine, I made the split-second decision to stop using logic and let my instincts take over. I had to have *some* survival instincts, right? Weren't all humans born with them?

Like a lead weight into the ocean, I dropped my weight instantly, sliding down to the ground where my toe brushed a large piece of brick, presumably shaken loose from the building when the structure started crumbling many years ago. Gripping it tightly, wasting not even a second, I shot to my feet again, ramming the top of my head into the underside of the vampire's jaw. Hopefully, it had hurt him far more than it had hurt me, because, *jesus,* it had hurt me.

"I hope you bite your tongue off, asshole," I growled at him, swinging the brick with all my might. The goal was the side of his head.

The blow landed, but did little more than briefly stagger his large frame. My vision swam from the throbbing in my own skull. I would not die there. I couldn't. Spreading rapidly along the back of my neck, unexpected warmth tried its best to snag my attention.

Footsteps approached from the side street—the same expanse where I'd rested just moments ago—and I recalled the body that emerged onto the street from further up the road. Fearing vampire reinforcements, terror rushed to the surface, boosting my movements with a surge of speed and determination that I hadn't known I was capable of.

I swung again, but not quite in time. His hand arced toward me with the syringe at the ready, aiming directly for the exposed expanse of my neck. The speed of his movements registered far too late. I managed a small adjustment to close the gap between us and the brick connected just as his pale hand leveled with my face, jerking sideways and up so that the needle scraped across the skin of my cheek instead.

Small blood droplets pooled at the cut, threatening to run down my face in a matter of seconds. The sudden clatter of the needle on the sidewalk startled me, distracted me, so that I didn't see the vampire's other hand until a solid fist was already making contact with my face. The pain was immediate. The knowledge that a bruise would be proudly overtaking my face at any moment only served to fuel my anger. God only knew how I was going to explain it to Luke and walk away without his insistence on being attached to my hip for the next forty years. Couldn't have a repeat occurrence with a shadow that menacing.

Repeat occurrence? Luke? None of that mattered if I didn't walk away, and soon. From the reactions, and the attack itself, it was crystal clear that the vampire's goal wasn't to kill me. The only true hope that gave for me was that he'd be pulling his punches.

I would not.

With a roar that would challenge any Obscure's—and I'd bet on that—I forced my entire body weight that last small step forward and toppled us both to the ground. He took the brunt of the impact, his form crumpling briefly against the cement sidewalk; it was all the hesitation I needed. Pinning his body against the concrete, my makeshift weapon at the ready, a heinous round of blows unleashed themselves through my arm.

I dared not stop until the pool of thick blood under us was satisfactorily large and contrasted nicely against the pale pink of brains peeking through the hole in his skull. Warmth gripped my knees, reminding me of the sensation against my back. For a split second, the fear that I'd wet myself crossed my mind. It was quite the opposite. The denim of my pants sponged up the blood as it reached me and my heart beat in rhythm with the pulsing in my head. I felt excited, satisfied, dangerous.

Relieved.

The footsteps, finally reaching us both from behind, ground to a halt in the scatter of pebbles along the sidewalk. I was quick to turn, face the direction of the intruder, and raise my brick in defense. Something wet and heavy fell from the hard surface in my hand, slapped the ground. New splatters of blood blossomed on the sidewalk, as well as my arm.

The pale face of a woman stared back at me. Her snow-white hair, tucked neatly into a bun, swung in the air as she shifted her head from me to the body, and then back again. She raised her hands slowly into the air, mimicking the sign of defenselessness. Her voice was small, matching her stature, though her presence was enormous even amidst the tension bubbling threateningly all around.

"I am not here to hurt you. I heard the noise and I came to check. That's all."

The tan blouse that hung over her tiny frame matched the color donned by the figure that had come into view at the far end of the other road, before I'd decided to turn back. I glanced at the pink rim around the bottom of her shoes. Sure enough, she was the figure I'd seen up the street. That wasn't good enough.

I remained silent while my body decided whether fight or flight would be the safest move.

"You know that's a vampire, right?"

Whether she intended it that way or not, I bristled at the patronization. Annoyance surged forward to meet her. "I was made aware of that fact when his fangs were inches from my face," I snapped in response.

She smiled then, a moment's hesitation before she bared her teeth to show me that she sported no fangs of her own. "They're not exactly easy to kill. I've been following this one for some time, waiting for an opportunity to present itself." Her eyes scaled me, assessing. She looked like a proud mother. "You're something quite special."

I said nothing, letting the words hang between us. There was no need to point out that the dead vampire was only dead because he was trying not to kill me. My mood was not much in favor of small talk anyway. Her demeanor shifted, hands nesting in one another under her breasts. Suddenly, nothing about her seemed small at all. Though her face was kind, her voice evoked peacefulness and calm, and she threw an air of authority that equally intrigued and unnerved me. My guard remained high and steadfast.

"You are Marie Morrison, correct?"

An involuntary step back put my heel flush with the dead Obscure's body. The firmness of it jolted me. Along my knees, the blood-soaked cloth was growing cold. "What's it to you?"

She extended a hand, as though expecting me to shake it, but thought better of the motion halfway through and retracted it. Instead, she reached into a back pants pocket with her free hand and took a large step back as well when I stiffened in response.

"My name is Ellie. I, like you, am curious about the Obscure and I also want to end the madness. There's a way that we can do both—learn about them, *and* stop them." She lifted a business card toward me slowly, holding it determinedly when I didn't reach for it right away. "We are the New Government. We know everything. We know that you're researching Obscure on your own, that you're looking into the murders. We know that a friend of yours was recently found deceased, and that there are some questions you have surrounding both her life and her death. We know that you're running out of money. I only want to offer you a job. You can continue all of this, and we'll pay you for sharing the information that you find with us. Let us help each other." A pause. "We may even have some of the answers that you're looking for."

Snatching the card out of her hand, I pressed it into my own pocket, making a purposeful show of not looking at it even for a second. Ellie smiled again, without teeth, and nodded gently. There was no intent for further conversation. Ellie seemed content with that, shrinking back into the innocent mask of anonymity that she'd first approached me with.

Seemed everyone had a secret.

Turning to leave, I looked once more at the body lying on the ground. It was a new world, alright; apparently, when life gave you Obscure, you became a murderer.

Chapter 20 - Luke

There was no sense in pushing Marie any further about leaving her home. She was a bull-headed woman and I'd known that; my approach had been all wrong, muddled by emotion. Genevieve had betrayed us, and as of yet I had no idea whether *he* had been a part of that. The priority was always Marie.

Since she had begun to trust me again, we could make progress. A knot settled heavily in the pit of my stomach at the half-truth I'd given. I ignored it.

With a quick succession of taps on my phone screen, I penned a response to Peter for his advanced notice regarding Genevieve's video and Leena's body. It seemed that there were still some people who were reliable and trustworthy. An extra envelope of cash would find its way to his office as a thank-you gift. Another thought struck me, guiding another message to him with a request that he alert me to my own name appearing in the media. At the bottom of the email, I reminded him that I still expected immediate notice of anything related to Marie. No emails allowed for that alert, though; it required an instant phone call, repeatedly, until he spoke directly with me to relay the information.

The news of Leena's death had been taken much more lightly than expected, which only heightened my worry for Marie's mental health. To make matters worse, not only were the Obscure a threat to her, but a troubling rumor about the New Government pushing out a recruiting campaign for eager humans had piqued my anxiety as well. Marie needed to stay far, far away from the New Government and whatever protections or bribes they would offer to her. I was sure they would do both. Unfortunately, it was impossible to share my knowledge about them without sliding down a slippery slope of questions and secrets, which I knew would only push her further out of my reach.

The solution was, simply, to remain physically by her side as much as possible. If she didn't like it, too bad.

But first, I needed to know what options were still available to me.

Punching in the phone number, he answered right away.

"I know," he said, exasperation evident in his tone, even above the disgust for me being the one on the other end of the line. "Genevieve did as Genevieve does."

"Does she know?"

"She suspects."

Tension sang through my left arm. I clenched a fist tightly to cut off the urge to swing at the first object within reach. "Did *you* know?"

Momentary silence.

"I should have, but I did not." His voice was tight, clipped. It seemed that he was more than a little perturbed at the fact that she'd left him out of her plans. It did little to placate me.

"Can you do this without her? I need assurances."

"I can only try. Let me put it this way," he said, forming the words with inflection that betrayed his facade of prior planning. "If it goes sideways, there is one guaranteed way to stop it."

"We'll be right back here again. That's a temporary solution, at best."

"I'll take it *all*."

The blood drained instantly from my face. Thankful that he couldn't see it, I took a deep, steadying breath. "You won't survive that."

"I'm aware, and it will be well worth it if it comes to that. Don't contact me again until it's time, or you risk blowing this whole thing. I will do everything in my power to keep Genevieve away, but the girl is up to you."

He disconnected abruptly. I left the phone pressed to my ear, stunned. I'd known the risks of involving him and I had been fully willing to sacrifice myself to ensure success. There had been no contingency for failure, no timeline considered in which Marie suffered as a result of the plan to save her life. Until the crumbling of my careful plan.

Because of Genevieve.

I'd put too much faith in him to be able to handle it all on his own. Was there another option?

There was only one way to find out.

Resolve flooded my mind just as restlessness flooded my body. I sprang into action, running between my vehicle and home to load the trunk with supplies. Nonperishable food, clothing, and a tightly locked briefcase were all hastily dumped together, along with a few other necessities. In my bedroom, I eyed the padlocked door which barred the only entrance to the mostly-underground basement. Below, nothing but secrets lay buried. Every piece of information that could possibly be used to unravel my past was tucked away just under my feet. It was a graveyard of my misdeeds, right under my own nose at all times.

With the uncertainty of my return hanging in my mind, the decision to add extra security was an easy one. Should anyone target my home, they'd be hard-pressed to gain access to the basement already. If they torched it instead, the evidence would go up in flame anyway. It wasn't safe for me to have kept the proof for so long, especially during the time that Marie had lived in my home with me, but it was something that I just couldn't let go of.

However, in a choice between Marie and the display of guilt below, Marie would always win. That's why, though it pained me to leave it so unguarded, even with a bump in security, I would do it for her.

Several hours later, when the modifications invoked as much satisfaction as possible, I pushed the worry from my mind and set off for Marie's apartment. Though she wasn't home when I arrived—where the hell did that woman go in the middle of death and destruction right outside her door?—I let myself in, as usual, and settled in to wait. That time, I had no intention of leaving. If it meant that I had to give up a little more of the information I locked tightly away, so be it. There was no going back from what I was about to do.

Besides, I'd already promised Marie a conversation.

Chapter 21 - Marie

The trek back home was much worse than the one out had been. Where my thighs complained loudly before, my entire body screamed for mercy. The cut on my cheek had definitely begun to bleed at some point, drying into a crust that I dared not touch for fear that it would begin all over again. The opposite cheekbone was swollen, pushing unusually dark bits of skin into my lower vision.

An ache had begun at the top of my head, but had quickly dropped to settle at the base of my skull instead. I all but limped my way back home in the pitch black of night-nearly-gone-morning.

When the apartment complex loomed into view, relief nearly caused me to collapse on the spot. Visions of steaming hot baths and ice packs danced in my head—lightly, of course, so as not to cause more pain. It wasn't until I heard it echoing against the cement walls of the parking garage that I even realized I was groaning gently with each step. Frequent walks may have prepared me for more vigorous cardio, but what could have prepared me for fending off vampire attacks?

A past Marie would have said: Luke. His strength, composure, and ability to handle himself would have more than avoided that entire scenario. Damn him to hell.

And speaking of, the son of a bitch was leaning against the kitchen counter as I kicked open my front door with as much finesse as a pissed-off bull.

Ah, shit. The rescheduled conversation.

A quick glance at his face told me that I was extremely late for our impromptu meeting. It also told me that the darkness of the room, back-lit with only a small lamp in the far corner, was doing a super job of hiding both my injuries *and* my shame. Realizing it, I halted my advance, closed the door behind me, and dared enter no further into the space. If all went well, Luke would talk himself tired and then leave, affording me the chance to nurse myself without his worried, angry eyes or his incessant lectures. It would be easy to turn away as he passed, hiding the worst of it from him; he'd be none the wiser. I just had to make it through the conversation first.

Unfortunately, my body had other ideas. Barely thirty seconds after the brilliant plan had taken root in my brain, the toll for the day's effort was collected from my strength and I collapsed.

* * * * * * * * * * * * * * *

Warmth gently pulled me from sleep. Blurry vision stopped me from wanting to move to check my surroundings, though I recognized the giant blobs of color as being the furniture and walls of my bedroom. If I was home and in bed, there was no need to rush off anyway. I was safe, although I was unusually warm. Perhaps a cool glass of water would help—assuming that water was running in the complex today. I really should have contacted the utility company for a copy of the ration schedule.

One by one, my muscles stung and groaned and twitched against my instructions to act. All the bits seemed to be responsive, if not entirely functional. That was a problem for another day. With the slow clearing of my vision came the equally slow acceptance that my left eye was well and truly impaired by the mound of swollen flesh below it. Even the wince that slit my eyes caused a rolling ache along my face.

The sun was high in the sky, which I guessed from the amount of light leaking into the room. A strong beam traced across the edge of the pillow in front of my body, angling back toward my collarbone. Well, that explained why I was warm, but who'd opened the blinds?

Fully intending to roll and face the window behind me, a shift of body weight did nothing more than toss the blankets around my feet. In fact, the movement felt strange. Not normal. Though I'd tested my capabilities cautiously and found myself in good enough shape to move, my body did not react to my commands. It was as though I'd suddenly lost the strength to control any one part of myself in conjunction with another.

Then it hit me. Vanilla swirled in intoxicating puffs, shooting straight from my nose to my brain where, no matter the suffering of my body, a wave of pleasure pulsated outward. An involuntary shiver slid through me along with an equally involuntary sound that escaped my lips. The deep thrum of a chuckle rose up from behind me.

119

I froze, finally realizing what had felt so unusual. The lack of reaction from my body made complete sense when considering the new information.

Ignoring the violent shake as I did so, I shoved a hand into the bed and forced myself into a sitting position, careful to retract the weight on my arm before it could give away just how unhappy it had been to take it in the first place. I would not show weakness beyond the careless abandon my body had already displayed. Luke sat up beside me, pulling back the arm that had rested so casually, and heavily, on my waist just moments before. The blankets pooled in our laps as we stared at one another, warm quicksand eyes to hard emerald ones.

"What in the hell are you doing here?"

"I'll answer that if you explain why '*in the hell*' you're in the condition you are."

The mimicry hit as intended. Truly, I didn't owe him a damn explanation about what I did in my own life, on my own time; conversely, he certainly did owe me an explanation as to why he was sleeping in my bed, with me, and without my permission. More than that, he still had yet to explain his presence in my house when I'd arrived. Sure, I'd missed our meeting. That didn't earn him a 'get out of trespass charges free' card.

"Get out of my bed."

He held my gaze a moment longer, a moment too long, before throwing off the covers and sliding off the mattress. I expected him to leave at my command—truly, I did. The head injury had probably caused minor brain damage or temporary insanity, because I definitely knew Luke better than that.

His strong hands wrapped around my wrists, mercifully freeing every part of me from the weight of my own body, and yanked me to my feet. If I'd been a car instead of a person, every warning light would have triggered at once to alert me that we were in desperate need of repair. But I was not a car, and I *was* as stubborn a human as they came. Though it hurt like the devil, I stood my ground and tipped my chin up in defiance, shaking off his grip to reject the offered help. Honest, I only trembled a little.

With a click of his tongue, a sound that made me bristle in response, Luke retreated from the bedroom. Clinking silverware and rustling noises filled the room almost instantly, blissfully followed moments later by the smell of bacon. Slowly, gingerly, somehow, the weary bones resting under my skin transported me across the hall into the bathroom. The mirror did *not* reward me for my efforts; much like myself, it did not hold back.

Dark, thick knots of tangles and blood stuck out from my head just about everywhere. A purple that bordered on black swam over the left half of my face, tinted toward the center with a million different colors that I didn't dare identify. The cut over my other cheek was clean, much more shallow than I'd thought, but deeper in the middle where the needle had briefly found purchase. Pressing fingers into rough, dry hair, I prodded the bump on my head, which stung and throbbed at the lightest of touches. The crust of dried blood surrounding it was studiously ignored.

I sucked air through my teeth, then blew it out in a heavy sigh. I looked like hell.

A fearsome gurgle from my stomach signaled another type of pain fighting its way to the surface. Looking down at it, I realized for the first time that the soft yellow tank top and leggings adorning my body were not the clothing I'd collapsed in. At the realization, pink rushed forward to color the one good cheek left on my face.

It wasn't as if Luke hadn't seen me undressed before; there was just something inherently intimate about dressing someone who wasn't capable of doing it themselves. The vulnerability of the action made me want to sneer—which I didn't do, because it bloody hurt. The blasphemous idea of Luke caring for me in such a state made my stomach turn in an entirely different way than the bacon had just seconds ago; the thought of him then sharing my bed again made it clench in yet another.

It was so very complicated, and so very not.

With one more deep breath to steady myself, I exited the bathroom toward the smell of greasy food. There, in the kitchen, looking as at home as anyone could, Luke transferred sustenance from pan to plate. He was still in the clothes he'd been wearing when I saw him, wrinkled and speckled with fuzz from the blanket we'd shared. The cuffs of his button-up were rolled to the elbow, his shoes and socks abandoned somewhere so that his feet made tiny slapping noises against the laminate flooring as he shifted around in the space.

In another lifetime the scene would have made me happy. In this lifetime it only hurt, which turned immediately into an unbridled, pent-up rage.

"What makes you think that you can just let yourself in here to play house?"

The face he turned on me was livid, borderline terrifying. It was not a face I'd seen Luke wear before. A spatula hung forgotten in his grasp, drops of grease wobbling at the edge in response to fury that shook his entire being.

"You want to tell me what you're doing messing around with vampires, Marie? You could have been killed."

"It's none of your business."

"You *are* my business."

"No," I growled, low and threatening. "I am *not*." Surging forward, I ripped the spatula from his hand, thrusting it across the room where it collided with something that sounded large, but I dared not look away from Luke's face. The emotion poured out of me, nearly a tangible weapon in its strength. "You think that you have to save me all the time, but you're wrong. You seem to know all about the dangers of vampires, but do you know what *I* did to *him*?" I advanced with my words, shoving myself into Luke's rather sturdy frame. My voice dropped to a whisper. "I don't need you. I don't even want you, Luke Therion. Get out of my house and get out of my life."

A pause notched my anger higher, which I threw at him as if it truly were a weapon. I lashed him with it, growing triumphant as he stepped back, recoiled from me as though he felt the blows. The face that held such danger only moments ago was suddenly stony, impassive, unreadable in the slightest. It took no more convincing.

With the bacon left to burn in the pan, the English muffins growing stiff over the cooling toaster coils, and the eggs congealing into a sloppy mess in the two plates set for us, Luke retreated from the apartment without another word.

Chapter 22 - Luke

Dear God, I was too late. Time had run out; there was nothing more that I could do to prepare for what was happening. Standing there, barefoot in her kitchen, she'd unleashed on me a strength I had hoped—no, prayed—that she would never discover. The only thing I could do in response was leave before she accidentally, or less than accidentally, hurt one of us.

With the new information, I couldn't call him to finish what we'd started; the plan had to change. I had to adapt. Genevieve was his problem, but Marie was mine, and mine alone.

Where I had been casual and gentle before, only training and the mission at hand remained. Instead of my lover, my friend, the thing most precious to me in the world, Marie had to become nothing more than my target. Immediately.

Pulling deep for every bit of the training that had earned me a place in her world to begin with, I began the slow and careful planning required in order to quietly tail her every move, while I formulated a new plan of attack.

Chapter 23 - Marie

It took only another five days for the wounds to heal enough that I could resume my bus routes and investigation. Luke hadn't attempted to reach out to me that time, which was a great sigh of relief in the stressful life that I had adopted. His over-protectiveness was suffocating and I was not a mewling kitten for him to baby when he got the urge. There was no longer an opportunity to rely on Luke's closely guarded secrets; answers to the questions at hand would have to come through my own hard work.

After a particularly boring circuit with still-increasing numbers of people roaming the streets and frequenting businesses, I requested that Carmen take a detour. Outside the for-hire journalism shop, I counted the bills in my pocket and pondered my tactic. The determination not to walk out empty-handed was all-consuming. It was practically a challenge, the first Obscure-related obstacle someone like me could take on, and I'd not lose. I wasted no time charging through the door and calling out to alert the journalist of my arrival. Just as before, he stumbled out from a back room with a look of surprise and a full head of disheveled hair.

"Do you remember me? I'm here for the articles we discussed. I got your call."

His face pinched, glasses bumping against his nose as they shifted. "When I had to leave you a voicemail three days ago and didn't get a return call, I didn't think you'd be back, honestly."

Annoyance threatened to spring forward, but I tamped it down with a clearing of my throat. Crossing my arms against my chest, I shifted my weight to one foot and tapped my toes lightly against the floor. "You worked faster than I had anticipated. Do you have what I need or not?"

It took only a moment of consideration before the chance at earning real money won out over whatever else he'd been thinking, and he raced over to pull a stack of papers from behind his desk. Bound together, they were quite cumbersome, and they thudded on the top of the desk with enough weight that it shook the floorboards below. A frown pulled at the corners of my mouth. I'd thought there'd be more of them after the many long months of death and Obscure. Magnified eyes behind thick lenses looked me over cautiously.

"Jeez, are you okay?" His head tilted side to side as he eyed what was likely the yellow and brown spot encompassing a large portion of my face. At least it wasn't black and purple anymore, and I could actually see properly.

"Yes, fine. How much is it?"

My impatience offended him; that, or my lack of social prowess in the face of polite small talk. Sniffling irritatingly, he sat down in his desk chair and motioned to the space under his desk. "There are three bundles like this. It's thirty for each bundle."

Shit. My hand scraped against the paper of the bills in my pocket. I could only afford one of them if I wanted to have any hope of surviving the next several days. The air conditioning kicked on in the room, swirling strands of hair into my face as we stared one another down. The nameplate sitting unobtrusively on his dirty desk caught my eye.

"Alright, Peter. Let me level with you. You need the money, but I don't have it because I also need the money." I gestured wildly to the open air around us both. "We all do. You've already done the work, so it's going to be wasted cost unless I purchase everything from you. My offer is this," I placed a hand possessively on the stack that sat atop the desk between us. "I'll buy two stacks now for forty and come back for the last, which I'll buy at the full thirty."

"Deal."

He'd responded too quickly, making me curse myself for starting the offer so high. Annoyed, I fished out the bills, leaving a singular twenty-dollar bill safely tucked into my pocket for groceries, and hefted the first bundle into the air while he ducked down for the second. As I made my way for the door, he waddled along behind me with the second stack in hand.

We boarded the bus in tandem, Peter from the door at the center and myself from the door at the front. He frowned when he realized that he boarded the further door, but said nothing as he made his way toward me, finally sliding the items into the first row of seats where I gestured. Then he backed away, down the front steps, and held out a hand for me to shake. Originally, there had been no intent to make physical contact with anyone, especially while still rattled after my encounter with the vampire, but I felt oddly sympathetic to Peter's plight, so we shook.

"Thank you for your business…" he trailed off, lifting the last word into a prompt for my response. I realized quickly that, having not set up my voicemail greeting, he hadn't learned my name. Fleetingly, the thought of giving him a fake one skittered through my mind. I decided against it. Peter could prove useful.

"Marie."

Peter nodded again, eyes widening slightly, then adjusted his glasses and retreated back to the relative safety of his office building. Through the opaque storefront window, I watched him sink back into his chair and eye the bills I'd left with near reverence. It made me wonder how long it had been since another soul had set foot in his office with a job.

Carmen, kind as she was, did not offer to assist me in hauling the heavy papers to my apartment when we arrived. She did, however, maneuver the bus against the parking garage and idle in silence while I raced back and forth to secure my prizes. It suited me just fine.

Safely home with at least a million hours of research ahead of me, I cut the taught binding of the first load and, with binders and highlighters and pens aplenty at hand, set to work.

Hours flew by in the whisk of rustling paper. At nearly halfway through the first stack, which had been the oldest of the articles, I'd identified at least five separate—albeit small—inconsistencies within the reported deaths that had plagued us for what felt like an eternity. One single sheet of paper housed the names of the dead whose postmortem specifics didn't seem to match the others. Some of them shared relative location while others had similar wounds. Others yet had matching physical characteristics. None of them clicked easily together in the 'ah-ha' moment I'd been hoping for.

Still, a great deal of strange wounds or curious notes pawed at my mind. Sure, there were always going to be human killers that had their own signatures and wouldn't fit into the kill methods of either vampires or witches, but it felt to me that there were missing pieces to the puzzle—giant, neon-signs-with-arrows-and-sirens types of pieces. There was more out there than we knew about, or were willing to admit to ourselves. I was sure of it.

A small stack of papers that I was sure correlated to vampire killings had been set to the side. All references to the killer were highlighted in a bright, screaming blue. I was pretty sure, based on the references in the articles, that most of the killings had been done by a woman. I crossed my fingers that I had just spent several hours learning that there was a distinct possibility that the leader of the vampires was also a woman, like Genevieve.

That, or I'd wasted a great deal of time pairing up kills that had nothing to do with one another, and could very well have been something other than vampire, or even witch, for all I knew.

Frankly, the idea had crossed my mind several times that Leena could have been a witch, but when I shuffled past the last of the reports in my load and had yet to find a description matching hers, I cursed and kicked at the nearest crumpled page. I needed the last stack of research to figure out the answers to my questions, which meant I needed money, fast.

There was no true deadline for the work that I was doing. No micromanaging boss would swoop down to slap me on the wrist for making my way slowly to the last stack of reports. I had no consequences for being unable to make progress. Yet, the idea that in the morning, with nothing more on hand to help me inch closer to the answers I was looking for, I'd simply continue the mind-numbing crawl through my bleak life, had lost its appeal entirely. I couldn't do it anymore. Marie Morrison could not sit idly by and wait for life to gobble her up.

Taking a break from the tedium, and delighting in a much-needed stretch, I found myself drawn to the silent television as it flashed images across the screen. Report after report after report of death and destruction played on repeat—always the same story with a new body or building each time. The news anchor was more alive than I'd seen her in several weeks. It made me smile, just a little. I reached for the remote to resume the sound, searching for the same alertness to ring from her voice and fill the space between us with hope.

Instead, the screen flashed immediately to a field reporter whose baby face and squeaking voice led me to question whether he was even of age to be employed, let alone qualified for field news work. Briefly considering the option to mute the screen again and wait out his piece, I decided against it and took a seat on the couch to satisfy my curiosity about him instead. He was nervous, nearly trembling in both the face of the lens and the operator behind it. The microphone wobbled in his grasp, sometimes bumping gently against his face. The resulting hiss of air was comical. The camera panned out slowly to provide a grand reveal of the location and the guest starring in the segment. Beside the man, a woman as calm as the sea before a storm stood patiently, a polite smile resting comfortably for the audience.

I froze, recognizing the face instantly. I punched the volume level up so far that the sound vibrated the stand underneath the screen.

"—rumors of the government rising from the ashes seem to be true, then."

"No," Ellie corrected, a sparkle in her eyes that told me she found the whole thing amusing. "We're not the same government you used to know. We're the New Government."

"But will you not act in the same way that the old government did?"

Ellie shook her head slowly. An awkward pause grew between them while the field anchor waited for her to elaborate. When it became clear that she didn't intend to, he pushed, likely spurred to from within the earpiece that he fidgeted with incessantly.

"Then what *will* you do?"

At that, a magnificent smile spread across Ellie's face. "We have been hunted and killed and terrorized by Obscure for long enough. The New Government seeks to end the war between the Obscure and the humans."

The incredulous tone that seeped into the reporter's voice was very likely *not* prompted by the channel's higher-ups. "How do you plan to do that?"

"The New Government will employ a specialized task force to handle the Obscure. We have experts trained on each and every creature out there, educating us on everything and anything Obscure until we know them inside and out. Our teams will live and breathe Obscure. They are our protectors, our wardens." She gestured behind her at the replica of the White House that stood tall and proud as a backdrop. "Our facility is equipped with holding cells for Obscure that will allow us to capture and question them until we have enough knowledge to protect ourselves against them. To stop them. As we know more, we will adapt our containment facilities to better suit each and every individual need. There is no more need to fear what we do not know; the wardens will give us the opportunity to cohabitate with Obscure, peacefully."

"And where exactly did you get this specialized army?"

Ellie's smile broadened, nearly a menacing grin. "That's the best part. It's made up of mere humans who, like us, want to end the suffering." She looked directly into the camera. "We've plenty of room if you can hold your own against an Obscure. We will give you the tools you need to find the answers you seek and make a difference—save lives, even. And we pay."

Nervous Man shifted from foot to foot. "Tell me, do you know what they're looking for? The Obscure?"

Her face never changed as she spoke, though she tossed him a glance as if to call him an idiot. "We intend to find out."

The screen changed again, moving back to the first anchor who recapped the story for those who'd missed it. She referred to Ellie as the *President* of the New Government. I was no longer interested in the television, however, as I'd already raced into the bedroom and stuffed a hand down into the back pocket of a pair of bloodied jeans that were stashed in my clothes hamper. My fingers frantically dialed on my cell phone, several years of heavy phone use coming to the rescue. After three rings, the line was answered.

"I was waiting for your call, Marie. Have you decided to join us?"

Swallowing against the excitement and fear that rose up in equal measure, I found my voice unsteady as I replied. "Yes."

"Wonderful. We'll see you in the morning."

"Wait, where do I meet you?"

"At the White House, of course."

The line went dead.

Chapter 24 - Marie

I'd done a book report on the White House once, many years ago in school. While there had never been a complete blueprint revealed, or a location or name for each room in the facility, I was convinced that whoever designed the replica had spent a great deal of time there personally. Not a single wall or shade or desk was out of place from the original, as I could recall it. It made me wonder where the army and the holding cells that Ellie boasted about were hiding, since those certainly wouldn't have been on any tour, had they existed in the original building.

She met me exactly as I entered the facility, as if she'd known the moment I arrived on the front lawn. Maybe she did. The crisp clicking of sensible heels down the tiled floors was the only indication of company, alerting me just seconds before she arrived. Though she appeared very much the same as I'd seen her before, her looming presence was no longer masked behind the facade of innocence. Ellie stood every inch the President she claimed to be. The sweeping hemline of her long, pleated skirt brushed my shoes as she halted in front of me—a bit too closely for my liking. The snow white of her hair was perfectly pinned into a complex up-do which only served to make me self-conscious over my own untamed mane. The urge to reach up and flatten down what were inevitable frizzy bits and split ends twitched in my fingers, but I resisted. Standing so close to such obvious perfection made me want to shrink back into the shadows. It was instantly clear to me, as I'm sure it was to anyone who saw her in action, how she retained her position.

Ellie eyed me from head to toe, not unkindly, then smiled and gestured for me to follow her. We zigzagged through narrow hallways, past more closed doors than my entire apartment complex housed, and— I was pretty sure—we looped back over the same stretch of hallway more than once. Photos clung to only the largest stretches of wall space, though all of the images looked strikingly similar—most of landscapes, luscious green and comforting. There was a distinct lack of signage. None of the rooms were labeled, such as 'bathroom' or 'Secretary's office', none of the hallways contained maps with a 'you are here' star, and there were certainly no arrows pointing visitors in the direction of any exits. In fact, the lack of orientation began to make my legs feel heavy, a large pressure in my head urging me to pause and seek out a landmark of some sort. I guessed my survival instinct was, indeed, alive and well, and entirely unhappy about being lost in an unfamiliar place with a woman who I was sure had to be hiding some dangerous talents to earn and keep her place at the table. As if in tune with my thoughts, we suddenly stopped short outside an unadorned door that looked exactly as all the rest had along the way.

A large wooden table engulfed the majority of the floor space inside the room. Twenty-five chairs sat neatly around it, most of which were occupied. Faces of all shapes, sizes and colors turned to assess me quickly before turning back to the front of the room, where Ellie had marched forward to take the helm. She gestured at the table, beckoning me to take a seat. I did, opting for one next to a male who looked at least three years younger than I was, and whose buzzed haircut did nothing to hide the tattoo on his skull underneath, which then made me second-guess his age. The only other option had been the chair next to a very off-put-appearing woman with hair the color of a good sunset. The idea of placing empty seats between myself and everyone else was extremely appealing... however, being that I was so far back from Ellie already, I didn't want to struggle to hear what she had to say. I was there to learn, there to work to stop what was happening outside the walls of the quiet headquarters of the New Government.

After a brief sip of water from a glass that seemed to appear out of thin air, Ellie began to speak.

"You are all here for a reason; that reason is yours—and yours alone—to keep. I don't care what drives you to become a warden, I care that you do the work well and that you follow instructions."

I shifted in my seat at that. Truthfully, I was not well known for doing as I was told.

"My name is Ellie, but I respond to 'President'. At the end of this very day, you will officially work for the New Government. We have lodging on-site, provided at no cost during the training period, and access to the food court, which is also available for free. We will take care of you as long as you continue to serve our purpose. In addition to the housing and food, you will each receive a monthly stipend of three hundred dollars for research and recreation. But," Her gaze swung across each of us in turn. "You must first complete your training. Make no mistake—it is not an easy task. Obscure are tough, fast, viscous creatures at times and you must be prepared to protect yourself and those around you. All of you were invited to the program because you have shown an interesting level of natural skill. If we're correct, and you continue to impress, you will become great wardens." A brief pause, met with the polite smile that I was beginning to recognize as President's way of softening words that may not want to be heard by the recipient. "However, should you fail your training, you will be *removed* from the program."

Silence settled around the room, cut only by the occasional shift of an anxious body. President allowed the silence to stretch far longer than I'd expected, her posture relaxed and her focus settled on the sheets of paper that sat before her on a small podium. At first, just as the others had surely done, I assumed that President would resume speaking shortly. Seconds ticked by into minutes with no sign of further communication from the front of the room. President remained face-down toward whatever had caught her attention. After several more minutes passed, a man near the front began tapping his fingers against the tabletop in impatience. Each of us silently memorized the others as the time ticked on, no one daring to break the spell of silence themselves or finding anything more interesting to do with their time than analyze the other people chosen for their own 'natural skill'. I suppressed a grimace at the memory of what 'skill' I'd shown President, and another at the thought that each of the people sharing the table with me would have to have done something similar. I sized them all up in turn, trying to imagine any one of them also bashing a vampire's brains in with a brick. The female I'd nearly sat with began swinging her foot gently under the table, almost imperceptibly, though it seemed to be a thinking gesture more so than a bored one; her face remained focused and analytical, searching the rest of the room. Another girl mid-way down the table began to twirl her platinum hair between her fingers, mouth pinched in displeasure between smacks and pops of bubblegum.

"Samson Frekt. Olivia Pommel," President's voice finally called out, jolting more than a few of us to attention. The hair twirling and finger tapping both ceased, replaced by two sets of surprised eyes. "You're both dismissed." They each stood abruptly, though in tandem, looking at one another across the table. Samson opened his mouth to argue, but President spoke over his forthcoming argument, allowing no room for disagreement. "We were mistaken; neither of you have the patience or the aptitude for this work. You're welcome to reapply at a later time, though I can't imagine that my findings will be any different then. You may go."

Tension built rapidly in the air. Instead of Samson, it was Olivia who stepped back and slammed her chair into the table, pointing an angry finger in President's direction. "That was a stupid test. If you'd just told us that was the goal, we could have acted appropriately. You said yourself that you saw something in us to begin with!" A booted foot stomped into the ground in protest, not quite as childlike as it should have appeared. "I want to be part of this—of ending the fear and slaughter. That's what I came here for."

President remained entirely indifferent to the outburst. She carried on her calm, poised demeanor, a small smile that dared hint at cockiness spreading across her face as she returned her attention to the papers in her hands. "Tyrone Bennett, please raise your hand."

A man on my side of the table raised his hand cautiously. His dark skin was nearly flawless, I'd noted earlier when I entered, but was crinkled along his forehead and the corners of his mouth with what I could only imagine was worry. Where I'd envied him before, I feared for him instead.

"Olivia, what is Tyrone's tell?"

Olivia's eyes went wide, the pale shimmer of makeup over her cheeks barely covering the rapidly darkening pink skin underneath. The sharp look she gave Tyrone only seemed to enhance her beauty, which faded ever so slightly as she dropped her gaze to the tabletop to contemplate the question. She balled a fist at her side, which shook from the tension, but no response was given. She glared briefly in Tyrone's direction once more before tipping her chin in silent defiance.

President merely nodded gently. "Karen Mossamite, then. Please enlighten us as to what Tyrone's tell is."

The woman across from me with the radiant locks raised her head proudly as she spoke. "He clasped his hands and rubbed his thumbs back and forth over them."

"Marie Morrison, what's Karen's tell?"

I took in the way Karen stiffened at the implication that she had a tell. The past few minutes replayed slowly inside my mind. "She swung her foot under the table."

I was rewarded with another of President's small nods before her attention returned to the two standing people.

"Neither of you can identify the tell of *anyone* else at this table, let alone *everyone* else at the table. Not only that, but had this been a mission of stealth, both of you would have given away your positions with tells that created sound. This wasn't a test of silence alone; it was a test of intuition. You have failed. Potential is not everything when it comes to war."

It took no more convincing than that. Both recruits exited the room quietly, greeted by a burly man just outside the door that presumably escorted them back to the entrance. A pang of guilt threatened to rise up in me, but was quickly squashed as President addressed me again.

"Marie," she said gently, imploring. "Do you like that name?"

"It's alright." The question was strange, prompting a surge of fear that raised the hairs along my arms. If it was another test, I wouldn't fail it. I needed the money just as much as I needed the answers the New Government could provide.

"I prefer Mare, don't you?"

Mare. Mare Morrison. It did have a ring to it, though I'd never admit to President that it sounded too aggressive and I preferred being called Marie instead. I simply nodded and shrugged at the same time, as non-committal and non-confrontational a response as I could provide to avoid a potential land mine hidden within the conversation.

She continued calling recruits by name and assessing the level of information they'd obtained in the time given. When she was satisfied, and we'd all been able to pass the first of her tests, she dismissed us to the first phase of training. Another physically intimidating and silent man appeared outside the door to lead us all, including President, into the lower level of the building, where we discovered rows upon rows of massive cages and all manner of restraints lining the walls. President explained the various specifics of the bindings and containment areas they'd created before handing us each an item that resembled reinforced handcuffs. They were thicker than normal handcuffs, just about everywhere, had no keyhole, and seemed significantly heavier than handcuffs should have been. I didn't share that information, knowing I might have been forced to provide the source of said information. I flushed slightly at the thought.

"These are Obscure restraints. Each type of Obscure will have some form of magic inside them; that's what makes them Obscure. Here's your first lesson: The magic that creates an Obscure is the same for every type; what changes is the way the host's body reacts to the magic. Different reactions cause different Obscure. It's possible that there are an unlimited number of them, but we have reason to believe that the magic is influenced by the source as well." She paused to pan the room in silence. "These restraints, once applied, will prevent the use of magic at all. It will render them no more dangerous than a human could be. The goal of any warden is to capture Obscure as you are directed to do so and return them to this facility so that we can question them. We'd prefer that there be no casualties on either end, but things do happen." Any icy chill caressed me as the hard look landed on us each individually, insisting in no unclear terms that President was not to be messed with. "We are not here to eradicate Obscure. Make no mistake—should we find that a heretic has joined our ranks, and the tools we give you are being used to fulfill your own personal agenda, we will eliminate you ourselves."

Several gasps sounded from the group. A quick glance around revealed that every set of eyes was glued to President, the physically scarier man behind her not even considered. I'd bet, secretly, that President would win just about any fight she found herself tangled in.

"One more thing. Remember the faces of those that you see here today. Outside of these walls, you are to tell no one that you are a warden. Even disclosing your status to another warden is grounds for dismissal. The safety of our force relies largely on anonymity. Knowledge of other wardens may prove useful in the field, should your paths cross, but not at the risk of exposure."

The threat hung in the air that 'dismissal' at that point was akin to elimination.

We moved again, further into the bowels of the underground fortress. Past the cages—of which there were more than any one person could count—and down a corridor to the right, a large expanse of what looked to be warehouse space rested. Along one wall, nearest to where we entered, a row of men stood at attention, patiently waiting. President greeted them warmly, introducing them to us as our trainers. I bristled at the fact that a woman had not been included among them. Women were just as good as men, and sometimes even better. Seeing as how President was a woman herself, it surprised me that she'd not been able to find a female capable of the position.

I chose to hold my tongue and school my face into neutrality, lest I draw in any unwanted attention. The trainers introduced themselves, then rattled a list of names for their assigned recruits and led their groups to a separate section of the space. The trainer who called my name introduced himself as Michael. He was quite lean and a bit on the short side compared to the rest of the trainers, but an aura of complete authority washed out from him as I crowded in to accept his greeting. We shook hands, which might well have simply been to allow Michael to flex the muscles I'd very much assumed he didn't have. Something told me that Michael was used to being overlooked and wasn't much a fan of it. Best to get that out of the way early, I imagined.

Tyrone and another male named Victor were both assigned to my training team, plus a few others. The relief I felt at seeing Victor's scrawny body up close nearly made me collapse. Until that moment, I was sure there had been a mistake in registration; the most athletic I had ever been was running to and from my problems, and while I kept a relatively thin frame, there wasn't much to it. Sizing myself up against Victor gave me confidence that I hadn't felt since walking into the building.

Michael laid down the ground rules: show up every morning, work hard until dismissed for the day, and expect to repeat the process until your instructor felt that you'd mastered enough to be released to field duty. The estimate given was twelve months, with the caveat that we were expected to find our specialty and strengthen it—just as much as the skills we were weakest with—before we'd be allowed to graduate to field status. After introductions, the instructors gave us a fifteen-minute break to change into some more athletic clothing that they'd provided us.

I changed quickly and sought out President, who'd remained nearby for what I could only assume was one hell of a show at the expense of us new recruits.

It took nearly a full hour of negotiation with her, but I'd not wanted to reside on-site during the training period, and I relented only at the offer that, in exchange, President would make my own home more comfortable after I graduated from training. With a few calls, the small issues of water and electricity rations were eliminated from my apartment building entirely. I was also promised all the answers that the program could provide once I was field-ready.

The last thing I negotiated was a copy of the blueprints for Wild River Penitentiary.

Once upon a time I might have said that the hardest thing in my life had been losing Leena, or walking away from Luke. Those events were nothing compared to what I would endure during the program. No longer would I need anyone to protect me.

I would emerge as Marie Morrison, fully trained warden for the New Government.

Chapter 25 - Luke

Idling several careful paces behind the behemoth of a passenger bus, memories crashed over me in a tsunami of emotion. It had not been so long ago that silent observance was the only way that I could fit into Marie's life, as I'd followed her every move without her knowledge. My mind filled with images of Marie's determined face and my heart filled with dread. I would *not* be going back to that life.

Marie was mine.

Whether she wanted to admit it or not, she belonged to me. With me.

There was nothing in my life that I craved more than her affection, and nothing I wouldn't give to reclaim it.

Nothing.

She stepped carefully, nearly cautiously, down from the bus as it halted. My heart leaped at the sight of her, and for more than one reason. While her beauty was always stunning, that particular stop was not one that the bus route typically honored. Marie had chosen to stop there, to exit the bus in front of the great expanse of lawn that stretched before her. I squeezed my eyes shut for a moment, sure that by the time I opened them again, Marie would be stepping back onto the bus and driving far, far away from the building and all of the trouble that waited just inside the bright white-painted lies.

But she didn't.

Instead, she continued her casual pace up the perfectly maintained walkway, and, to my horror, the bus pulled away to continue on without her. Surely, she was only stopping to pop in for a moment and she'd catch the bus on its next loop around. Frozen in disbelief and terror, my limbs refused to react, to snap myself out of my car and grab her before she crossed the threshold. What business could she possibly have there?

I'd tried so very hard to keep her sheltered from all that was the New Government, without betraying my own personal knowledge of it. Perhaps that was my mistake. Had I come clean about my involvement, would she still have found herself there? Shit. There was no telling with Marie.

A horn blared behind me, impatient at the idiot idling in the road for no reason. Yet, I couldn't rip away my gaze as her slender, perfect form yanked open the door to my own personal version of hell and strolled inside. Even as she vanished from view, the driver behind me trying to maneuver around my stalled SUV, none of it seemed real. Everything I'd worked for was about to come crashing down around us all. She had managed, somehow, to find the one place where I couldn't watch over her or protect her.

Finally, painfully, I pushed the button for my emergency lights and veered to the side of the road, allowing the small line of traffic to pass with more honks, shouting, and several rude gestures. Didn't they know what was happening? It was war, and it was far from over. Looking once more to the empty doorway, the realization bloomed fresh pain; if Marie didn't step back through that door momentarily, the war was, in fact, just beginning.

Hours passed, slowly, agonizing. I waited for all of them, never taking my eyes from the sickening brightness of the replica building, even when darkness spread through the sky and the glowing white turned from cheerful to eerie in the lack of sun. Denial rode me hard, snarling at my growling stomach or fatigued eyes if I dared consider moving on. I was convinced that any moment, precisely the moment I gave up, Marie would emerge, angered at her lack of progress with the institution and seeking a way to get back home.

Yet she never did.

It had been too many years since I'd had to maintain surveillance akin to stalking, and I was exceptionally out of practice. Exhaustion tugged at me when the sky bled back to pale pastel shades and announced the new morning to the world. My own emotions had leaked out along with it, leaving only pain and fear to battle back against the will to simply give in. Finally, mercifully, I closed my eyes and tilted back my head, opening them again to greet the dark pink clouds overhead through the sunroof. I hadn't cared that the New Government would have seen me here, clearly staking them out, but perhaps it was better to leave before they decided to send someone out to address it, lest things got ugly. Killing a warden wouldn't get me any closer to Marie.

In fact, I wasn't so sure that I *could* get any closer to her after it all. She'd be on her own, not only bringing danger to herself, but to me as well.

To all of us.

Orange tones traced themselves through the sky, chased quickly away by the deep red of the approaching sunrise. It made me chuckle, though not in amusement. It seemed that even the skies knew of the impending bloodshed.

To the air, I said: "Was this your doing? Are you trying to show me that you know I've failed us all?"

No response came. I hadn't truly expected one.

The grief would come—and soon, I feared. It was best that I be home when it did, away from anyone who could get caught up in my all-consuming pain. Christ, failure never got any easier to swallow.

Truly, though, what would a few more bodies be to the many who would fall in the coming months? Marie would emerge a warden; I was convinced. All hope was already lost.

Gritting my teeth, I finally let my vehicle drag me away. There were preparations to be made.

Part Three

Chapter 26 - Marie

Old, rusted, and terrifying were probably the nicest words I could think of to describe the vehicle that ambled to a stop in front of me. The man behind the wheel paid no mind to the upturned lip I sported, though that may have had to do with the large sum of money the government had given him to chauffeur me to my destination. The ride, I assumed, would not be a smooth or luxurious one, and I could live with that; what truly troubled me was whether I would make it there at all.

As I slid into the back seat, the driver eyed me briefly. Though he was dressed very casually, in clothes that almost seemed a size too large for his frame, the gaze he flicked over me was that of a professional—merely a glance to ensure I was safely tucked in before he stepped on the gas, not a second too long or too short, and with not a dare of a linger anywhere except in the general direction of my person. The thought made me stare hard at his reflection in the rear-view mirror, as though the intensity of my willfulness to read his mind would grant me the ability. He would, undoubtedly, feel the pressure of my attention, but he made no gesture to suggest such a thing.

Definitely a professional.

Admittedly, there was no surprise in learning that President had sent a babysitter. As it was my first solo mission, I'd assumed there would be eyes on me at all times. Mustn't let the newbie get killed on the first day, after all. What a waste of eight grueling months of training that would be.

Still, they didn't have to send the male model GI Silent Joe. He may not have been clocking my appearance, but *I* surely hadn't missed the way his flawless tawny skin glowed against deep hazel eyes and a head of lush, dark hair. You wouldn't want to get me started on the corded muscles that bunched up under the short sleeves as he gripped the wheel for a turn. I'd have bet my whole first month of stipend that a nice set of abs and a firm butt were hidden just under his unassuming outfit. At least the view was nice during the slow, lurching trip.

We rode in the first light of morning with nothing but the sound of the road to accompany us, save for the swishing noises my clothes made against the cloth seats when I adjusted position. Though the journey itself was only just over three hours by car, the silence made me want to bash my head in within the first fifteen minutes. I resorted instead to lifting the briefing notes out of my bag to look them over again. And again. And again.

Geraldine Vasser, appeared fifty-two, suspected werewolf, wanted for questioning in connection with the death of her neighbor, Andrea Gregor. The very limited number of notes I had received on Geraldine indicated that she lived alone in Carson City, Nevada, on a property of just over an acre in the hillside. Andrea's home was two lots down from Geraldine's, similarly sized, and sat closer to the entrance of the neighborhood—which also served as the exit, as there was only one road to and from the homes. When Andrea's body was found by next of kin, ravaged and barely recognizable, suspicion landed on Geraldine, being that Andrea's doorbell camera showed both her arrival to Andrea's home approximately forty-five minutes prior to the estimated time of death, and her exit less than thirty minutes after the fact.

Several photos of the body, from the crime scene and autopsy alike, were provided in the file, along with a headshot of Geraldine. Not an expert by any means, I'd not been able to pick out from the wounds what had specifically set President on the trail of a werewolf. Though most of the body remained untouched, various bits were crushed with an as-of-yet unidentified hefty object. There were also a handful of wounds that looked, to me, like chunks of skin ripped out with human teeth. Expecting claw marks and dog bites when I'd learned I was tracking a suspected werewolf, the reality of the target was frustratingly disappointing.

Michael's voice rang through my skull: "Never underestimate your target. They all appear human, until they don't."

Setting my jaw, I forced myself to scour the text over and over again. I wanted to know what President knew. The singular photo of the presumed Obscure smiled back at me from the pages on my lap. She was anyone's mother with her silvering blond locks pushed into a messy bun, dark circles that hung low under tired eyes, and a warm smile that still managed to make you want to smile in return. Could that be the face of a werewolf? Could it be the face of a murderer?

Shifting my attention to the view outside the window, I mentally compared the autopsy description to that of the newspapers I'd pored over the past several months, as the strips of pale green and sandy brown terrain skipped by. While I had yet to return to Peter's office for the remainder of my loot, I had used the time instead to comb over the articles again and again each time I learned a new bit of information. The piles that had once been sorted by 'Vampire' and 'Witch' and 'Strange' and 'Probably human' consisted solely of various piles of Obscure-responsible deaths, with only a small stack of articles that likely belonged to a killer of the human variety. I could easily tell the difference between a witch and a human killing where I hadn't been able to before—even those humans who intended their kills to be pinned on the Obscure.

At least three bodies floated to the top of my mind, each having missing chunks of skin and pulverized parts alike. Originally, I'd taken them for troll kills—at least until I'd learned that trolls didn't eat their victims. Then I'd moved them to vampire kills. Being as vampires also had a strength advantage, it was a logical leap to make that they'd been too rough during a struggle and both flattened bits of their targets and perhaps taken too aggressive of a bite out of them as well.

I knew better... probably.

Geraldine wasn't proven a werewolf until she either admitted it or she had been labeled so after interrogation at the headquarters. Innocent until proven guilty, and all that.

The fact remained that *someone* had killed Andrea, and that someone was likely a werewolf, according to the experts.

I snapped back to the present as the vehicle slowed, my companion catching my eye in the mirror.

"I'll wait here for you," he said, settling into his seat and cutting the engine. There was finality in his tone, no more discussion was needed or would take place. Half of me wanted to make either a very rude remark or a very rude gesture in response to his authoritative attitude, but I refrained. I had definitely learned something during all those months of training.

Without a word I snapped the file shut, shoving it into the bag that I slung back over my shoulder as I exited the car. Perhaps I shut the door behind me a little more forcefully than was necessary. Baby steps.

The dusty road sign at the end of the street advised me that I'd been dropped at Sycolin Lane. Based on the map my cell phone had so graciously provided, I knew that Sycolin Lane backed to the houses on Richardson Road. In front of me, a ranch-style home with a perfectly manicured lawn boasted a 'for sale' sign. The keys jingled in my pocket as I stepped toward the front door. President hadn't wasted any time; I'd had the keys in hand less than two hours after suggesting the cover. Apparently, the New Government had a bit of reach across the entirety of the country, not just in our neck of the woods.

I also hadn't missed the appraising look she'd given me while she watched me skim the file for the first time and asked what my plan was. She hadn't known it yet, but the second she'd handed me my first mission, I'd known that when I handed the file back to close the case, I intended to collect on some of the answers she'd promised me nearly a year ago.

Stepping through the front door, I quickly stashed the keys and my bag in a hall closet and marched directly to the back door, steps echoing strangely in the empty space. Opening the sliding glass door felt like dropping a plate in a busy restaurant—much louder than necessary and bound to draw everyone's attention. Despite my fears, the distance between homes ensured that I was left to my own devices. I strolled the perimeter of the yard casually, as though assessing the quality of the land in relation to the price of the lot. I poked at the old wooden fence surrounding the yard, I kicked at rusted playground equipment lying on the furthest edge of the lot, and then I hunkered in the corner that was darkest under the rising sun so that I could peer through a gap in the fence posts.

From that vantage point, I was staring directly into Geraldine's yard. The house was quiet, though several lights blared on through windows mostly darkened by curtains. I strained my eyes hard, to no avail, as the distance was too great for me to make out any movement inside the small home. Resting a hand against the restraints in my back pocket, I took one last sneaky look around to be sure I was alone, and then I vaulted the fence. It took less than thirty seconds to jog across Geraldine's yard and press silently against the back wall of the house. No sound greeted me. The first few windows that I peeked into gave only small images of wall or furniture around the badly fitted blinds. The rest revealed nothing at all.

On a whim, I pushed at the back door and found it coincidentally unlocked. Again, the stomach-dropping sensation gripped me as I shoved the glass door ajar and slipped inside. Sure that Geraldine would fly out at me from every corner at any given moment, I paused for a steadying breath. Still, it was eerily quiet. Tiptoeing room by room confirmed that my target was not on the premises.

I stood in the middle of the kitchen, hands on hips. There was no way I was going to fail my first mission. *Think, Marie*. Where was Geraldine?

Taking another sweep through the home for clues, I found only an extremely unhelpful calendar from the previous month that indicated a schedule consisting entirely of Yoga classes on Tuesdays and Saturdays. Being that it was Wednesday, and early morning, I didn't imagine that Yoga was occupying anyone's time just yet. Though, that did give me an idea.

Stalking back to the front of the house, I peered carefully out through the crack of the living room window until a bright red sedan shifted into view in the driveway. Oh, Geraldine definitely wasn't at yoga—or anywhere else, for that matter. Geraldine was home, or nearby enough to be in capture range. It was just a matter of locating her.

Shifting the restraints out of my pocket and opting to hold them at the ready instead, I reveled in the feeling of badassery as I stilled myself in the middle of the room to listen for even the smallest of sounds. The tall grass blew against the siding from the breeze outside, whooshing gently with no real rhythm. The fridge gurgled in the kitchen, just as the air conditioning started up and began to blow air through the vents. Curtains rustled against furniture, walls, and blinds, which in turn clunked against window frames.

Frustrated, I willed myself to patience. Sound and sight had both failed me. What was left?

Quickly mapping a layout of the home in my mind, I walked the rooms one last time, stopping in front of a shut bathroom door that I'd checked twice already. I frowned. A decent length of wall stretched between the bathroom and a nearby bedroom, but a large amount of space between the two was unaccounted for. A small alcove next to the tub in the bathroom led to a tiny linen closet, set in line with the depth of the bathroom, but the bedroom's closet was only a third of the depth of the rest of the wall.

With a tight grip on the restraints, I crouched in the closet and searched for an opening or switch of any sort that may lead me to the hidden area behind. After several minutes of unfortunate, clumsy fumbling, I stepped back into the doorway and resorted to Plan F—as in, 'Fuck It'.

"Geraldine," I called in as authoritative a voice as I could muster. "It's clear that I've found your hidey-hole. You can either come out on your own, or I can start blasting holes in the walls of your nice little home until I drag you out myself." Silence. "While you may not mind that so much, your neighbors might get curious about the noise, and then I'd have to detain and question them all in relation to this matter. I'm not sure how they'll feel about living next to someone suspected of murder, who's getting her house blown to bits."

Could I really blast holes in the walls? Probably not; at least not without first sorting through the red tape, and Geraldine would be long gone by then. Did it at least sound convincing? Hopefully.

"Listen, I just want to ask you some questions about Andrea. That's all. I don't think that's worth getting your house all busted up over. Your neighbors won't have the slightest clue if we do this the easy way. I'll give you two minutes to make your decision."

It didn't take two minutes.

Immediately, shuffling noises erupted behind the wall, which rotated sideways with both ease and weight behind it. Geraldine stepped out into the room, eyed me warily, then turned and hefted the wall back into its original position. I snapped one half of the restraints onto one of her wrists before she was done, trying desperately not to panic at the fact that she'd just moved what appeared to be three solid inches of steel wall without any effort at all.

Her eyes went wild. She yanked her cuffed wrist backward, pulling me along and proving just how much strength she had hidden inside her tiny frame. The realization was a gut punch, but a welcomed one that snapped me back into the mindset of the mission.

Using the momentum of Geraldine's flailing, I tucked my legs under me and dropped my body weight onto her, taking us both to the ground. The movement surprised her, but she recovered instantly, grabbing my hand with the other half of the restraints and swinging my entire body into the ground beside her. The wind was knocked instantly from my lungs.

"I didn't do it," she screeched, fear and anger thick in her voice. "I swear, it wasn't me!"

Struggling for air, I reached for the knife I kept tucked safely against my stomach in a special elastic holster. The goal was to pin the sleeve of her arm to the ground while I slapped on the second cuff and sapped her of her otherworldly strength. Geraldine had other ideas. The second her eyes registered the knife, she rolled on top of me. I adjusted my trajectory mid-motion from an offensive maneuver to a defensive one, raising my knife-wielding hand instead to push Geraldine off of me. For the effort, the blade made contact with her pristine face, slicing open a line from mid-cheek to ear. Taking the opportunity that her pause of shock gave me, I held the cold metal against her throat while blood dripped from her wound onto my face. Her free hand was also tightly grasping my own neck, the strength I hadn't managed to negate being used to slowly crush my windpipe.

"Tell your partner to back off and I'll let go."

My brows furrowed a moment before a figure stepped silently into the room. I rolled my eyes upward, trying to see the newcomer upside-down and determine how much more danger I was in. It took only seconds to register his face and the gun he had pointed directly at Geraldine's head.

My chauffeur.

I locked my eyes to his and opened my mouth to reiterate the request, but the grip on my throat choked off the words and Geraldine's blood was dropping into my mouth, drowning me via the small amount of air I was able to take in to breathe.

The man assessed the situation quickly, raising his arms and hanging the gun from his thumb through the trigger guard. I was probably the only one of the two females in the room who knew that he could still aim and shoot before Geraldine so much as blinked—at least, I was hoping that was the case. A lot was riding on my assumption that he'd received the same training I did; the training that had taught me the speed which I'd just used to save my own life.

True to her word, the vice around my neck was released, though her hand remained clasped there in warning. Anger surged through me as I gagged on both the metallic taste of blood and the remnants of fear alike. Her skin was hot under my touch, the stagnant kind of heat like what permeates your kitchen after a day full of high-temperature baking with the afternoon sun beating its way in through the windows. I was sure the anger had also boiled my own flesh, or at least had created a storm behind my eyes, judging by the stricken look that overcame the other woman's face.

With a swift burst of speed that surprised even me, the knife dropped from my grip, narrowly missing my own face, and I coiled my fist to punch Geraldine directly in her already bloody face. Her body sailed off of mine, colliding with the metal wall she'd hidden behind just moments ago. I rolled, secured the second half of the restraints onto her free wrist, and abruptly emptied my stomach into the corner of the closet since it was finally safe to do so.

Obscure blood tasted more awful than I imagined human blood ever could. Duly noted.

Chapter 27 - Marie

The ride back to HQ was far worse than the ride out had been. Had someone told me that hours ago when I first stepped grumpily into the car, I wouldn't have believed them.

Geraldine sat in the rear of the vehicle, cuffed and alternating between being a bawling and snotty mess, and a whimpering, twitching one. The cut on her cheek had been deeper than I'd thought, refusing to slow even the smallest bit over our travels. By the time we pulled up to the enormous white building, the long stretch of green lawn swallowing up what the luminescent walls didn't of our vision, most of the cloth interior under our captive's body was either sticky and dark or wet and dark. The novel idea of werewolves was that they healed quickly from anything other than silver; did that mean that Geraldine wasn't a werewolf, or that storybooks had disarmed us with misinformation?

Three heavily armed figures stepped toward us from the walkway between the buildings. I vaguely recognized the female of the group, her high ponytail in shades of campfire stirring my memory. The words formed on my tongue before I remembered that I couldn't address her by name or status—that I wasn't *allowed* to recognize her—so I swallowed them down again bitterly and settled for locking my gaze to her form in the hopes that she'd feel it and return my look with her own of recognition.

No such luck.

Geraldine squealed and kicked as though her life depended on it, nearly toppling one of the wardens as they extracted her from the back seat. No one so much as blinked at the blood-soaked seat cloth or the still-dripping cut on her face. Was it a confirmation of the deception fed to us through fables? I made a mental note to ask Michael about it when I saw him next.

A sturdy whoosh of air greeted me as I shoved my way through the building's main entrance, the mission file in hand and my bag lying abandoned in the passenger seat. I'd nearly forgotten it after the capture and flushed a heavy shade of pink when I was reminded by my mysterious driver.

Speak of the devil.

My chauffeur hovered behind me, the weight of his presence just heavy enough to grab my attention as his footfalls echoed my own. Part of me wondered whether it was intentional, and that part grew exponentially larger as I turned and exchanged a look with him. Nearly concerned, a look of intrigue splayed across his face while his shoulders bobbed in a harmless shrug.

"So, you *were* my babysitter."

A tiny sliver of a smirk was all the response I received. Tension sang between us, neither wanting to break first in the unwitting battle of dominance I'd spurred on with the hard look I pierced through his stupidly handsome face. I'd never been one to back down from male dominance games, despite the fact that I lacked the physical equipment to qualify for the challenge in the first place. He shifted ever so slightly toward me, a fist balling and then stretching back out. The threat of physical violence was growing thick between us until he abruptly dropped his eyes and saluted, stiffening to a rigid board of hardened warden flesh—some of which was peeking out from underneath his t-shirt as it fluttered across his stomach. It took more effort than I'd like to admit to drag my gaze from that exposed skin. If anyone asked, I'd blame it on the overwhelming amount of testosterone he exuded.

I'd also been right. Abs of steel.

"Give me your report," snapped President's unusually stern voice.

I whirled, mouth agape to relay the mission before I realized that the command was not meant for me. Of course not.

"The target was apprehended with minor incident. No intervention was necessary, and the drop time was approximately fifty-nine minutes."

President swung a hard gaze my way. "Too long," she chastised before returning her attention to my chauffeur. "Injuries?"

"None to report on the asset. The target sustained several."

A long silence stretched between the three of us. Breath caught in my throat, unwilling to come forward and face the scene unfolding. I was certain that President would turn her anger on me at any moment; an anger that both surprised and alarmed me when compared to the babbling brook demeanor she'd held during every encounter prior to that one.

Finally, mercifully, our leader spoke again. "Report on the injuries."

"Laceration to the left cheek. Two cracked ribs on the lower left side. Minor concussion. All are non-healing."

I blinked rapidly, unsure that the conversation still centered around my mission. Geraldine certainly had been cut on the cheek, but I hadn't harmed her ribs *or* concussed her. Had something happened to her after our altercation? I measured up my travel companion silently, trying to recall if there had been a moment of privacy stolen between him and our captive, but I'd rode in the front with him the whole way back and I'd kept watch over Geraldine the entire time. There was no chance I'd have strayed my attention for even a second between capture and delivery, lest my first mission end with the target escaping. Failure was not an option, and so I had been careful. Apparently not careful enough.

Several more words were exchanged between the two of them, but they never reached my ears. A tsunami of thoughts tumbled from one end of my mind to the other and back again. Maybe Geraldine had been right to fear capture. Was there a hidden agenda in the capture of Obscure, or was there perhaps a fanatic among the wardens? How had she sustained injuries that I hadn't caused when I was the only one to make contact until just moments ago?

Was he lying? No, lying to President wouldn't benefit anyone. My teeth chomped against a bit of my inner cheek, both in thought and an attempt to keep my thoughts from spilling into the air unwittingly.

It took several minutes to realize that President and I were alone and she had been watching me expectantly for an undetermined amount of time, as though she knew the thoughts in my head before I even made an attempt to voice them. A knowing smile softened her face, all trace of the previous anger tucked neatly away. She gestured for me to follow and led the way through the maze of halls that I was sure I'd never be able to fully navigate alone. It was clear to me that, while the majority of the building retained the original structure of the real White House, the interior layout had been severely modified to dissuade any unauthorized trespass. One could learn the route if traveling it often enough, but there were strict guidelines in place to dictate which personnel could access certain parts of the facility, and as we crossed the threshold into the Presidential suite, I was sure that I was not authorized for that part.

President pulled out a chair as she passed it, gesturing me to take a seat while she settled into her own behind a desk nearly the size of a car. She tapped briefly at the computer between us before shifting the monitor my way and revealing the screen to us both. There, in an image that my own eyes could process, sat Geraldine and the three wardens who had escorted her from my custody. With a flick of her wrist toward a device I couldn't see, sound blared to life.

The burlier of the two men paced back and forth across the screen, hands shoved forcefully into his pockets. He never slowed or stopped, as though his entire purpose was to wear a footpath in the thin carpet along one wall of the interrogation room.

"If you can't come up with an explanation for your presence at the victim's house," Karen said slowly, calmly. "*At the time of the murder*, we have no choice but to detain you until you can." I could see only the back of her fire-red hair as she spoke, which swayed with her words as if to emphasize them.

Karen flipped through several pages in a file that sat on the table between them. Out of the stack, she drew a photo and slid it across the tabletop. Geraldine's own face stared up at her, courtesy of the doorbell camera from Andrea's home. Geraldine only whined, which seemed to annoy the pacing man, who picked up speed. The remaining warden merely sat unmoving, the back of his head the only proof that he even existed at all.

"We know that you're a werewolf," Karen continued. She pointed to the laceration marring Geraldine's otherwise kind face. "Why hasn't that healed yet?"

Silence, save for the footsteps echoing against the claustrophobically small room, of which all three visible walls were captured in the camera view.

"Did Andrea know your secret? Did you do this because she was threatening to out you? We are well aware of what happens to outed Obscure. Was this to protect your identity?"

All at once, Geraldine's face twisted. The pitiful woman who'd cried alligator tears in the fetal position for nearly three hours was no more. A lethal smile split across her face and something about her bone structure shifted before my eyes, though I'd not been able to pinpoint what exactly had changed; she was just suddenly, *more*. In place of the generic sitcom mother stared back the Big Bad Wolf who'd already eaten grandma. She growled deeply, training her gaze on the form darting back and forth across the room.

"You humans will never understand."

The rumble of laughter that spilled from her lips shot the hairs on my arms to attention. Even the unknown distance between us did not diminish the intensity of the warning of danger that slithered up my spine.

Something else also rose within me to meet the adrenaline— excitement.

Knowing that President's attention was likely split between the scene before us and my reaction, I schooled my face. If she didn't look directly at the goose flesh creeping its way along my skin, it would be impossible to sense the anger and fear coursing through every fiber of my being. And yet, I also felt *exhilarated*; betrayed by Geraldine's facade, but ready for action.

Through the monitor, Karen slapped a hand down on the table and leaned forward, no hint of fear in her that could be conveyed through the camera's view. I tried not to flinch at the sudden noise. Geraldine only glowered, entirely unaffected by the display of aggression. I noted that her wrists were shackled, a long line of chain links disappearing from view under the table. Still, it probably wasn't smart to get too close, so I held my breath as Karen's face inched toward Geraldine's, anticipating a violent scene unfolding in my mind's eye. Her words were low and slow as she spoke them, spilling from between her lips as though they were heavy and she was tired of holding them in.

"Please, enlighten the rest of the class. What, exactly, do you think that we don't understand?" Karen's face may not have been visible from the camera angle, but the menace dripping from her voice painted enough of a picture that I stiffened, reacting to the threat unintentionally, as though it had been directed at me, personally, though I knew that wasn't the case. "You're pretty weak, as far as werewolves go. Is that why you can't heal? Not enough power, baby werewolf?"

A snarl ripped through the room—both the interrogation cell and President's office alike. I slid my eyes to President's side of the table and inhaled sharply as I met her gaze, which was riveted not to the screen, but instead, to me. A moment passed between us before I could manage to look away again, nearly sucked into the expression of fascination shining in her eyes. Surely President had seen interrogation happen previously, through endless variations; could it have been a test of sorts? Was she watching for my reaction to see if I could handle it; that I was cut out for the work required of a warden? My teeth ground subconsciously against one another as the thought skittered through my mind that each of the new wardens may have taken a turn in that very seat, watching the interrogation of their own first solo mission target. It seemed too simple an exercise after the sufficiently rigorous training we endured just months ago. There had to be more to it than observation; it was President, after all. It was the New Government.

Michael's voice filled my mind. "Be prepared for *anything.*"

The sting against the back of my head resurfaced with the memory, a reminder of the unexpected blow he dealt to punctuate the lesson—with the butt of a gun, no less. Shooting me would have been physically painful, and yet less agonizing than the hit that I took to my pride at the time. The point was that a gun was useful as a weapon in more ways than just by firing bullets.

Use your weapons to their fullest extent. That's what I learned. That's what I'd do.

My mind sifted quickly through the options in front of me, trying to find the hidden meaning in my presence with President at that specific moment and the best possible way to prove my skill; to prove that she was not wrong to choose me. If nothing else, should I fail the test—whatever the hell the test actually was—I'd learn something new from the experience. I pushed to a stand, my chair easing across the perfectly polished wood flooring with barely a whisper.

"I'd like to speak with Geraldine."

Something passed across President's face before it curled around a pleasant, unruffled smile, the corners of her eyes crinkling slightly under the shift. She, too, stood. With the push of a button, the computer screen faded to black and she led me wordlessly out of her suite and down the stairs I'd traveled endlessly over my days of training. The familiarity helped to bolster my resolve. Instead of taking a right toward the training halls, however, we continued straight through the rows of cages in silence. When we'd passed what felt like the thousandth set of bars, the space finally opened into a room lined with doors that looked very much like vaults from the outside, complete with cog-shaped handles in the center of each. I counted ten of them just from my position at the entrance of the room.

President marched directly to one of the closed doors, peering briefly through the high glass window at the top on her tiptoes, then knocked lightly twice and produced a key from her pocket that slid home to unlock the door. As it swung open and revealed an entirely smooth opposite side, my brows knitted together. If the door was locked only from the outside, and there were no guards waiting to open it, how did the people inside get out?

There was no more time to ponder it, as President stood holding the door wide for me with a patient expression that I wasn't entirely sure would remain patient for long if I dawdled. The pacing man paused, confusion bare on his face as he eyed me in the doorway. Karen spared only the briefest of glances in my direction before returning her attention to Geraldine, along with the seated man who never shifted his attention at all.

Stepping cautiously over the threshold, steeling myself not to flinch as the door shut firmly behind me and the key slid the lock home once more, I hesitated. Was it wise to have trapped myself in a room with three near strangers and a werewolf? Probably not, but it was far too late to turn back. I'd finish what I started.

Geraldine's hair was frazzled in many places, flyaways swirling in the air as her head whipped back and forth between the increasing number of wardens in the room. It did feel a bit crowded with the five of us crammed into a room the size of a small closet. I glanced at the bright red locks at the other end of the room as a sigh pushed its way through my lips.

It was surprising to have seen Karen appear at the delivery point, which made it even more strange to see her sitting across the table from my first target, though I didn't dare let the shock show. I had been sure that she'd failed the program. While the wardens who started together hadn't all trained together once we'd broken into teams, some days our teams shared space with other trainers and their trainees, which meant a glimpse at some of the other recruits and the ability to measure their progress. I used it as a benchmark against my own progress, always pushing to stay ahead of not only my own team as much as possible, but all of the others as well. Because of that, I graduated from the program earlier than most of the rest—but not before one particular session where the entirety of both classes watched as Karen was escorted out in the middle of training by a man I hadn't seen before. She hadn't returned after that.

Seeing her at Headquarters, looking at home in the cramped quarters of the interrogation cell, raised more questions than it answered.

Geraldine made a small noise—sort of a cross between being startled and pinched. She tried to rise from her seat at the table but the chains were apparently too short, so she hunched instead and gave me hungry, angry eyes.

"*You.*"

"Hello, Geraldine."

"What do you want?" The words dripped with malice, each barbed as though, once spit from her mouth, they could be honed into a weapon against me.

"I have some questions for you."

I tried to move further into the space but quickly realized that there were too many bodies already. The silent seated man patted Karen on the arm, then stood and escorted her toward the door. The pacing man followed. The crowd of bodies against the door prevented me from being able to see what they'd done to unlock it, and the idea of being trapped alone with Geraldine momentarily froze my feet to the floor. Then she laughed again—an ugly, evil laugh that burned my blood as it brought to mind the crime she stood accused of. Fear was eaten alive by rage. I took the closest seat and clasped my hands on the table, trying to pin together coherent thoughts amidst the swirl of curse words I wanted to stab her with instead.

When I'd asked to speak to Geraldine, I'd done so in the hopes that it was President's true test. Becoming a warden meant that we would give our lives in an effort to bring peace to the humans, and that meant seeing the mission through all the way to the end, whatever that end may be. A deep, steadying breath soothed the fire in my veins enough that I could think clearly again. When I spoke again, it was with sympathy and genuine curiosity. I hoped it translated.

"What does it mean to be a werewolf?"

I looked up quickly to catch Geraldine's face as the question registered. Her scowl softened, her lips released from a toothy snarl into a gentle slackened jaw. As intended, my words disarmed her.

"I know what we're taught here at the facility, but that isn't all of it. I want to know. What do you *feel*? What's it like?"

Even the rigid set of her body relaxed as she sunk back into her seat. The rattle of chains tried to drown the sigh that escaped her as she did so, but I could hear it just the same.

"It's difficult to describe to a human." There was a finality in her voice, and I thought she would leave it at that, but her own hands clasped on the table, mimicking mine, and she leaned forward a bit to continue her words more quietly. "I was human too, once. *Before*. I've only been this way for a few years." She shrugged her shoulders lightly, looking up to the metal ceiling as though she could see through it to the sky high above. "Maybe fifty or sixty. They do pass quickly once you're nearly immortal."

Nearly immortal.

The words shot a bolt of ice through me. I shifted in my seat, which Geraldine either didn't notice or didn't care to point out. I'd bet that the others were watching the scene unfold, and they would surely notice. *Keep it together*, I chastised myself.

Geraldine continued as though she was speaking with a friend, a casual sadness overtaking every bit of the anger she'd held before. She seemed to shrink into her words as they left her, transforming her from the monster she was just moments ago.

"At first, it's scary. The magic inside you, it's strong. It feels like bugs underneath your skin." She moved to rub her arms but the cuffs didn't allow the movement. She settled with smoothing fingers over her opposite wrist instead. "Then you get used to that. You think everything's going to be fine afterward. You're strong, you have all of these," The word escaped her, so the werewolf merely shook her head and moved on as if it was not needed. "You wonder why it's called a curse, but then it hits you. The undeniable urge for a *pack*."

Wide, fearful eyes darted back and forth across the room. Tension suddenly rose off of her in waves, pitting the sadness against frustration and rolling them together into a clear threat of violence. "The magic, it wants you to be around... humans, your former pack. It taunts you and teases you with it, and if you don't oblige, there's unimaginable pain. It gets worse and worse the longer you fight it, until you just can't fight it anymore."

"Do you, you know, shapeshift?"

"Oh, no, no. Thankfully, no." Her face contorted in an effort to hold the peacefulness we'd achieved.

"So to become a werewolf, you are a human who is *cursed*? By what?"

"A witch, of course."

Oh, right. Of course. Witches. "And the curse, it forces you to be close to humans, right? So why kill them if you're supposed to think of them as pack?"

A sad smile crept across Geraldine's lips. Tears welled in her eyes, marring the color of her irises behind the ebbing salty water. "Because they smell like food; the most delicious of delicacies you could ever imagine. That's the curse. You have to fight it, but it's so hard. That's why I killed her. I didn't mean to, I swear. I just went for a visit. The urge was pushing at me, causing me all sorts of pain and when I got there, when I stood in front of her, it all changed. I was so tempted and it's so hard to control when you're new."

Tears poured freely down her face, falling to the metal table between us with light taps against the silence. Afraid she'd turn back into the mess of snot from the backseat, I quickly reached across the table and offered a gentle squeeze of her hands. I knew the moment we made contact that it was a mistake—and a rookie one at that—but it was too late to take it back and despite my bravado, I *was* a rookie. Something shifted rapidly behind her eyes. She yanked her hands back as though my touch had burned her, as if I'd intended to use the moment of weakness to harm her instead of learn from her. Her features twisted with anger, the rigid set to her spine lifting her head high.

"You did this to me!" she screeched. "You will not torture me any longer, you monster!"

Chaos followed. Geraldine launched herself upright, but where the shackles previously constricted her movement, they instead crumbled under her immense strength. Thanks to my recent months of training, I registered the lightning-fast movement of her right arm, which, finally free to move as she wished it to, plunged directly into her own chest cavity without a hint of hesitation. With all the speed I could muster, I lunged forward to take hold of her arms, intent on stopping whatever gruesome display was unraveling, but as I tugged the limb free of her body, my eyes caught sight of something very much out of place.

There, in Geraldine's hand, was a vice-like grip of her own heart, no longer connected to her being.

It took only seconds for her body to go limp in my arms, the weight dropping fully into me, causing me to stagger hard to remain upright. Hands that were not my own were instantly on my body, but I didn't register whose or for what reason. Warm wetness washed over me, soaking the majority of my clothes, which clung uncomfortably nearly everywhere. The werewolf's corpse was lifted away by several more pairs of hands, and I let it go, knowing that there was nothing more I could have done in that moment anyway. A voice rang in my ear, close to me and trying hard to grab my attention. I couldn't force myself to acknowledge it, to break from the barreling train of thought that threatened to flatten me if I dared attempt to slow it down.

Geraldine had taken her own life; but why? Her last words looped in my mind, pushing apprehension and confusion through my veins with each repetition.

Someone had been torturing her, and she believed it to be me.

Chapter 28 - Marie

My cell phone rang, startling me from my thoughts. The apartment was quiet, as usual, but where I once found relaxation and peace, the silence seemed only deafening. Most of my neighbors had left the area, meaning even the noise from beyond the walls had turned tail and run. President may have been able to pull strings and restore consistent power and water to the building but it hadn't made a difference to the other residents, who still fled for whatever greener pastures they imagined. The once-bustling complex felt like a ghost town, haunted by the memories of families long since torn apart. Maybe they'd have stayed if they'd received the same offer that President had made me on the bloody sidewalk what seemed like ages ago.

With a snap, I closed the binder I'd been working in and pushed it aside. My brain didn't appear to have the capacity for research—or perhaps just not for the particular subject I'd chosen. The words 'werewolf' glared out at me along the shiny spine as I pushed it away and lifted the phone screen to my face. The letter 'P' flashed brightly across the face. Speak of the devil.

Lifting the phone to my ear, I forwent a greeting, opting instead for silence and patience. Chit-chat wasn't necessary; President knew that I was there and she would have no time for small talk anyway. Whatever test it was that she'd thrown me into on the day of Geraldine's death, I must have passed, considering further contact could only mean that I was receiving a new assignment. At least she'd given me the grace of a few days' time to gather myself, though she'd not known that it had been spent careening down a destructive path of ravenous information-gathering. Or did she? She seemed to know quite a lot that she very likely shouldn't have.

"Mare," came her voice, small through the phone line and utterly fragile-sounding despite the fact that we both knew it was a front. Why she bothered anymore was beyond me. She could have saved the energy for someone who was still buying the innocent facade she was selling.

Marie, I corrected in my head automatically.

"A car is waiting outside for you. The file you need is inside. You have only five hours this time."

Dial tone.

Wardens were strong, resilient, and nearly indestructible if trained properly, but we were not heartless. It had been less than seventy-two hours since Geraldine's body dropped. Andrea's murder had been closed, officially, and the news outlets hastily reported that the New Government had apprehended the rogue Obscure responsible for the crime. There was no mention of *her* subsequent untimely passing, I had noted. Though I was the one who brought Geraldine into custody, I tried hard not to feel guilty over what had happened. Regardless of what urges Geraldine felt, she'd committed murder and needed to face justice for it—and in a way, she did. The method was what had haunted my sleepless night since.

Sighing, slinging the small pack over my shoulder that lived mostly next to the front door for situations precisely like last-minute assignments, I slipped on my shoes and headed out. The thought crossed my mind that Silent G.I. Joe might be behind the wheel, and that brought a small smile to my face as well as a slight bounce to my step. At least it meant the view would be decent during whatever travel would be required. Yes, it was time to move on. Geraldine had died; it was just something that happened in the line of work I'd pursued. All that was left was to move on and catch the next bad guy, save what would be their next victims. Pushing away the thoughts of my previous assignment, focus began to settle over me. It was time to be a warden again.

The vehicle waiting for me was a vast improvement over the last one. A sleek black metal body shone to a perfect polish, right down to the darkly tinted windows that shielded the interior from curious eyes. It idled along the sidewalk just outside the parking garage, purring. My steps slowed as I approached, a low whistle of appreciation slipping out, both for the car and for Silent Joe, who emerged from behind the wheel in nothing less than the most expensive suit I'd ever seen. Well, next to some of the ones I'd seen on Luke, that was.

Wordlessly, he rounded the front of the vehicle and extended something to me that lay curled in his fist. Immediately, I held out my own palm to receive it. A set of extremely light keys changed hands, the metal warm from being cradled in the man's palm. He nodded once, curt, and retreated to what I then saw was an identical car parked not far behind the one he'd exited.

Mine.

Hot damn.

The interior was as flawless as expected—all dark leather and fully loaded. The GPS navigation screen was nearly as large as the TV screen in my living room. Okay, maybe not quite, but it did feel that way to someone who'd not owned a car in many years, and certainly never one as fancy. On the passenger seat sat three pairs of Obscure restraints, a thin manila file, and a bag that, once opened, revealed itself to contain a handgun,—a Smith and Wesson M&P, to be exact, which meant it would fit perfectly into my small hands,—an upgraded version of the knife I kept tucked away on my person at all times, and a baton. The sight of the knife brought a smile to my face.

The makeshift kit seemed to include all of the weapons I'd proven myself to be most proficient with during training. It was, in essence, personalized. Replacing the shoddy knife in my belly holster with the newer one, confidence washed over me. It was the one weapon that had kept me head and shoulders above the rest of my class; the weapon that, I believe, secured my graduation. A laugh pulled itself from my throat as I stroked the cold metal and the memory replayed—my fellow trainee, Prakeet, and I grappling through the hand-to-hand section of training. Prakeet wasn't often assigned to me for those exercises because he was significantly taller, stronger, and heavier than I was, and the few times we'd been matched initially, I was easily overpowered and had a myriad of injuries to prove it. That time, however, I decided that I would not lose again. When Prakeet pulled me into a choke hold, as he often did, I slid my rickety knife from my boot and stabbed him directly in the thigh—or, I would have, had Michael not seen the flash of the blade and stopped the fight before I made contact. Regardless, I'd won the match and the look of surprise and appreciation on Michael's face had been entirely worth it.

Rule number six of being a warden: Use *every* advantage. We were not just fighting with weapons, but with our lives.

I picked up the file and thumbed through it as quickly as possible, absorbing the information with only a glance. Thankfully, the location was close to home—only twenty minutes away by car—and the file was nearly barren. A dark-skinned man smiled up at me from the photo clipped to the inside cover. His head was bald, shiny, and his toothy grin seemed genuine, borderline pleasant. He seemed like the type of man you'd find hurrying through the streets of the business park, grabbing a quick bite to eat in a pristine suit between back-to-back meetings; entirely professional and comfortable with the chaos of a hectic life. I could picture him at the head of a large conference room table, speaking animatedly about his topic of choice. Leadership oozed from the glossy surface of the photograph. The only other page in the file listed him as a vampire, but did not identify the crime he'd committed or for what he was wanted in relation to. The word 'DANGEROUS' was scrawled across the top of the page in red ink, the handwriting so perfect that I assumed it had come from President herself. That was an interesting fact to note, which I promptly filed away for future review. Was President personally assigning missions? Had the mission been hand-picked for me—and if so, why?

"Alright, Mr. Hakim Kaplan. What did you do?" I frowned while I plugged his home address into the GPS, moving the screen with my fingers to scout the area around the residence before beginning the journey. "And why only five hours?"

There were no answers for me in an empty car outside my apartment. Glancing at the clock, I set off toward my destination.

The streets were quiet as I rolled the vehicle into Hakim's neighborhood. It was an appealing area—the homes, while some still sported the telltale signs of vandalism, were all two-story cookie-cutters, freshly painted prior to the destruction. It was easy to picture manicured lawns and children hosting lemonade stands on the street corners. Thankfully, no one remaining had suddenly developed the urge for a spontaneous jog, so the risk of civilian interference was low despite my lack of planning for the approach. Having no true time for reconnaissance on such a short deadline, and having seen no obvious alternate intrusion point via the GPS map of the area, I angled the vehicle directly into Hakim's driveway and marched up to his front door. Snuggled tightly into the front of my pants, the shiny new Smith & Wesson pressed its cold metal against my flushed skin. Adrenaline hummed to the surface as I readied myself on the small stoop.

Without any delay at all, as though he'd been standing at the door in anticipation of my arrival, a man answered, surprising me slightly despite my supposed preparedness for the mission. I recognized him instantly from the photograph, his bright smile meeting his eyes just as it had before the camera when the image was snapped.

"Can I help you?"

"Hakim Kalplan?" I asked, remaining as polite as possible in the hopes that I wouldn't spook him. The restraints practically burned a hole through my back pocket at his proximity. How easy it would be to whip them out and slap them on him—mission over. But knowing that he was a vampire ensured that I wouldn't underestimate his speed. The man nodded. "I'm with the New Government. We'd like you to come in to answer some questions for us."

His grip tightened briefly on the frame of the door, then released. He sighed heavily, opened the door wider, and beckoned me inside. "I am in the middle of something, but if you'd please come inside, I'd be happy to answer your questions while I finish."

It was a bad idea—horrible, in fact. Yet, Hakim turned on his heel and disappeared immediately into the void of darkness just beyond the door. I cursed silently to myself and stepped across the threshold, glancing at my new watch on the way. I'd taken too much time already and there remained just over four hours until the mission had to be completed. Mission completion included delivering the target, which was another forty-minute drive to headquarters.

Shit.

The interior of the home lacked any visible light source, even boasting heavily covered windows that dared not allow even a peek of sunlight through. Narrowing my eyes, I recalled both the fables of vampires hating sunlight, and the way that Hakim had stood, unaffected, in the doorway of his home while sunlight beat against his bare skin. Keeping a hand close to my back pocket, I took a steadying breath and advanced into the home. Michael had taught us about vampire speed and that the myth of drinking blood likely came from the fact that it was most reliable to bite their victims in order to draw out the magic; but the New Government had no hard and fast evidence one way or another on the effects of sunlight. I was in the dark—literally and figuratively.

My only available path seemed to be down a central hallway, rooms opening to either side with doorless archways, and a wide staircase about halfway through. I glanced up the staircase, noting that it curved back over top of me and didn't allow much vision into the upper floor without first ascending. There was a fifty-fifty chance that he'd taken the stairs to the second floor. I paused for a moment to get my bearings; to make a decision. Continuing forward down the hallway, past the staircase, the other end of it spilled out into yet another open area—one containing the kitchen, informal dining room, and what appeared to be the living room. Hakim stood in the kitchen, fidgeting with a pan over the stove, and did not acknowledge my presence as I stepped into the space behind him. It unnerved me that, though he moved about the kitchen, there wasn't a sound of pan shifting against the burner or footsteps on the wooden floor. The scrape of drawer glides was mysteriously missing, as was the rattle of the contents inside.

Silence enveloped us. My hand shifted closer to the restraints, an odd feeling of foreboding draping itself over the room. Over me.

"Unfortunately, this cannot wait. I'm giving you the option to surrender peacefully. I'll ensure that you are taken discreetly, so as not to alarm your neighbors, but we have to leave now."

He turned then, a sickening grin of danger and amusement catching me off guard, but he didn't advance. Instead, he disappeared; entirely gone, vanished. I cursed, loudly and severely unladylike. I pulled the knife from its hiding place, deciding that the element of surprise was not going to do me any good in the scenario and that firing bullets at something that could vanish wasn't exactly helpful either. It had to be a goddamn vampire, didn't it?

A wicked laugh descended from behind me, echoing down the hallway and back again. I scouted each of the rooms in front of me, just in case, before turning back down the hallway and taking the stairs slowly toward the upper floor. The sound had definitely traveled downward at me. Another hallway greeted me at the top, though that time the rooms boasted tightly shut doors, both to my left and to my right. Fan-fucking-tastic.

Choosing the closest door down the left side, for no reason other than proximity, a firmly placed boot below the handle forced it to reveal its contents—emptiness, darkness, and silence. I would *definitely* be blasting music in the bastard vampire's ears on the ride to headquarters. Each of the remaining doors down the left side opened to reveal the same, tipping my frustration further into rage with every one. Hakim could have easily left the residence ages ago, meaning I was doing nothing more than wasting time on an already short deadline.

Was it a distraction while Hakim fled, or was he playing games with me, watching me fail over and over again?

Turning, resolved to return to the vehicle and wait him out, he suddenly appeared at the opposite end of the hallway.

"Catch me if you can, warden woman."

That time, he didn't disappear. I stalked forward, gripping the knife tightly but keeping it as hidden as possible against my thigh in the dark. Arms spread wide in a gesture of arrogance, fangs peeking from behind slightly spread lips, he beckoned me forward.

It was a trap and I knew it, yet I had no other choice. When there was barely five feet of distance between us, I lunged at him. The sickening sound of maniacal giggling penetrated my ears, reverberating in my skull so powerfully that I halted all movement to shrink back and protect myself. It was no use—the sound cascaded through me, agony screaming through my body on its heels. I'd never felt such white-hot pain from a sound before. What in the hell was happening? If it was a vampire power the New Government didn't know about, we were in deep shit. It seemed like the vampires kept a hell of a lot hidden from us. I could see that Hakim had earned every bit of his 'dangerous' file tag.

Forced to drop to a knee just inches from Hakim's prone form, he crouched to level our gazes.

"You kneel before me so easily. You're not much fun at all."

Then, I felt it. As the pain became familiar, numbing, and my body adjusted to it as it had been taught to do, I could sense the presence of the second individual. The location was vague, unclear amidst my senses screaming for relief and battling back the hurt slowly. My bet was that I'd find them hidden beyond the door Hakim stood guard in front of. It seemed the safest place to be. I sucked in a deep breath, held it a moment, and released it quickly as I swung the knife in an arc and buried it into Hakim's arm.

Wide eyes skittered away as he howled in pain, the door behind him flying open at the sound.

"Didn't think I could move, did you, you bastard? I'm not as weak as you think."

A female stood in the doorway, looming over Hakim's form, which had more to do with her enormous presence than her physical height. She was small, young, and her short hair made the face of rage that it framed all the more severe. In her arms, she cradled a stuffed animal against her chest. At a quick glance, I'd have placed her around seven or eight years old. My initial instinct was to treat her like a victim, but my training knew better, pointing her out as the source of the magic permeating the air all around. The girl was dangerous too.

She was also, apparently, emotionally driven, as she'd dropped her magic the second Hakim's howls had driven her out of hiding.

Wasting no time since the pain had receded, I moved forward again, releasing a set of restraints from its home in my back pocket. The girl registered the movement, locked her eyes on the metal in my hand, and dropped the weight in her arms to fling them both in my direction. It was only then that I realized the thing in her arms had not, indeed, been a stuffed animal. Bulbous eyes turned to watch me from a face covered in curly white fur. Its mouth was far too wide, showing off dozens of flat, broad teeth. It stood barely a foot high, jumping from one tiny fuzzed foot to another as it cackled madly, but no sound emerged. Its tiny body shook with silent laughter.

Two things happened at once. Hakim disappeared again, reappearing immediately behind me, where he locked a strong grip around both of my arms and pressed my back against the length of his front. At the same time, a blow struck me from the front, whipping my head to the side and knocking the restraints from my grasp. Above my head, Hakim—who stood nearly a foot taller than I—grunted as though he'd also taken some of the blow.

Huh. Perhaps he had.

Not wanting to wait for another strike, and knowing that with the presence of the magical girl and her beast, I was sorely outmatched and outnumbered, fear began to trickle through me. My survival instinct rose to greet the fear, devouring it in an instant. The file had said nothing about the girl or the creature, whatever they were, but I resolved to not let it impact my mission. Once I'd sampled a taste of what I was up against, I was ready.

I dropped my weight, hoping to snap free from Hakim's hold, but had no such luck. The vampire merely leaned down, allowing my weight to draw forward his upper body and bend it over me. He still wore an ugly smile, though blood dripped from his nose and smeared against his teeth. My brow furrowed as I contemplated the idea that the girl's magic had done that to him.

Not daring to hesitate even a second, I quickly propelled my feet straight underneath me and launched myself upward, my head connecting directly with Hakim's face. He roared in pain, the girl screamed, high and shrill, and the creature began to run circles around her feet as I yanked my arms free of the vampire's grip. The restraints sat just a few inches away, having seemingly bounced off of the wall with the impact. Snatching them up, I rolled behind Hakim's body, using him as a shield against whatever magic was heading my way from tiny fists of fury.

I reached forward with an open cuff, but Hakim straightened before I could reach his wrist. He bared fangs so white that they nearly glowed in the dark. I realized, a moment too late, that I'd just handed him my own wrist in the process of trying to catch his. He whirled, snatched my arm with both of his, and sank teeth into it before I could so much as move to defend myself.

That time, I was the one that screamed.

Chapter 29 - Luke

She was in a hurry; apparently too much of a hurry to check for a tail. I followed, leaving more than the required space between us, just in case she wised up to it. She'd been gone for months, but surely that was not nearly long enough to have learned everything she needed to learn. I'd assumed, as anyone would, that she'd failed her task at the great white building and returned home with her tail between her legs. I was sure of it because of the way she shuttered herself in her apartment for nearly three days after. I had been ecstatic, relieved that the nightmare was over and things could return to normal—to the plan I'd so carefully laid out for us both—but then she'd emerged as if nothing had happened at all. In a rush that piqued my curiosity and my fear equally, she set off on a task that I couldn't help but tag along for, whether she knew it or not.

We traveled together to an upper-scale neighborhood not far outside of our hometown. I couldn't stop myself from admiring the car she drove along the way; it was very nice, and very expensive. The sun shone off of it like it had been waxed and buffed regularly, not exactly new but still meticulously maintained. How had Marie managed to afford such a thing, and who had been caring for it? The Marie I knew barely kept her house livable. There was no way she'd been tending to that car—not with it still in the condition that it was. Not even a warden's stipend would cover something that shiny and new, even with it being a model from a few years past. Glancing out again at the homes we passed and noting that she'd begun to slow in front of one around the corner, I frowned. It was possible she'd made a friend in the formerly affluent community, and the car had truly belonged to them instead.

She pulled into a driveway and got out promptly, heading to the front door to knock and tap her foot impatiently. That was my Marie, always impatient. I couldn't hear what was said from so far away, but she exchanged brief words with a tall male figure and then followed him inside the home.

Fear sang through me, though I had no reason for it. Instinct had my metaphorical hackles raised despite the innocence of the exchange. Pausing to step back from the situation, I had to admit that rushing off to see someone in a neighborhood she'd never been spotted in before was no reason at all to be alarmed. Still, something about it was off.

Marie had returned home after months behind enemy lines, but I knew for a fact that warden training was grueling and Marie just hadn't been built for such a thing. The possibility hadn't crossed my mind that she'd actually passed the training, in what could be considered record time, and would be out in the field so early on.

My teeth ground together. It was also possible that my feelings and past memories of her were clouding my judgment. Objectively—was Marie capable of becoming a soldier?

Christ. The answer was yes.

So...

Was it warden business? Surely not, as she'd followed the man inside as though they were friends.

Yet, she'd left the front door wide open in her haste.

I killed the engine and stepped out of my own car, working my way cautiously toward the house they'd disappeared into together. It seemed like a quiet community, the kind where you'd see loads of children playing outside together on scooters and with sprinklers in the yard. Or, at least you *would* have, before the wars. The silence that settled over the neighborhood instead was both familiar—as it mimicked nearly every neighborhood in every city around the country—and unsettling. In a lesser area, the contrast would be less noticeable, less eerie.

Approaching Marie's new car carefully, I dipped my head against the tinted windows to peer inside. Only barely visible, on the passenger seat, was something in the vague shape of a sheet of paper, just thick enough to be concerning. A file folder. It sat closed, shouting in all but flashing exclamation marks that it held something interesting just beyond the thin paper cover. *Definitely* warden business. Jesus, Marie. I shifted my gaze to the door again, the feeling of dread growing by the second.

And then she screamed.

Speed that I hadn't used in ages pushed me through the open door and to the base of a large staircase in seconds. Overhead, the unmistakable sound of a struggle drifted through the air. I flew up the stairs, barely pausing long enough to assess the situation before barreling into the man whose teeth were sunken into Marie's exposed arm. She screamed again, likely from the force of the fangs being violently ripped from her flesh, but it was a better option than allowing him to continue while both of us danced around the specifics of extraction.

Marie's eyes landed on me with a look of surprise and fury as the vampire and I rolled over one another on the ground, each grappling for control. She hesitated only briefly. Confusion flickered over her face before she made a decision and turned her attention in the opposite direction of us. I could only hope that she'd decided to leave the vampire to me, as I'd intended. Truly, I didn't know what manner of being she faced instead and whether I'd made the right choice to pick one enemy over the other, but there wasn't time to change that decision. What was done, was done. It was time to survive.

I focused all of my attention on the being below me and forced everything else out of my mind. Marie would have to handle herself, and I couldn't afford to let my worry over her distract me from my own survival. If she'd managed to become a warden as I feared, then she had to be strong enough for whatever she faced in the dark of the hallway just beyond what I could see.

The vampire hissed at me, bucking under my body before realizing that I, too, held a hidden amount of strength and he'd not be going anywhere any time soon. He swiveled his head, a sickening crack sounding as his neck extended well past where it should have, and he sank fangs into my own arm instead. I roared, gripped his shoulders and lifted briefly before slamming him back down into the carpeted ground. The plush fibers softened the blow, but not so much that he didn't feel the pain of his skull connecting with the firmness of the wood below. With a wail that was echoed from a much higher-pitched voice behind us both, his teeth retracted from my skin. Two large, deep holes remained. Every few seconds, the muscles twitched from the trauma and spasmed the fingers of my left hand.

I gripped his skull with my good hand, pulling his head as far forward as I could manage while still on top of him, and slamming it back down again with all my strength. The bloodcurdling scream he bellowed made me shudder, and it struck me that the goose flesh spiraling along my skin wasn't entirely in displeasure.

"No!" Marie yelled from behind me, voice strained with frustration. "Don't kill him!"

The words pierced me, made me falter so that my grip slipped almost completely from the vampire's head as I strained it forward. Hell, *he* was her target. Of course he was.

I hesitated, weighing the options. If she failed the mission, would she be ejected from the program? Would she be free of the New Government's hold?

No, probably not. Once they got their claws into someone, it was both tough and dangerous to dig them out.

If I ruined things for her, would Marie hate me? That was an easy question to answer—it was a large, resounding yes.

Christ.

I tempered the blow, aiming instead to cause enough pain to buy a few moments of time. In a rush of air that chilled me briefly, Marie's body soared by to collide with the wall just beyond my reach. Under the force of the blow, and partially Marie's weight, the drywall buckled, dumping her to the ground below. I chanced a glance behind me but couldn't see her opponent through the rain of dust and debris that showered us. Something bumped against my shoe. Marie stood, not bothering to brush herself off, and pulled a gun from somewhere I didn't register in time. She aimed it like she meant business. I looked down, spied the restraints resting against my shoe, noted the clean lines they'd dragged across the carpet from where she'd slid them to me, and quickly secured them around the vampire's wrists. Though I'd seen them from afar, I had no idea what exactly they were meant to do or what effect—if any—they'd have on our vampire friend. He hissed at me again, baring fangs in preparation for another strike. I hoped that it wouldn't do much with the restraints on him, but it would still hurt like hell and it seemed poor form to let the bad guys beat you up after you cuffed them. I rolled away. Coming to my feet, I also hefted him to his before tossing him down the stairs. He'd hurt, but he'd survive.

Turning finally to Marie, I found her pointing her gun directly at the chest of a small girl. The golden halo of hair around the delicate features shifted something deep within me. It kicked loose a long-forgotten memory that I dared not revisit. Blood flashed across my vision, blurring the lines of reality and memory so deeply that, for a moment, I smelled only sunshine and the overwhelming aroma of copper. Tamping down hard on the image, I forced it back and stared at the child who stood defiantly, confidently, in the face of Marie's weapon. A child who was still alive.

"No," I breathed to myself, finally catching sight of the creature dancing around her short legs. "That's most definitely not a small girl." Not good. I stepped forward to assist, but Marie shifted to block my path, never taking her aim or her eyes from the threat in front of her. Apparently, my help was unwelcome since the vampire had been subdued. Apparently, I had also been very wrong about the level of training that Marie had received in her short time with the New Government. There were no more questions as to whether she'd become a dog of the enemy; the stance, the confidence, and the pure power she exuded told me all that I needed to know.

"I don't know why you're here, but you've interfered enough. Go home, Luke."

"You don't know what you're dealing with," I said, continuing to inch closer. "About any of this."

She turned then, swinging the gun, which I knew she would have aimed at me if she'd been allowed to finish her movement. I simply would not permit her to do so, grasping her wrist mid-stride. The girl before us raised her arms, tears streaking her small face, and yelled as she released a wave of magic directly at the both of us. I lunged at Marie to cover the short distance between us, managing to take the brunt of the blow, but the gun slipped from her grasp and flung awkwardly in the unpredictable gust to bounce to the tiny pink shoes across from us.

Marie swore, racing forward with just shy of enough time to stop the girl from picking up the weapon and aiming it at her. At the distance between them, there was no way she'd miss the shot. It was barely six inches from barrel to forehead. I froze, the knowledge that I couldn't stop what was happening paralyzing me in a flood of grief and denial.

The girl smiled, showing off a missing front tooth despite the tears that still leaked down her chin and soaked the collar of her white dress, which was mostly no longer white. Marie faced her without fear, without hesitation, her face set in determination. She merely stood, slowly, unwilling to die in any position other than on her feet. I admired her for it; I could feel the change in her from the determined, yet woefully under-skilled woman she'd been just months ago. But it was not enough to save her, and when she died, I would not fight being the next target. I would follow her, even in death.

Marie had other plans. She didn't appear to enjoy having her own gun pointed in her face, which was an understandable, albeit useless notion given the circumstances. Rage boiled to the surface—I could see it in the way she clenched her fists and narrowed her eyes. Something passed between them; a shift of the air around us all raised the hairs along my body. The girl hesitated at what she saw in Marie's face, unsure for a moment whether she should pull the trigger or run far, far away.

Then, my fear was for another reason entirely.

I no longer feared for Marie, but instead for the girl and I. Marie was nothing if not an act-now-and-seek-forgiveness-later type of woman. Sometimes her fury shone so white-hot that she managed to do more damage than she intended to, and everything in me snapped taut in anticipation of one of those moments. There was absolutely nothing I could do to stop it.

The air tensed around us, the vampire groaned from the foot of the stairs, and Marie let loose a howl that stopped even the creature's strange dance at the feet of its master. The hair along my entire body tried to rip itself free of my skin and run for the hills, goosebumps prickling along every surface as my stomach dropped to the floor simultaneously. Without warning, I was knocked back, smashing into the corner of the wall where my skull cracked heavily against the metal of the corner bead. Stars flashed across my vision and I slumped to the ground, stunned from the impact as much as the scene unfolding in the hallway of a stranger's home. In front of me, through blurred vision, I could just make out Marie standing above the crumpled form of the little girl, whose creature also lay limp against the floorboards where it had just seconds before been scurrying in earnest.

Satisfied with what she found, Marie stood, her auburn hair speckled with flecks of dried paint and covered in large spots with drywall dust. Her left wrist bled profusely from the savage bite mark, and I could make out the dark patches of even more blood around her ear as her hair shifted with the movement of a slight limp. She tossed me a look that was none-too-friendly, assessing me as I swiped at the back of my head and came away with blood of my own. We both eyed the bite in my arm as well, which bled much less enthusiastically than Marie's did.

"You'll live, I'm sure."

It struck me that, even in her condition, Marie still managed to be the most beautiful thing I'd ever laid eyes on. No amount of dirt or gore could change that. I wondered, absentmindedly, if she'd still be gorgeous to me once the New Government turned her into a monster. I also wondered if she knew what their plan for her was. Had they discussed it? Had Marie *agreed* to it?

Without so much as another glance in my direction, she descended the stairs. I rushed to stand, to follow, only to find myself disoriented and unable to walk. The only thing that seemed to be functioning on any usable level was my voice, though even that betrayed the quiet pain I felt. If only she'd known that my pain wasn't physical, nor for myself.

"Marie, you have to stop this. You don't know what you're getting into."

I heard her pause, turn around, though I couldn't see her or the look on her face as she registered my words. The moment hung between us in silence before she exhaled a sigh to signal the reluctance of her response.

"Then tell me. What was that girl and that… *thing?*"

Sucking in a breath, I pressed my lips tightly together. There was no answer I could give—not without the risk of allowing her to dive deeper into a world she should very much stay away from. We'd had the conversation at least a hundred times since the wars began; that there was a world of secrets I had to keep locked away, for everyone's good. Unfortunately for her, they were also mostly for *her* good. The refusal to respond was as much a wedge between Marie and me as it was a gut punch to myself. I wanted desperately to tell her all the things I couldn't. She'd understand someday, but it was not that day and that meant I had to hold her contempt for a while longer.

"That's what I thought. I'm going to end this, whether you like or it not," she said, finally, and she continued down the stairs.

The groans from the vampire and the subsequent grunts in Marie's low tone told me that she'd complete her mission regardless of the mess she left behind; there seemed no intent to clean it up. At the very least, I'd likely managed to save her life, if only for the moment.

I struggled over to the form lying on the ground at the other end of the hallway, pressing my fingers to her neck for a pulse. Nothing. There was no need to check if the beast was alive; it wouldn't be. Perhaps it was too late for change, after all.

"Jesus, Marie," I whispered to the nothingness around me. "What are you becoming?"

Chapter 30 - Marie

Whoever said that work perks weren't all that amazing was an idiot; the blueprints helped immensely. While I wasn't sure exactly where Jesse's cell was located, I'd been able to pinpoint two separate areas of vulnerability that would get me inside the penitentiary without much fuss.

From there, it was just a matter of time.

Lazy, useless guards loped through the grass surrounding the facility, eyes trained on one another and the importance of sharing furtive glances more than seeking out impending trouble. It was a wonder why none of the inmates had broken themselves out already.

"Stacy finally called," the taller guard said. "I'm telling you, Steve, she's gonna give it up."

Steve chuckled, pausing in his route to smooth down the front of his shirt. "So where are you taking her?"

"My place, of course!"

The two laughed together, Steve clapping the other on the back momentarily before they parted ways and continued their circuit of slow walks and flashlights in the night.

Idiots.

Didn't they know they were supposed to be looking for people breaking in just as much as those breaking out? It was surprisingly uncomplicated in either direction.

Breaking through the fence was the easy part. The power rations were supposed to have avoided the jail, but I'd seen the lights flickering several times during my visits with Jesse and knew that while the power never went completely out, it did drop to emergency systems only on a frequent enough basis for my needs. They simply couldn't power the whole building all of the time. Patiently crouched under the bulk of a nearby bush, waiting, I grew more and more irritated at the supposed protectors of the facility. Each time they passed one another, they spoke exclusively about how the unnamed guard planned to bed Stacy while putting as little effort into the relationship as possible. There wasn't a single thought given to Obscure or prison safety.

I put my life on the line for morons like that.

I almost hoped that I would get caught so that I could tattle and get them fired.

Almost.

Finally, the exterior lights flickered, allowing me to snip another section of fencing and stomp it down into a sizable hole. I dove through the opening just as the lighting regained its full glory, catching my ankle against a stray piece of metal.

The resulting zap was hardly the worst thing I'd encountered in my life, but that didn't stop me from having to bite down on my knuckles to keep from making a sound. I sat, momentarily stunned, in the grass inside the fence line when I heard the sound of footsteps approaching once more.

As quickly as I could manage, I scurried to the outer edge of the building and hunkered into a dark corner among the shadow of the night sky. Steve passed by, yawning, without a care in the world. The trail of his flashlight never even threatened to expose me, though I sat less than ten feet from him. When he'd strolled his casual ass around the corner, I darted out and toward the maintenance room on the exterior wall.

The lock was child's play, thanks to a set of skills I'd never admit to possessing under questioning.

Inside, I gripped the tallest ladder I could find and angled it under the air vent, shushing it when it rattled under my weight, as though it could obey. With careful fingers, I unscrewed the vent cover and pulled out the filter, staring directly into the abyss that was the vent piping.

Claustrophobia, look at me go.

I reminded myself silently that Jesse's execution date was only a month away. If he wasn't rescued soon, it would be too late to save him at all.

I would not let a man die who'd saved my life.

With a heaved sigh, I climbed the rest of the way up the ladder and shimmied into the vent, praying that it would hold my weight. Only fifty feet to travel before I could relieve myself of the cramped space. It couldn't be all that bad, could it?

But it could.

My knees banged against the thin metal as it fought not to bow and pop under me, no matter how gingerly I moved. The skin of my hands slapped and stuck against the material. It smelled like dust and mold. And yet, I crawled for all I was worth.

Eventually, the piping opened up and I found myself over the vent to the break room—my intended destination.

I dropped through as quietly as I could, though the screws couldn't be removed from the inside and I was forced to wait until the room was vacant before I kicked the cover free from its housing. Hastily, I pulled the hidden screwdriver from my pocket—one of the few tools I actually owned—and replaced the vent as quickly and inconspicuously as possible, despite sagging where one of the screws had stripped itself in my initial descent.

I sent up a word of luck that no one looked up, then hurried to the sink, hefted both a plate and cup, and dropped them at my feet.

Right on cue, a guard barged into the room and caught sight of me.

"Oh, I'm so sorry. I was trying to wash up and it slipped right out of my hands." I said, giving my best apologetic expression. "I'll clean it up, don't worry."

The guard narrowed his eyes at me and stepped further into the space, another appearing at his back just outside the door.

"Ma'am, what are you doing in here?"

I let my expression fade to annoyance. "What do you mean? I was *told* to wait in here."

The first guard blinked at me for several seconds. "Told? By who?"

"Atley, of course!" I placed my hands on my hips and added a bit more exasperation, letting it show exactly how unhappy I was that they weren't up-to-speed. "He was supposed to be getting my prisoner for me?" The blank looks the guards exchanged sent me into a spiral of fake fury. "Oh my god, you have no idea what I'm talking about. I'm a warden—you know, from the New Government? I came here for Jesse Rowe, to collect him as a suspected Obscure and take him to HQ for questioning." Kicking several of the pieces of dish out of my way, I stepped forward and glared at the guard in the back. "The paperwork has already been processed at the front and I've been here for nearly thirty minutes now. Do you intend to bring me my prisoner at any point tonight, or is this some sort of game?"

The first guard squared his shoulders, challenged by my anger. He squinted at me, eyes hard. "Aren't you the one who's been visiting him? Seemed rather friendly, if you ask me."

"Of course I've been friendly when I visit him. You think he's going to cooperate if we're hostile? Jesus, this is why I'm a warden and you're not. You know what," My cell phone appeared in my hand and I began pushing buttons to make a call. "Forget it, I'll wake her up and have President come right down here, herself, and sort this out. I hope you're prepared for that."

The guards exchanged a look again as I raised the phone to my ear, Leena's number ringing loudly enough for them to hear it even though they, thankfully, couldn't see the name on the screen. The closer guard leaned back and whispered to the other, who disappeared instantly.

"Wait," the remaining guard said. "Just wait. If you've already been cleared through the front, then that's good enough for us. We're getting him for you now. I'm sorry about the mix-up."

Triumph rang through me, but I was careful to school my face. I ended the call and scowled back at him, still clutching the phone as though I might end up making the call again after all. "That's what they said thirty minutes ago."

He held his hands up in defense. "Atley's gone home for the night, so I'm sorry about that. I'm not sure what happened."

I knew that already, and sincerely hoped that Atley found himself in the boss's office first thing in the morning as retaliation for the judgment he passed during my visits with Jesse.

The second guard reappeared, alone, and whispered to the first, whose face became utterly impassive. Not a good sign.

"Is there a problem?"

"Actually, there is. Jesse isn't in his cell. It appears as though he's escaped."

Time moved at a snail's pace. The words hit my ears what felt like minutes after I watched the movement of the guard's lips. All at once, sirens and lights began to sing and flash through the interior of the building. My heart dropped to the floor. My mind reeled.

Gone?

Gone *where*?

"This has to be reported to HQ right away. This is now a possible escaped Obscure. Do you have *any* idea where he'd have gone?"

The second guard stepped forward, cramming himself into the doorway. "No, ma'am. You were the only visitor we ever saw him have."

Christ, what the hell was happening?

I thanked the men, allowed them to escort me back out of the building while they threw the rest of the facility into a lockdown, and once I was safely tucked back inside my car, I let the fear take over.

Jesse would have made contact with me if he was on the outside. But did he know how?

I'd never given him a phone number or address—there'd been no need to.

Shit, shit, shit.

But Jesse wouldn't have escaped without me; not when he was so adamant about staying to die and cleansing himself of his sins. That left only one option.

Someone had taken him.

I strangled the steering wheel while I weighed my options. I couldn't look for him without raising suspicion in every possible way; it wasn't an official mission and I couldn't make it one without calling attention to myself. President would sniff that out in a heartbeat and then I'd have to explain it all to her from the beginning. It wasn't even a feasible train of thought if I wanted to keep myself from being interrogated in that exit-less room while President watched from her computer. No way.

I'd simply have to wait for him to find me, and pray that he was capable of holding his own against whoever had gotten their greedy claws into him.

Chapter 31 - Marie

July slapped me in the face much like an overdue bill—entirely by surprise. The weeks had flown past without any regard to the goals I'd made prior to joining the New Government. While I had finally managed the time to visit Peter's office for the remaining stack of articles, of which I tipped him handsomely for holding all the while, I couldn't yet bring myself to review them. Leena's death, I knew, would be included in them—yet the determination that had spurred me into becoming a warden had simmered to just barely a light boil of annoyance under my skin. Truth be told, I was content, if not tipping toward complacency; I didn't feel any urgency in dragging forward the past I'd left behind when I transformed myself from a tired, useless homebody to a soldier-for-hire in the Obscure war.

And… I could also admit that the gig was starting to get a little stale in places. The money never stopped, nor did the amenities to the apartment complex, despite the fact that the last three of my targets came willingly and without incident, which made me feel as if I hadn't been earning my keep. The thrill of the chase, the hunt, the catch, was sorely missed; in truth, it felt less like work to end the war and more like I'd sold my soul to join 'President's Witnesses', going door-to-door to speak the word of saving humanity. Yet, it was a better life than I could have hoped for if I'd not made the leap off the precipice of the mundane.

As such, the newspapers sat in the corner of the room, pressed against the back of the couch where they only nagged at my conscience if I stopped to consider them. Usually, I chose not to. It worked for me if I didn't look too closely at my motives.

The secret binders of information nestled in my bookshelves grew by the day—and by the mission—as my interactions with the Obscure freed new tidbits of their personalities, abilities, and weaknesses. I was still no closer to learning anything of the girl I'd killed several months back, or the hideous beast she'd coveted like a pet, and the urge to ask Michael— or, frankly, any more experienced warden that wasn't President—about it had nearly pushed me to the edge several times; but that single niggling bit of curiosity, I held back. I collared, leashed, and tightly caged every syllable of the question any time it sprang to mind. Admitting to having seen the girl would, in the end, also be admitting to killing her, and I'd learned very quickly, and very indirectly, that President was growing irritated with the number of bodies left in the wake of my completed missions. That was precisely why I'd reported the Hakim Kalpan mission as a 'success without major incident', and neglected all mention of Luke and of the child. To their discredit, no one had asked the right questions that would have ferreted out any complications during that particular mission. That was their own fault.

Though I did owe a begrudging debt of gratitude to general carelessness for the inadvertent heads-up about my faults. So, *thank you very much* to the Receiving wardens who chose to gossip about me, and about President's displeasure with my aggressive nature, where they thought I wouldn't hear. Unfortunately for them, they'd chosen to do so during my last target delivery, and while they'd assumed I'd gone inside to debrief. Their observation skills left much to be desired if they truly thought I'd done anything less than intentionally avoid walking into that sterile building for as long as humanly possible.

Amateurs.

Come to think of it, I hadn't seen Karen again since the first werewolf mission, though I truthfully hadn't looked very hard. Though I'd been lured into the grasp of the New Government with the promise of answers, it was mostly a pile of questions that kept me cozy at night. That may, in part, have been the reason that I'd found myself strolling through the bright white door of the building on a day that I had not been expected, and planting myself in the foyer until the crisp tap of kitten heels made their way down the hall in my direction. I had to admit, they did sound authoritative. President emerged, glorious as always, wearing the tight smile I'd come to recognize as hiding a great deal of annoyance she didn't feel it particularly advantageous to display. Perfect, I was annoyed too.

"Mare," she greeted me, stopping much further away than she usually did.

Marie, I corrected silently. Out loud, I said: "President. I have some questions for you. I believe a condition of my enrollment here was that I'd be receiving answers."

She inclined her head slightly, but did not offer me to follow her back to her office as she usually did when the conversation turned personal. It struck me as odd, made me reconsider the timing of my delivery. Should it have waited? We held an uncomfortable silence with one another for several beats. I'd gone through a hell of a lot of trouble to scrape together my own research, utilizing hardly any New Government perks to do so. I was entitled to what I was promised.

To hell with it. Squaring my shoulders, I lifted my chin as President had done.

"I'd like to know about Karen Mossamite. She was removed from our training class, but she's here, somewhere, still working for the cause. I understood that an inability to complete training was an automatic removal from the program."

At first, I thought that President had no intention of answering my question. She merely stared, coaxing a thin vein of icy fear from the depths of where I'd buried it not so long ago. I knew just as well as she did that the question was off-limits, none of my damn business. There were very few rules among the wardens, and what I was asking was a hard and fast one. No wiggle room.

Rule number three of being a warden: Never, ever, under any circumstances, disclose your status as a warden. Technically, seeing one another at headquarters counted as disclosure, so the unspoken rule was that we never verbalized it—any of it. Ever.

Yet, there I stood under the scrutiny of President as I asked her, to her face, to inform on the status of another warden. The cat-and-mouse game we'd played since the first day in the conference room had grown tired and old. The more I learned about Obscure and wardens, the more sure I was that I'd only seen the surface of President and of the truth beneath the establishment she'd built around herself—only the bits she'd wanted me to see. That was no more. My deal was that I'd given my body, my safety, and my life over to the cause; I'd risk everything about myself to stop the death and the war, and in return, all of my burning questions would be answered. Thus far, the scars along my psyche and skin were proof of payment on my end of the deal, but it went no further than that. The questions festering for over a year still raged within me, growing and merging into a beast inside that wouldn't be tamed. I was no longer willing to be a mindless minion at the beck and call of a greater power that didn't see fit to repay their debts.

President was the first step in regaining control of myself. I only needed the protection of the New Government, not their trust. It was nothing short of a giant risk, but I needed to know how far she'd let me push her, no matter how sure I was that she'd simply stare me into submission, never daring to entertain my antics. But then, she did. Perhaps she only wanted to see me squirm first; perhaps that was my payment for the information.

"Karen Mossamite," she said, rolling the name around in her mouth as though she was unfamiliar with it—as though she had to reach for the information she fed me. We both knew it was at the tip of her tongue the moment the question was out of my mouth. "She was found to be more useful in the Interrogations section of the New Government. She's got quite a bit of raw talent, and—like *someone else I know*—" A pointed look made me narrow my eyes in response. "—must still strive to prove herself valuable in order to retain her position."

Alright, so she'd answered the question. What then? Push her. Push her until she couldn't be pushed any more.

I ground my teeth together, sucked in a shallow breath, and blurted the next question with as much confidence as I dared. "When can I stop picking up the low-hanging fruit and actually make a difference in this war?"

Something swam behind President's silvery irises briefly, too fast for me to decipher it. Her head tipped to the side, curious.

"These Obscure that I've brought in, they're not calling any shots. Sure, they can provide some insight into their kind, but they can't stop the war." I paused, straightened my spine. "I'm here to end the killing. You know I'm capable, so why am I still working the newbie files?" I stepped forward, closing some of the distance between us. She didn't move back. "The vampires are wreaking havoc out there. Stopping them would blow a hole in the Obscure army; it would weaken every other Obscure's hold over the humans. We should be focusing our talent there. You know who their leader is, don't you? You have to."

"Well, I see that you're feeling quite comfortable in your new role," President chastised, assessing me. The expression she held was not one that I would have considered to be friendly. "You may *not*," she added in a no-nonsense snap of teeth, "Summon me at your discretion. You must earn the answers that you seek. That's how it works."

Suddenly, I caught sight of a file folder pinched between two of her fingers and resting neatly against her front. Had that been there the whole time? She held it out to me, delicately, without a hint of uncertainty that I'd take it from her, but as my own hand closed around it, hers did not release. Our eyes met and held for a moment, driving home the point she'd been trying to make—that she was very much in charge and very much unhappy with me. Well, at least I knew where I stood in no uncertain terms.

"I was hesitant to give you this mission, seeing that three others have already failed it." She hadn't needed to say that by 'failed', she'd meant 'died'. Wardens didn't *fail* anything. That was the job. "But you seem to think that you're ready to play with the big dogs."

Running my fingers against the edges of the thick paper folder, just shy of enough pressure to cut into the soft skin of my fingertips, I contemplated giving into the curiosity and opening it right away, like an excited child tearing into a present. That, perhaps, wouldn't be the best course of action while being handed a mission that had already claimed the lives of three others. To keep the anticipation from my face, I stared straight ahead at a painting that hung just over President's left shoulder. The bright greens of grass and trees filled my vision as she continued to speak.

"If you can manage to survive this, I'll answer any question you want. But I warn you, Mare," her tone dipped low, turning her voice to a whisper of gravel. "You're holding in your hand the file on the current head of every vampire in existence. The Kingpin—or, *Queenpin*, if you will. One wrong move is all it will take for your name to join the list of lives she's claimed, and I can promise you that all the bravado in the world won't do you any bit of good against her."

A nod was all I could manage in response, not daring to meet her stare for fear that I'd betray the shiver of eagerness sliding through me.

"Good luck. You'll need it." She spun to leave, but abruptly turned again to face me. "Oh, and do be careful. I hear that a prisoner on death row has escaped from Wild River."

There was not an ounce of hesitation as she turned on her short heels and strolled back into the maze of hallways that I was certain only she could navigate with any bit of ease. The conversation, though it excited me, left a sour taste on my tongue. I wanted to be happy that she'd chosen me for the assignment, but the truth of it sat like a lump in the back of my throat. I wasn't given the mission because she'd had faith in my ability to complete it. The task was an ultimatum, a means to an end. Either I crippled the vampire's leadership structure, effectively turning the tide of the war in our favor, or I died trying.

Either way, President walked away the victor. What made it worse was that she seemed to also know all about Jesse already.

The urge to call her back and confront her about the options burned in my stomach, but I resisted. It would do me no good. Deciding not to stick my foot any further into my mouth—was that the cause of the foul taste left there?—I retreated with my metaphorical tail between my legs, though it chafed me to do. I did receive what I had come for, so it had been a worthwhile journey. What to do with the information was another matter entirely.

Back in the quiet sanctity of my car, I nudged open the file. A beautiful face was the first thing to greet me from the small photo clipped to the inside section. The woman's skin was milky white, flawless, and all but glowing next to the deep red of her lips. Behind the photo sat a thick collection of papers, stapled securely to the folder so as not to be lost. Each of them, as I thumbed through, was stamped 'use extreme caution' in large red letters. It seemed that my vampire friend, Nika Volkov, was viewed as quite a dangerous woman. Nearly each of the sheets of paper under her photo contained a dozen names of presumed kills—mostly human, but dotted throughout with Obscure. On the topmost page, three names had been handwritten in small print.

Oscar Sanchez.

Baptiste Bernard.

Anders Hollin.

I hadn't known any of the wardens listed, but I didn't need to in order to be certain that the vampire would be a tough cookie. Unease slid through me briefly before being replaced with resolve.

Nika was in no way what I would have considered my typical mission target. The danger that I'd been placed in during prior missions had been due to either my own naivety or sheer happenstance—most of which, I'd chosen not to admit to the New Government. As far as they were concerned, a great bulk of my targets were either easy captures or near-miss fumbles under the care of new hands. Growing pains. Sure, some of those fumbles had ended up as dead Obscure along the way, but that was accidental overkill as a reaction of self-defense. None of those missions had been half the amount of danger as the head vampire would be. Nika was in another league entirely, and the fact that I'd been assigned her case directly from President was either very, very good, or very, very bad. Already knowing that the intent was the latter, I contemplated my chances to turn it into the former.

There was only one way to find out how it would end. A smile that I hadn't intentionally beckoned creased my face. Hadn't I just been wishing there was a bit more fun in my life? Ask for excitement and you shall receive. Or something like that.

Scanning the other side of the folder, I spied the last known address for Nika, a description of the vehicles she most commonly traveled in, and a *blank field* where the mission deadline should have been. Apparently, I had all the time in the world to bring the murdering bitch into custody.

Plugging the address into my car's GPS, I was surprised to find that it belonged to a tiny commercial lot and not to a residence. A brow lifted in interest. I was liking Nika's case more and more.

A quick internet search of the address on my cell phone gave me a cornucopia of interior photos. Apparently, it was a bar. People really ought to be more careful of what they put on the internet, especially when flirting with the danger of Obscure and illegal activities. It was a small building, housing not much more than a seven-seater bar counter, a pool table, and a restroom. There was, of course, the chance that it had a basement that wasn't shown in the business photos, but it seemed more likely for Nika to be an owner or frequent patron than it was for her to be living in the musty basement of a place like that. In fact, if she'd been draped in a crown for her photo and listed as the queen of just about anywhere, I'd have nearly believed it. Even through the camera capture, she exuded poise and luxury. If nothing else, she was a woman who enjoyed the finer things in life and had no qualms about surrounding herself in such. In fact, there was a good chance that her kills were covetous; that she'd sought material belongings from most of the victims she claimed. She certainly seemed the type, last known address aside. I'd bet money that there was a reason she kept the ratty bar in proximity.

An idea rolled around in my head, growing like a snowball as it collected thoughts along the way. Nika was so extremely dangerous for the reason that she killed simply because she could. She killed for the fun of it.

She enjoyed murder.

She'd *perfected* it out of passion.

Never mind that the realization should have scared the wits out of me. I felt nothing more than fidgety anticipation for the hunt. It was finally my time to face a big, bad Obscure; *that* was what fighting a war was all about.

Pushing the gear shift into drive, tires squealed as they rocketed me forward toward the Amber Tavern.

Chapter 32 - Marie

It was exactly the same as the photos. The dirt brown exterior that I'd assumed was simply badly captured in the images had been, indeed, the exact shade of dried mud in person that had been depicted online. The atmosphere also held precisely the same amount of appeal as it had in the lifeless, still photographs. Still, I took the last empty seat at the bar—in the dead center of the action, no pun intended—and studiously ignored the thinly veiled threats hidden behind glares from the other patrons.

So, it was an invite-only affair, apparently.

The bartender moved to stand in front of me, more blocking my view of the back counter than giving any pretense of customer service. The scowl he wielded against my best tourist smile was definitely going to earn him an abysmal Yelp review at the end of my visit.

"Hi. A gin and tonic, please."

We stared one another down, neither willing to be the first to break in the contest of stubbornness we'd begun. Unfortunately for him, I was in a foul mood after facing off with President and if he didn't hand me liquor, *pronto*, someone was going to regret it. The world stilled under his gray-blue irises while vivid images of the many different ways I could end his life with only the items on the bar between us danced through my mind. The noise from the other guests fell to a hush, each pair of eyes that hadn't already been boring holes in my back from the moment I'd walked in had found their way to me in the midst of the power struggle that seemed to also serve as entertainment. At least someone was serving *something*.

I tipped my head to the side, refusing to allow my smile to waver even the slightest, and arched my eyebrows in the universal sign for 'Can

I help you with something?'. The weight of the attention focused on me was immense, nearly palpable; if any one of them could have lifted my stool and tossed me out on my ass with it without asking for more trouble than it was worth, I was sure they would have.

"Ashton," a voice crooned, suddenly loud, slicing through the silence in a strange mixture of sultry and authoritative tones. "Give the woman her drink."

The bartender snapped to attention, moving as though he hadn't just been glaring daggers into my very soul for daring to place an order. With quite a bit more force than necessary, my drink was eventually dropped onto the hard counter in the general direction of my place at the bar. I didn't miss the roll of liquid over the edge of the glass or the hasty retreat that he made as soon as he'd completed the bare minimum of required interaction. Five stars for enthusiasm.

"Thank you, Ashton," I sang sweetly at him, gripping the slippery glass and tipping it in his direction. Here's to you, asshole.

With a tiny sip that I most definitely made a show of taking, I swung around on the stool and raised my glass again, that time to Nika Volkov, who stood wearing a look of amusement and interest as she watched me from the short distance across the bar.

"And thank you, as well. I wasn't sure I would ever get my alcohol."

There was no way she'd walked through the front door without making a sound, and yet I knew with undeniable certainty that she had not been leaning against that wall when I first entered the room. She laughed, just one harsh bark, before straightening and making her way toward me with slow, deliberate steps. If she thought that I was feeling in any way like a scared rabbit under her show of stalking fox grace, she was in for a surprise.

A thin hand extended itself between us, fat rings with equally chunky jewels glittering strangely in the low light. "Nika," she purred.

With a smile that nearly slipped from admiring to smug—but not quite—I took her hand in my own and gently squeezed.

"Mare."

A spark of unidentified emotion soared through me at our contact. The idea that she could pull me forward and sink her teeth into me at any second made me pay closer attention to her potential strength. It also threw vivid images through my mind which were better left unexplored. She was the enemy, after all, even if she was more captivating in person than I'd originally given her credit for.

"What an interesting name. I like it."

Snapping her fingers at Ashton, who heeled on command like a very good boy, she beckoned for a drink of her own and slid her hip against the bar top next to me while she waited. Unlike me, she didn't have to wait very long.

"How do you get that kind of service around here?" I asked, taking another sip to drown the rest of the comment that tried to fight its way to my lips.

"You own the bar," Nika said with a laugh that was most definitely not genuine.

Ding, ding. Point for me.

I eyed the ceiling and walls with only the smallest amount of disgust that sat buried inside. "You ever think about updating the place? This could be an investor's wet dream."

She looked at me then, truly looked at me, for the first time since she'd spoken. Her eyes roamed over my form, taking in the tidy athletic leggings and pristine, brand-name sneakers. They flicked over the understated ring adorning my right hand and the thin gold necklace that encircled my throat almost like a collar. No doubt she was scouting for any sign of wealth, any hint at all that I'd make a good target for her collection. Sorry, sister, but you picked the wrong one. The tables had turned and she was sitting on the wrong side of them. To be fair, there was nothing inherently *poor* about my outfit that would have turned her away. I'd already been dressed in some of the newest of my clothes, and the sneakers had been pretty expensive when I bought them just last week. The jewels were cheap, imitations that I'd hoped would pass well enough under dull bar lighting to hint that there may be taste and allowance for better pieces tucked away at home. Admittedly, while they were nice, they weren't worth killing over.

As expected, Nika chose not to acknowledge my question. Instead, she collected her glass—which I imagined was pointedly dry on the outside, unlike mine—and returned to the shadowed corner of the bar that she'd materialized in. I waited several minutes before daring a peek in her direction, and was unsurprised to find that she was just suddenly no longer there. Not wanting to give up my cover just yet, I downed the rest of my drink and plunked the glass on the table, sure to shoot Ashton a wink in return for the face of vast relief he sported when he realized that I was planning to leave.

With a few bills dropped on the bar, which were calculated early on to be just barely over the cost of the drink, I gave each of the other patrons direct eye contact and a sweeping finger wave as I hopped merrily from the stool and exited. As the door swung closed behind me, the sound of rushed conversation swelled up, muffled by the glass that separated us. It was probably too ostentatious for a covert mission, but I'd enjoyed myself. Frankly, if there was any chance the mission would be my last, I was damn well going to get a kick out of it on the way down.

There was zero chance that I wasn't the cause of the ruckus rising inside the building as I strode away from it; the strange, unflappable woman who appeared out of thin air and hinted at investing in the bar before taking off just as quickly. I'd had the drop on them, but that wouldn't last. They'd all be ready for me the next time I showed my face, including Nika. But that didn't matter because I had her interest. It was barely going to take a gentle shove to tip the predictable vampire into my plan. With any amount of luck, the mission would be wrapped up before the week was out. What kind of losers had they assigned to Nika before I came along?

Chapter 33 - Marie

I spent three weeks frequenting Nika's bar only to find Nika conspicuously absent for all of them. Ashton and I had finally made it to a first-name basis, which he sneered at me every time I slid myself into a seat in front of him. It was truly more amusing than it was insulting, as the word slipped through his lips sounding vaguely French and I could only imagine that was *not* what he was going for. The trouble was that while the banter may have very—and I do mean very—slightly ingratiated me with the other patrons, the only true headway I'd made with my regular visits was tripping onto the beginnings of a slippery slope to alcoholism.

Two times I'd attempted to spark conversation with the other bodies in the seats beside me and both times I was met with tightly closed lips and a look that very clearly said that no one would miss me when I was gone.

I could only give the ruse another visit or two at most before the routine either became a staple in my real, actual life or I had to give it up entirely and fall back to the Plan B that I hadn't yet devised. My mood was pensive as I parked and trudged up to the glass front door, peering inside as it whooshed open to flood me with ice-cold air conditioning. I'd have to give it my all or go home empty-handed.

Danger hummed in the air all around as I crossed into the room once more. Eyes drifted my way, then immediately floated off, no longer interested once I'd become nearly as permanent a fixture as some of them had. Or, so I thought. As I marched forward to take my usual spot—the only one always left open at the direct center of the bar, as though it held some unseemly curse that had yet to be mentioned to the new girl—all attention shifted wholly to the man sitting on what had quickly become known as *my* stool. Perhaps no one else thought of it that way, but I certainly did. A stranger's dirty hams did not belong there.

It did not escape me that all noise ground to a halt just as my feet did directly behind the stranger's back. Smirks hid behind dirty glasses raised to eager mouths while I sized up the situation. The rump seated in my territory belonged to a man who was easily twice my weight; what I'd call bulky, but not fat. He didn't reek of weight racks and steroids, but he wasn't a shrimp either. My eyes narrowed at his broad backside. There was a 'good 'ole boy' vibe emanating from his every pore, soothing any confrontation that dared spark in his direction. Very under-the-radar, only interesting to someone cautious enough to see it as a red flag—someone like me. He was *too* average, almost as though he entirely banked on being overlooked. Well, if his intent had been to keep a low profile, he'd chosen the wrong place to park himself.

Likely sensing a disturbance in the atmosphere, the offending hunk of flesh and bone spun to face me. Icy blue eyes, cold much deeper than in color alone, raked across my form as he lifted his glass for a sip and a second to stall while he drank me in. I shot a well-deserved death glare at Ashton for daring to give the new guy a drink when he'd all but forced me to brawl him for one just a few short weeks ago. And I'd thought we were becoming such fast friends.

"Hi," I said to him, slapping on a mask of innocence to match my tone. "I think you might be sitting in my seat." I pointed down, directly at his crotch, in case he needed further clarification as to which seat was mine or which part of him was currently out of place.

"Sorry, didn't see your name on it." His blasé retort sparked a fire of anger within my belly, even before the half bashful, half cocky smile he flashed at me afterward. Without waiting for a response, he leaned forward slightly and ducked his head as though sharing a secret just between the two of us. "What is your name, anyway?"

Arms folded across my chest like a spoiled housewife, foot tapping out a Morse code warning in annoyance—after all, I had to act the part since I had been flashing expensive pieces around and gushing about the windfall inheritance I'd just received over my last few visits—I tipped up my nose to stare down it at him. "It's Mare."

Something swam behind the deadness in his eyes, replacing it for barely a second before the shutter of indifference came down again. The harmless smile remained firm across his face, but it slipped a little into a grin that projected so much more than pleasure. A chill slithered through me at the sight of it. I pressed my arms to my chest, hard, to focus through the sudden spike of adrenaline. Though I'd not yet pinpointed what was off about the man, the predator in me had sniffed out a challenge in him and didn't seem to care that a dick-slinging contest would be just about the absolute worst thing to do under the cover I was using.

He turned back to the bar, quickly downed his glass, and stood, taking an intrusive step toward me as he did. Our fronts brushed. Everything inside me sprung to life, screaming against the threat that his nearness promised. The old Marie would have backed down, would have withered in the heat of the challenge presented. The new one held her ground, mimicking his smile, inch for inch.

"I'll be taking that chair back now. Thanks for warming it for me."

The man only nodded and looked me over once more—head to toe and back, like he was assessing the quality of a prized pig and calculating the price it would fetch in the next livestock auction—before departing the building entirely without so much as a backward glance or parting snipe. I relaxed into the chair by millimeters, wound tight from the tension that threaded the air. A thump on the counter before me revealed a neat, unsloshed glass with what could only be a gin and tonic cradled within. Ashton looked at me for a long moment, face as blank as ever, before giving me his back in the telltale sign that I was no longer worthy of his time or attention. I'd grown accustomed to it… though, admittedly, he did make me fight a bit harder for the drink on a normal day. Apparently, it was a special day; one where I'd rated silent, half-assed service in place of no service at all.

An hour passed with no real change before I allowed the thoughts of missions and President to invade. It had been a nice distraction to earn my place at the bar, even despite the fact that it was a ratty place that held no real benefit for me. For a while, I'd forgotten that I was a soldier, that there was a war going on outside. I'd allowed myself to pretend that the godmother of all nasty little vampires wasn't just outside of reach, having spent more time in my proximity than I'd bet any of her victims ever had before they were disposed of. It was easy to think that we were rebuilding ourselves when the streets had begun to fill slowly with cars and pedestrians, the businesses unboarded doors and windows, and conversations turned from death and terror to an intentional omittance of exactly that.

But the war was far from over. My place in the bar was a temporary one, a means to an end that was only satisfied when the vampire bitch was at the mercy of the New Government. There was no more time for daydreaming while humans continued to die.

I'd bragged and flaunted all I could to make myself an appealing target for Nika, and still she hadn't taken the bait. Either none of the jackasses at the bar were relaying the information to her about my potential as a mark, or Nika had already vetted me and found me lacking in some way. Whatever the reason, I couldn't walk away from the opportunity presented until I'd tried everything in my power first.

I decided to up the ante. At the rate that I was going, I'd end up broke and attending AA meetings on the weekends faster than I'd be closing out my mission. It was simply unacceptable. With an internal cringe, I called out to my very least favorite bartender with the one thing I knew he wouldn't ignore.

"Ashton, dear, I think we need a toast. Please, a round of shots for the bar. On me."

I added the last with a gigantic smile that I hoped was more endearing than terrifying. The line between suburban trophy wife and clinically insane was very, very thin. He obliged, thankfully, doling out shots of amber-colored liquor that I hadn't identified before he'd ferreted the bottle out of sight. Damn, it was probably the most expensive stuff in the place.

Hopping off my stool to stand in the center of the room, I lifted my own shot glass and swung it through the air in the direction of each of the patrons in turn. "To Nika, wherever she may be hiding. We wouldn't be here without her."

Reluctantly, they all raised their own glasses before shooting them down just as I did.

"Another?" I asked, feigning excitement that I hoped would rouse the same reaction. The grumbles of agreement and interest spurred me on. An eager nod from a rotund man at the far right of the bar had me drifting in his direction.

"Where is Nika anyway?" I chastised, as though he had personally been left in charge of her and hadn't done a very good job. "She should be here to celebrate with us."

He seemed unsure how to answer, his thick fingers scratching through the hair of an unruly beard as he considered me. A nervous habit. I motioned my empty shot glass at him, miming that I'd be seeking another round for the bar and wondering if he'd be interested. The swamp green of his eyes lit instantly. The offer seemed to loosen his lips.

"Went up north, I think. Said she'd come into some money, herself." A Scottish lilt edged his words, suddenly making the copper locks under his chin noticeably more intriguing. He shrugged like he didn't know what Nika's words meant any more than I did—but I *did* know what they meant.

While the wardens mostly worked out of the headquarters office in California, many of them set off to work remotely, covering the remnants of the states that weren't easy to reach from headquarters on short notice.

Being that Obscure operated anywhere and everywhere, the New Government felt it prudent to keep a watchful eye on the happenings even in the furthest, most decimated corners of the continent; which included cataloging the various groups of humans who banded together and set down roots in rural areas as a survival tactic, as well as planting an on-call warden to patrol the areas discreetly. Upon graduating warden training, I'd been debriefed on the most noteworthy communal gatherings across the nation, which included a very wealthy group—for all the good it did them in the state of the world—from one of the most famous non-profit organizations prior to the start of the war. Likely, they'd combed their contact lists when shit hit the fan and decided that they'd do better together, which had led to Alaska becoming the wartime version of the wealthiest 'city' in the country. There were supposedly three very skilled wardens assigned to that area, but even with the best-trained eyes available, accidents happened. Especially when you didn't always know what to look out for.

If "up north" didn't mean that Nika was gunning for Alaska, I'd eat my own fist.

I recalled that while scanning Nika's file, I'd been surprised to note that Alaska wasn't listed under her victim localities, despite my prior knowledge that the murder count in that particular community was high, putting the residents on high alert. It was possible that Nika was still responsible in some capacity and simply hadn't been caught. I couldn't imagine that she'd task a fanged minion to do the work when what she loved so much about it all was the kill itself. How many times could you really target a commune of billionaires without it being suspicious?

A tightness vied for control of my shoulders as I considered the implications of Nika's sudden venture to America's great frontier. There was zero chance that she was doing anything other than adding to her body count at the same moment that I stood charming the patrons of her ratty bar. She hadn't even considered me enough of a threat, nor sufficient enough bait, to hesitate before rushing off for larger prey. How insulting. The incipient flame lit by the stranger's standoff, and then quietly subdued, burst forward as a warning rush of heat within me. I would not stand for the offense.

When morning dawned, Nika would learn what it felt like to be hunted—to be the mouse instead of the cat, for once.

I smiled at the man before me, sickly sweet, and thrust my empty glass into the air, demanding another shower of alcohol from Ashton. Four rounds later, with a warm sloshing in my belly and a hole in my wallet, I stumbled out of the bar, satisfied with what I'd learned. It said a great deal that many watched silently, not caring to stop me despite the entirely convincing act of drunken helplessness I was tossing around as I exited.

It was apparently best to make a move on Nika *before* the ramshackle tavern was scrutinized under an alcohol-related violation and the gorgeous Russian high-tailed it to somewhere much less fun. Or would she? Something told me there was sentimental value in the establishment—if a shriveled black heart was even capable of holding affection.

I continued to stagger to my car, digging with large, false motions for the keys in my back pocket as I did, just in case anyone felt the need to watch me through the badly tinted windows or the smudged glass of the entry door. Training insisted that the cover remain firmly in place until the very end. Not that it would be hard to explain away my sudden sobering in the dark and deathly silent parking lot.

It took only fifteen seconds of standing poised at my door with keys in hand before a large pair of arms wound themselves tightly around me. Two seconds was all the reaction time I was allowed before I found myself effectively pinned. One strong arm took a death grip across my jaw to seize control of my head movement while simultaneously smothering my mouth. The second arm wrapped across my lower abdomen to clutch my hip and press the short line of my back into their unyielding front. I felt us both shift backward into the shadow of the trees surrounding the parking lot. Slowly, calmly, exhaling just enough to keep my heart rate even, I waited. Hot breath enveloped my ear.

"I know what you're doing." The voice hissed, so close that their lips brushed against my earlobe. The sound was impossibly loud, and I cringed away from it despite myself. "Stop coming after Nika. I won't ask again."

The arms tightened painfully, squeezing just hard enough to leave bruises along my hip and jaw before they were suddenly gone, along with the person they belonged to. Expression fully sobered and teeth clenched in annoyance, I scanned the edges of the shadows anyway, though I'd known from the second he released me that he wouldn't be there. That was alright, though. He may have taken extra care to ensure I couldn't confirm my suspicions, but I'd recognized that voice immediately. It was the stranger from the bar, Mr. 'I didn't see your name on it'. Huffing annoyance into the dark sky, I wondered what his stake was in the situation. Brazen enough to confront me, but coward enough to cloak himself at the same time, he practically stank of secrets. If nothing else, several small bits of information slid into place as his personality and mannerisms meshed with our most recent encounter, painting a picture in my mind.

I hated to admit it, but the familiarity of him irked me. Oh well. Only one thing truly mattered: if he thought he'd gotten the drop on me, he was in for a rude awakening.

With the adrenaline fading from my system, I unlocked the car and slid into the driver's seat. Once again, fear had abandoned post, leaving a tingling thrill in its wake. Since when had I become so addicted to the feeling?

I wasn't sure, but I also wasn't sure that I wanted it to stop.

My hands moved of their own accord to smooth down my clothes, lingering when they passed the most sensitive spots. As my fingers carved their way down my body, the memory of my initial panic flared to life, sending chills across my skin.

Through the windshield, I could make out the vague shapes of the bar patrons inside the building. What would they say if they knew who I really was? What I was really doing there?

My hands sank lower, dipping into my waistband on their journey. I hissed in a breath, caught in the flash of heat that seared through me and settled between my legs. The stranger's arms were suddenly replaced in my mind with Luke's, the same bruising strength used to pin me against him. My eyes never left the window to the bar as I slid my fingers into my panties, unsurprised by the wetness already there. The peaks of my nipples rubbed against thin fabric, the friction puckering them to tight points.

Someone could walk out at any moment and catch me.

I almost hoped they did.

A soft whimper fell from my lips as my head dropped back and the vision of a hand that was not my own took over.

One finger swirled carefully against the already sensitive bundle of nerves, sending electric jolts through me with each caress. Another heavy moan tumbled free, my free hand moving upward underneath my top to knead at my breast.

Nika's face swam into my mind, catching my breath with a glimpse of her fangs. I could almost feel the sharp points dragging so delicately across the skin of my neck, her ruby-red mouth leaving a trail of lipstick behind. A phantom bite parted my lips on a sigh, the pain and pleasure melding to something I knew instantly would become an addiction.

My hand moved faster, bore down with a little more pressure as the fingers of the other hand began to tug lightly at my nipple. Rocking the car alongside it, my entire body bucked from the sensations. I didn't even care if it drew attention. In my ear, I swore that I could hear Luke's voice, the deep timbre of it burrowing deep inside me.

That's my girl. Don't stop.

In an instant, I exploded, the climax taking me by surprise and ripping free a cry of ecstasy. Shock waves of pleasure pulsed outward, stealing away every bit of control against the sated bonelessness that enveloped me. Only my heavy pants remained for several moments. Then the vehicle settled as though it, too, had finished with me, and both Nika's and Luke's presences faded away as the excitement and fear did as well.

God, what they'd say if they only knew.

Chapter 34 - Marie

When I returned home, I debated packing a travel bag for the frozen adventure ahead. In the end, I settled on a few hours of sleep, changing into something slightly less than suitable for the wealthy Alaskan commune I was about to infiltrate, and pacing in the living room while I debated my next course of action. The sorry stack of newspapers that rested behind my couch was suddenly all I could think about as I passed by them for the thousandth time and they finally managed to grab my attention. It was no more just a tickling in the back of my mind, but also a roaring desire to finally close the chapter of my old life so that the book could be burned in its entirety.

It took no more than ten minutes to sift through the thick pages and extricate the ones specific to Leena, and I found a surprising amount of disassociation as I read them over. Where I'd expected tears and anger or grief and despair, I felt only the pull of analytical calculation: find the Obscure, draw out its secrets. Close the case, move on. Turn your back on your old self, forge ahead.

The papers couldn't tell me anything more than I already knew about Leena, other than the location of the body and the wounds sustained, though I knew right away that the culprit would be a werewolf. All the months spent researching, followed by the months seeing the carnage first-hand had finally come in use for something. *Boring.* What I didn't know—and wanted quite badly to—was the flavor of Obscure that Leena was. For a while, after coming to terms with the fact that Leena *was* an Obscure, I'd classed her as a witch. The magical woo-woo she'd performed in my house that night all but nailed the lid closed on that box of questions; however, since learning about the existence of fairies and trolls, as well as so many other surprising factions of Obscure, the glowing tattoos and the plant magic had set her apart from the rest and I'd quietly, unintentionally, moved her back into her own bucket.

But what the hell was she?

Frustration bit at the edges of my patience. Nika was out there, coordinating attacks and eating humans, and my godforsaken brain had insisted that Leena's strange abilities needed to be dealt with *right away*. Didn't my brain know that I was trying to cripple the war?

Scanning the articles again, I noted the locality where her body was found and rushed to my car, the four-hour round trip seeming much less heroic when all I'd been able to retrieve from the Police Department was the damned plant and her backpack, which constituted the entirety of the personal belongings found with her. Apparently, they'd almost missed the plant until the team's rookie questioned the neon yellow pot sitting nearby and mentioned how nicely it matched with Leena's backpack and aesthetic.

The damned plant.

Instead of returning home, I veered off course and beelined for headquarters, hoping to catch anyone at all that I could dump the issue onto and get back to the real work. Yeah, President may have warned me about asking questions I hadn't earned the answers to, and yeah, I'd yet to earn much of anything with Nika making a grand disappearance right under my nose, but to be truthful, I really didn't care. President wasn't the one on the streets soaking up the action, and if she wanted to dismiss me from the force for daring to ask questions that helped me understand what she was pitting me against, screw her. She could find a new warden to kick as much ass as I did. Good luck to her.

The building loomed into view, the pristine white stucco doing its job as a beacon a bit too enthusiastically. I parked in the half-circled drive where the target extraction took place and glared at the two wardens gossiping outside who had paused to check out the disturbance. Both ducked their eyes and dropped their voices to excited whispers in response.

"I heard it ripped his arm off," the first one said, her hand cupped around her mouth as though it would stop the words from echoing against the cavernous covered walkway.

The second warden sucked in air before leaning toward the first one slightly. "I'm not surprised at all. President said he's the strongest witch we've ever seen."

I slowed my walk up the front path, intrigued by the conversation and hoping to catch more of it before I closed myself inside the building. The first warden spoke again.

"Just don't go anywhere near him. Michael said even the restraints aren't nullifying all of that power. He can still do *some* magic."

"What about the cell?" The second warden squeaked. "That's not working either?"

If something more was said, I didn't catch it; I was hurriedly making my way through the bland double doors and scurrying down the steps with my hands tightly clamped around what I hoped would answer the only burning questions remaining. The basement was quiet, empty. That wasn't entirely unusual but it was ominous. My steps echoed against the plethora of metal adorning the room between the cells and the vast wall of Obscure restraints. It wasn't often that the area was traversed during the day; the interrogation unit remained at the far end of the building, hopping from room to room as they extracted information from various sources, and the trainees and instructors stayed down the right hall from morning until night, beating the living hell out of the new recruits and not letting up until they resembled something of a warden. Still, it felt wrong to be traipsing through, as though any second an alarm would sound and President would appear out of nowhere and yell "gotcha".

Not that it would stop me either way.

I hustled through the rows of empty cages until, finally, I came across a singular occupied one. I looked left, then right, and then approached it cautiously.

The man hunched inside was barely old enough to be called a man. If I had to guess, I'd have said he was maybe nineteen—twenty at most. At first I dismissed him, sure that he couldn't be the witch I was looking for simply due to his age and stature, but the shackles accessorizing both his wrists and ankles—definitely not standard procedure—had me stopping just a hand's span away from the bars. The dark mop of hair atop his head was stringy, unwashed. Blood stained the bottom quarter of his jeans, though I couldn't see a wound. Head dipped low in between his bent knees, his small back rested against the opposite bars. Though he appeared to be a broken young man, he certainly did not behave like one. It didn't take words for him to acknowledge my presence. The tightening of his shoulders did it for him. As I dropped the object in my hand onto the ground between us, he lifted sage green eyes in interest.

"So you're the powerful-as-fuck witch?"

His gaze continued to rise, taking me in from the bottom up until they settled on my face. Everything about him was slow, cautious. Smart.

"Well, prove it, then. Tell me what this is."

Something flashed across his face—amusement maybe—and he opened his mouth, then promptly snapped it shut again. A moment passed before one corner of his mouth lifted and he said: "That's a plant."

I knelt, knees framing the plant in question as we both stared at the garish yellow pot. "Someone did something to this plant." I waved my arms in the air, signaling the 'woo-woo' that I couldn't quite describe. "It's not normal." Pressing the pot forward by an inch, I gave him the opportunity to reach through the bars and touch it, which he accepted with less haste than I'd hoped for. He recoiled almost instantly, spat on the floor in disgust as he wiped his hand along the hem of his shirt to cleanse it. Did Obscure have cooties?

"That's weak magic. Worthless." He spat again.

"I dunno. Seems like you might be afraid of it, actually."

A harsh bark of laughter scraped through his throat, but his eyes were all but amused. "I'm afraid of nothing. I am the most powerful witch you will ever meet." He sniffed to punctuate the sentiment.

"You're, what, *nineteen?*" No effort was made on my part to hide the patronizing tone or the expression of doubt.

"Wrong," he said in a low whisper, gripping the bars with both hands and leaning his face so close to them that I was sure for a moment he was trying to sniff the leaves on the other side of them. Based on the small smile twitching his lips, he was pleased to look so young. "I'm well over six hundred years old."

Rumors had been swirling for months that witches often appeared much younger than they actually were. The New Government had yet to get their hands on a witch who'd confirm the rumor, or explain its origin. Apparently, that was about to change.

"Why do you *look* nineteen?"

Thin arms folded over an equally thin chest. Defiance rolled off of him, crashing into me with earnest. For such a self-proclaimed god of magic, the fact that he looked like a college student only detracted from his believability. He'd have to do better than give me words if he wanted me to accept his claims. He knew it. We stood in silence for several moments.

"Witches only age as they use their magic. The more magic they have to use, the slower the aging process. Magic cannot be replenished, so once we use it all up…" He mimed a knife across the neck before settling an unpleasant gaze on the item just outside the cage once again. "That," he pointed an accusatory finger at it. "Is *not* witch magic."

Brows raised in question, I straightened and looked down at the offending magical plant. "What kind of magic is it, then?"

He spat yet again, less enthusiastically. He was probably running out of spit. "Filthy druid magic."

Mouth already open to ask what the hell a druid was, the sound of approaching footfall gave me pause. Judging by the distance, someone had just begun descending the lower portion of the stairs. I had maybe three minutes before they were on us. In a hushed whisper, I spoke urgently to the witch. "A druid hid something inside it, I think. Can you get it out?"

"What do I get in return?"

The steps drew heavier, louder. They were stepping into the hallway. While I technically wasn't out of bounds to be in the facility, I didn't particularly want to explain to anyone else why I was encouraging a captured witch to use the very magic that escaped all of our efforts to contain it. "What do you want?" I said it carefully, unpromising.

"A favor, once I'm on the outside."

My gaze slid over the pointed leaves, lush despite the absence of Leena's care. Had the police been watering that thing? Damnit. What was it worth to me, to finally be done with it and on my way to Nika? What was it worth, to finally kill off the old version of myself in favor of the new one?

"Done."

He waved a hand in the air, curling his fingers in on themselves several inches away before tugging his clenched fist toward himself. Lo and behold, a thick metal object appeared as if from thin air and crashed to the ground with a sound that had the footsteps running quickly in our direction. I bent to retrieve it, stashing it between the elastic of my belly band and the soft skin of my abdomen. A hidden magical item, right at home next to my knife. Scooping the plant, I turned to leave just as the witch's hand snaked out for a fistful of soft cotton blouse.

"Wait," he hissed quietly. "Wait. My name is Theo. What's yours?"

For a moment, I considered shaking him off and making a break for it. It seemed significant to him that we exchanged names. Important. Could it have something to do with his ability to collect on the favor I'd promised? The moment passed as the figure finally emerged from the opposite end of the hall, gaze fixed hotly on my back. I leaned forward, the name rolling from my tongue as easily as it had each time I'd taken it before, under the guise of a cover.

"Mare."

Then I turned as his grasp relented and he shrunk back into the cage, and I speared myself with the furious eyes of President. Bring it on.

Chapter 35 - Luke

The cheap wooden chairs were ice cold, a product of the air conditioning being cranked far too high to compensate for the wave of heat outside. I rested my arms on the small table, but it wasn't comfortable. I guessed that was what you got when you were the boss who'd handed over control. Sophie was absolutely capable of running the thrift shop I'd inherited from my parents, and she did so with pride, knowing that it allowed me to continue working at the architectural firm where my passion truly rested. But that was all about to change.

On my way over, I'd emailed my clients and boss, advising that my pending projects would need to be reassigned because, effective immediately, I resigned. It was hard, but not the hardest thing I'd done in my life. Not even close.

No, that challenge might have been sitting right in front of me, waiting yet to be handled.

The plan was to meet at my shop, Reborn, because it was the most comfortable place for me. I needed to be someplace safe in order to muster the courage to do what needed to be done, and Reborn reminded me of family and of home. There was no better feeling in the world, nowhere I'd rather have chosen to have my life fall apart.

With Marie's continued involvement with the New Government, the world still spiraling into oblivion, and new Obscure coming forward every day, it was only a matter of time before things took a very, very wrong turn. It was best to be ahead of the trouble, no matter what the cost of that preparedness would be.

Hard green-brown eyes sized me up in silence from across the table. We'd spoken briefly over the phone before we met, and I'd known even then that she'd be no-nonsense. To the point. That was exactly what the situation called for, and while her name and contact information had originally come from Genevieve—the traitorous wench—I didn't have many good options left besides pushing the plan forward into action. That meant trusting Rebecca.

"You do understand that this is going to make you a lot of enemies, correct?"

I gave her a solemn nod. Yes, I understood completely, which was why I'd quit the job I absolutely adored *before* the pitchforks came out. But she wouldn't have known that—couldn't have, as I'd just done it moments ago, and I had yet to mention that fact to her. Would she still have asked that question if she'd known?

Rebecca blew out a slow breath, her cheeks puffing as she did. "You can't go back," she said, swinging that iron gaze across my face for any hint of uncertainty. "There is no going back." It was a challenge, one meant to give me a final out in case I was in any way unsure about taking the leap. I respected her for it, though I had no intention of backing down.

Nothing about the plan terrified me more than Marie throwing a wrench into it. For years, I'd laid out our entire lives and worked toward nothing less than exactly that—we were supposed to have been married, moved into my house together. Then once the war started and the plans changed, I was supposed to have convinced her to flee with me to the only safe place that existed. No matter what fresh hell the world fell into, Marie and I were supposed to be happy together.

Supposed to.

I couldn't dare be surprised that it hadn't gone to plan; Marie was nothing if not entirely unpredictable. Still, it was the next best thing. I would do absolutely anything to keep her safe, even the unthinkable. Nothing else may have been in my control, but the action I was about to take certainly was.

"I can prevent a lot of people from dying unnecessary deaths. The information I have about the Obscure needs to be shared, New Government be damned."

I didn't like to swear, especially not out loud; it was true that Marie brought it out of me often enough, but I was raised in an atmosphere where such things were improper. A man ruled with a strong fist, but was caring and loving to his spouse and children, and exuded only the manners he wished to pass on to them. Swearing was, most definitely, not a trait I wanted to showcase, especially with my name about to be topping every media outlet in the world.

Rebecca's hands rubbed a small circle into the face of the table for several minutes while she chewed over my words. It was obvious that her mind was elsewhere, an equally glassy and vacant expression settling over her features as she undoubtedly weighed pros against cons and judged my trustworthiness.

I thought briefly about Sophie, how my actions would impact her, and wondered whether I should have given her a heads-up. I trusted her immensely, enough to let her run Reborn in my absence, but it was something I simply had to play close to the chest. The element of surprise was partially a motivator for it—knowing that I'd put the New Government on their back foot, and Marie as well, would give me *immense* satisfaction; oh, and also the opportunity to regain control in the war. So, yes, I'd sacrifice myself to stop the killing. To put the humans back in a position of power. To finally put the New Government in a position where I could knock them back down again.

The only question, and hesitation, came from whether Marie would be too angry with me for any hope of redemption. Always, my plans had adapted and revolved around two things: her safety, and our togetherness. The ache in my chest told me in no uncertain terms that I already knew the answer, whether I wanted to admit it to myself or not.

"Alright," Rebecca finally said, jolting me from my thoughts. "I'll run your story, but you have to answer every question I'm going to ask you. No partial truths, no withheld information 'for the sake of' anything. I want it all." She paused, sitting up in her seat and straightening her spine as though the decision bolstered her confidence. "*I'll* be the one to decide what's too dangerous to publish. From there, it's all you."

That was all that I could ask of her—of anyone, really. The world was ready for the truth; it was on me to deliver it.

She pulled a camera recorder from the small bag slung across her shoulders and placed it on a tiny stand between us, facing me to capture every detail of our conversation. For nearly an hour we maintained a rhythm—Rebecca asking questions, my answering them, and then Rebecca asking more probing ones about my answers, digging for the deeper truths. Genevieve was right to have suggested her. She was going to give the story the exposure and the depth of information that it needed. It still felt strange, trusting a woman who was recommended to me by a double-crossing tramp, with the most delicate—and in some instances valuable—information the humans would likely ever receive. There was no more room for misdirection or half-truths or even blatant lies. Both the New Government and the Obscure needed to be exposed for what they really were. I had planned to do exactly that. Marie thought that she was the only one fighting the war, and that the only way to do it was under the thumb of President, but she was about to be proven very, very wrong.

When she'd finished interrogating me, satisfied with my responses and the amount of information she'd been able to receive, Rebecca replaced the recorder in her bag and leaned back in her chair, her arms folded neatly across her chest.

"Well, that was certainly something." Her face twisted into a scrunched version of discomfort. "I'm not saying that I don't believe you, because with the level of detail you've been able to provide," she sighed and patted a hand over the bag where the evidence lay tucked inside, safe and sound. "You're either being honest, or you're plain crazy." The words settled heavily between us. Perhaps she expected me to be offended, to make a remark in outrage or bang my fist on the table. I did none of those things, because I'd expected her reaction. I knew what she was asking, even before she'd spoken the words.

Her voice wavered slightly as she stood, subconsciously seeking higher ground to steel herself. "I'm going to need proof."

I was okay with that. Rising from my own seat at the table, I leaned forward, my palms on the small tabletop taking the brunt of the weight as I stretched across and whispered directly into her ear the things I could only know if I was telling the truth. When I pulled back a moment later, her pretty face was slack, lips parted more than a little, and her hands had fallen limp at her sides. The unflappable reporter was, apparently, flappable after all.

There was no surprise on my end when she snapped her mouth closed with a click and took a moment to compose herself before announcing with finality that she would, most certainly, be running the story and would be in touch to alert me of an air date. I was also not surprised when she paused halfway through the door to turn and advise that the story would likely be airing very, very soon.

Chapter 36 - Mare

Though President's office was quite large, I couldn't help but to feel boxed in as she settled across the desk and shot me a look that I was entirely sure was meant to kill. Well, that was fine, because I wasn't a fan of hers at that moment, either. I was itching to flee the room that was suddenly mostly filled with tension and tongues pinched between teeth, and it spoiled my mood even further than the strangeness of the encounter with Theo had. Leena's metal object dug into my abdomen from its spot in my belly band, reminding me that I had better things to do than partaking in a pissing contest with President. In fact, I had a war to win.

Her lips pursed but she remained silent. A thoughtful gesture, maybe even a tell. The dead gaze she dragged painfully slowly across my body was both insulting and unnerving. I'd never seen her that way; she'd been innocent—a facade, I knew—and authoritative, but never frightening. The idea knocked around in my mind, sat at the tip of my tongue so that I could taste it for the truth. Was I frightened of her? I wasn't so sure.

I shifted slightly, reluctantly, both annoyed at myself that the gesture gave away how much the situation was affecting me, and also annoyed at President for wasting my time. Nika was out there, murdering and stealing. Yes, I definitely had much more pressing matters to attend to—like *my job*. We were in a war for fuck's sake, unless she didn't care.

"What exactly were you doing with the witch?" The tone indicated quite clearly that she knew exactly what I was doing with the witch and was none-too-pleased about it. It was absolutely a test, because there was no way she'd known what I was doing. If she had, she'd be asking an entirely different set of questions. We likely wouldn't be casually chatting in her office, even with the amount of electricity in the air. Yet, it was a test I couldn't afford to fail. My answer was going to determine my fate in her eyes. Surely she had an idea what I was up to, but the fact that she was testing me for my response revealed that President didn't have her finger pressed quite tightly enough against my pulse to satisfy her. It was an interesting tidbit of information.

I paused, tapped a finger on my mouth in an obvious stall tactic that would probably only agitate her further, but I needed to buy time. The best lies were the closest to the truth, so I needed just a few moments to weave my lie with facts and make it virtually undetectable. President would forgive hesitation if it was beneficial enough to the cause.

Or to her.

I could work with that.

Leaning back in my chair, I pasted an expression of reluctant submission on my face—I drew my eyes just a bit wide and refused to meet her gaze, scrunching my lips as tightly as I hunched my shoulders to my neck. Then I released it all on an exhaled breath.

"I was extracting information about druids. You knew I came here, to the cause, for a means to learn about my dead friend. Well, I did. I knew that witch would have some answers because you don't live *that* long without knowing a little bit about everything." Punctuating the words with a loose shrug, I silently willed President to let it go. There was no fight there, at least not one that would end with any winners. Our fight was beyond the bright white walls we sat inside.

"And you thought you'd just go visit an Obscure in custody without backup and without permission?"

"I can handle myself."

Her brows rose high on her forehead. She, too, leaned back in her seat. "Yes, you seem quite capable of fatal damage."

I couldn't help it. My head snapped up at her words, a glare already locked across the desk. The small smile playing at the corner of her mouth was twisted and cocky, which only further spurred my anger at the accusation. I tried to restrain it, but the words still came fast and hard, barking out as if I could weaponize them and stab her right in her smug face with the threat I infused into every one. "Do you have a problem with me protecting myself? Isn't that what this very organization spent all those months perfecting in me? You hand me names and I stop them from hurting anyone else. I am doing what I was *made to do*."

She said nothing in response to my outburst, which allowed the rage to burn brighter. I pulled in all of the memories over the past year, everything that had felt off about the New Government, and slung them at her, if for nothing more than to see her reaction, to possibly catch her off guard. Every oddity clicked into place on a theory I'd been chewing over for weeks and I held nothing back as I vomited it back up into the pristine space between us. "Do you regret bringing me on board, President?" The name was a curse uttered from my tongue. "Is that why you've sent Luke Therion to follow me around like a bad memory, reporting back to you about my every move? You can't stand that I'm not bowing at your feet. It eats you up inside. Well? Do I not live up to your expectations? If you want me gone, just say so. Don't be a coward about it."

President rushed to her feet, knocking back the chair she'd been sitting in, which only glided backward slightly on the perfectly polished floors. "If I wanted you removed, Mare, I would have done so by now. This is your last warning before I begin to take a more drastic approach to your insubordination. Unfortunately for you, you may have willingly joined the New Government, but you are not given the option to willingly leave. You will leave when we are done with you, and not a moment before. Your life belongs to us, and I would think that with the questions you still seek answers to, you'd not be so quick to give it up." She gestured to the door, then returned to her seat as though the anger in her words had never existed, that it had only been a figment of my imagination that I'd briefly held the power to invoke such a reaction. "Dismissed, warden."

Bile rose in my throat. The urge to push my luck and force her hand was so strong that I swayed when I stood, my mind and body at odds with their decisions about my next move. If I'd learned anything over the past year of service for the New Government, it was that President was not at all what she seemed, and it was very, very likely that I couldn't trust her. What did that mean for the Obscure that I had been turning over into her possession? That was something I'd have to worry about another time. No matter what her true motives were, I couldn't deny the fact that the New Government had put me—as well as many others—in a unique position to tip the scales of the world in our favor. If nothing else, it seemed genuine that the outcome was intended to be an end to the fighting. In the meantime, a druid artifact and a vampire murderess were both calling my name while I played a rousing game of 'whose is bigger' with my boss.

For the record, I was 100% sure that it was mine.

I let myself out of the office, stomping through the halls on memory and intuition alone, hoping to god I didn't get lost and wind up back at that woman's office again. How embarrassing. Thankfully, after several minutes of blind turns and silent prayers, the foyer loomed into view and I burst through it on a mission to drive myself, my new plant, and all of my burning questions back home. I stopped at the apartment only long enough to pack an overnight bag and throw myself back into the car—sans plant or druid artifact—for the long drive to the Alaska wilderness.

If nothing else, I needed time and space to clear my head of the muddiness of the day and focus on my mission.

Thankfully, the settlement I was headed for had taken up residence in Anchorage, which was as close to the border I'd be crossing through as I could have hoped for. Once upon a time I'd have worried about having to pass through Canada—the only driving route that existed between the lower forty-nine and Alaska—as I had no valid passport and, truthfully, also no remaining patience for delays either. But with the state of the world, even with the slow progression to a new version of normalcy in recent weeks, no one had bothered to patrol the Canadian borders for identification in quite some time. In fact, we'd received a lot of intelligence reports from wardens in the northern sections of America that indicated a flood several months ago of Canadians, fleeing their own country for sanctuary in ours. Too bad ours was just as bad. I wondered briefly what came of them, our much more vulnerable frozen brethren. Did they have their own system in Canada? Had we pushed wardens into that land to patrol?

Thoughts for another time.

The drive was long, made longer by the fact that there were very few landmarks or attractions left on the two-day drive that I stretched to three for the sake of my own sanity. It grew colder the further north I traveled, forcing me to crank the heat as the miles ticked by. Thankful for the last-minute stop out of California at a singular run-down gas station that still had plenty of food, gas cans, and gas, I hadn't needed to venture off course often. Unfortunately, the time passed slowly when the only distractions available were the blurred white mounds outside the windows and the heavy, swirling thoughts inside them. Both left much to be desired.

Despite the abundance of planning, the trip took nearly four days instead of three, as the majority of the third day was spent venturing around the Alaska/Canada border for a functional gas station when the last of the gas cans in the trunk had been tipped into the tank. I did eventually find one, but not before every curse word known to man—and a few newly created ones—had left my mouth. I could tell by the relatively barren shelves and distinct lack of dust layers that it was a frequented location, which told me more surely than my GPS had that I was very, very close to my destination.

Taking the opportunity to scout on foot proved very helpful, as a large hill less than a mile behind the gas station afforded me the higher ground to peer out onto a large section of the city of Anchorage. It took less than thirty seconds to spot the difference between the abandoned homes and the occupied ones from my near-aerial perch. It was especially easy to pick out the most tactful approach from that vantage point. It was a wonder I hadn't seen any signs of other people or creatures in the snow at my feet.

It appeared that the community of gazillionaires had spent a great deal of their time erecting a "fence" out of lumber and various other items that they pilfered from what I could only assume to be the locally abandoned homes. The result was a lopsided, hideous beacon alerting anyone within eyesight that someone felt they had something inside worth protecting—besides the cornucopia of large homes that stood nestled within the radius of the commune. Idiots.

Two sections of the fence line were toppled, either under poor construction or a breach of some sort. It wasn't immediately obvious which. Figures moved in patrol patterns around the interior, but between the way they turned their backs to the walls as they passed one another for a quick chat and the irregular pacing patterns, it was clear that they were amateur security. I was momentarily caught between feeling sorry for the idiots and wanting to take full advantage of it. I decided to settle somewhere in the middle where it was safest. I *was* messing around with the baddest of the vampires, after all.

Trekking back to the vehicle, I paused before directing the car onward to scout the area on my GPS map, picking out the roads that would lead me most easily to the community while also avoiding the likely less traveled, and therefore more snow-covered, roadways. Choosing a path, I set out. During the last minute of the drive, my options laid themselves out before me for consideration. I could announce myself as looking for a murdering Obscure and ask for the community's help in locating her to bring her to justice, but I'd risk receiving absolutely no information from them at all and possibly scaring off any other Obscure who might already be covertly positioned within the community. It didn't seem like a good idea on several levels. I could also sneak through the fence opening and scout on my own to gather information, feigning ignorance if caught. That, too, seemed risky. If anyone got violent, I'd give myself away immediately as a trained fighter and I'd also shut the door tightly to any further cooperation. Either of those options would possibly also heighten the awareness of other wardens in the area. Bad options aside, I was only left with deception and acting as bait once more.

Deception was always a good play. I let the lies surface in my mind and ruminate as I slowed the vehicle along a particularly icy patch of road. I pulled over to the shoulder and cut the engine about a mile before reaching the settlement and assessed my clothing choice. I'd opted for an outfit that I'd worn to Nika's bar once already, but I'd added a fur-lined coat and heavy, fashionable boots; it hinted that I had money, but didn't give away exactly how much. It wasn't flashy, but I wanted their attention and commiseration, not their envy. Leaving the car exactly where I parked it, I set off on foot toward the city's outskirts and, more specifically, the fence line, making sure to kick up as much snow as possible on my way so that I appeared unprepared for the blizzard-cursed environment. Silent and tactical was not the way of the wealthy and spoiled.

It took only thirty minutes to wind my way through the wreckage of the suburbs and arrive at the location I sought. I approached the gate, a door of wooden planks that stood just a few inches taller than the rest of the fence, which put it around the height of an average human man, and found it closed tightly when I pushed on it. The noise alerted one of the roaming makeshift guards, whose shoes crunched on the snow as they hurried over to see what the commotion was. A head peeked cautiously over the top of the gate, eyeing me suspiciously. I smiled at the crop of jet-black hair and narrowed blue eyes.

"Hi, I'm sorry to bother you. I've heard of your settlement and I'm looking for a friend of mine. I think she might have come this way. Can you help me?"

The head said nothing and made no move from its watchful place above the fence posts. Even the bottom half of the face remained hidden behind a shield of splintered wood. It was much harder to judge expression with only the eyes and forehead. What was he thinking?

"Please, I'm not looking for shelter. Just my friend. I drove several days to make it here and my car just broke down that way," I gestured behind me, down the messy trail of footprints and then to the bottom of my pants, which were sopping wet from contact with snow that nearly reached my knees. "I think it's fixable, but I'd just like to know if you've seen my friend and then I'll be on my way."

Another full minute passed, me shivering in my wet clothes while the man simply watched, but then his head disappeared and the gate cracked open enough that he slipped out just a few inches to address me. He cradled a rifle that he didn't look entirely comfortable wielding and kept a good amount of distance between us. "I can't help with your car, but tell me what your friend looks like. It's not likely that she's here, but we may have seen her if she stopped by."

I fumbled in my pocket and pulled out Nika's photo, holding it between us as far as my arm would extend. He squinted hard and leaned forward, surely unable to see much of the photo since it was barely the size of my palm and at least six feet stretched between us. Yet, his eyes widened in surprise and he nodded at me enthusiastically.

"She was here about a week ago, looking for shelter. We don't take in strangers, so we suggested she head West where she might be able to find an abandoned house to bunker in. It's not exactly safe out here, but there wasn't much we could do for her."

Nika, you fox. To the man, I clasped my hands in thanks. "That's wonderful news! Thank you so much. I'm sure she's just laying low nearby. I really appreciate your help."

He inclined his head at me and stepped back, toward the gate. Apparently, I'd used up the day's quota for friendliness because he mumbled something that sounded a lot like 'good luck' and retreated once more into the settlement, closing the gate firmly behind him. Silence greeted me outside of his crunching footsteps, making me wonder by what fashion the gate had been locked, as I was sure that, had I pushed on it again, I'd once more be met with unyielding fence. Oh well. Curiosity killed the cat, or something. I waited to see if the guard's head would pop up again to watch me, but it never appeared. Out of the corner of my eye, in the uppermost level of a three-story home near the edge of the fence, the glint of metal caught my attention. I dared not turn in that direction to reveal that I'd seen it, but I was betting that, somehow, the rich bastards of the community had managed to get their hands on a sniper rifle that was pointed directly at me. Well, it was a good thing I'd discarded my earlier options.

Pulling the coat more tightly around myself and shivering in place for a moment, I stomped my feet and clapped my hands to promote warmth. Then I turned tail and made my way slowly, intentionally clumsily, back to my car under the watchful eye—and likely also under the trained barrel—of the richest bastards I'd likely ever meet. I rammed myself behind the wheel, cranked the engine over, and blasted the heat while grumbling to myself. That settled things, then. Nika was most definitely in the area, very likely watching the whole damn community, and was probably already aware that I was hot on her trail. The element of surprise was definitely gone, and the fact made me grumpy.

Punching the gas, I pulled a U-turn and retreated back the way I'd come, intending to take the westbound road that had branched off several miles earlier. I made it only another two miles before a figure stepped out of the snowy tree line ahead of me, bright red coat and dark hair standing in stark contrast against the whitewashed landscape. I slowed as Nika strode out into the road, blocking my way, and smiled at me. Apparently, she wanted a word.

Just as I'd suspected, she *was* watching the settlement, probing for a weakness she could exploit or a newcomer who'd serve her purpose just as well. Stopping the car, I stepped out and smiled back at her. My cover was blown, but that was just as well. It was always a risk to have followed her in the first place. I knew that going in. I was tired of sitting around and allowing President to think that I was incapable of handling myself when it came to the high-value targets. Finally, I'd show her. All it would take was one simple capture, and my target was standing right in front of me, smiling as though we were old friends. Perhaps we were.

Though, with the murderer's face just feet from me and without the guise of innocence, I wasn't entirely sure that my intent was still to capture.

Chapter 37 - Mare

Chill was beginning to seep into my legs from the rapidly freezing moisture surrounding them. I stood my ground, matching the dangerous gaze that slithered along my body along with the cold. With almost everything nearby covered in at least a foot of dense snow, sound was muffled and dampened, shrinking the noise of the car door slamming shut into barely a thud. Even the silence sounded warped—low, and enticing you to strain to make out what was happening around you. It was very much like I'd assume a padded cell would sound in a psych ward. Everywhere you looked was bright white, marred only occasionally by the tops of trees or the dark patches of road and rock where vehicles passing through had compacted the snow enough to reveal what was underneath. Birds chirped somewhere deep into the forest from where Nika emerged, the area otherwise tranquil and calm. Well, besides my breathing, which lifted in visible puffs of air and filmed my vision for several seconds at a time.

"So nice to see you again, Mare. To what do I owe the pleasure?"

Her accent was thick, much thicker than I recalled it being when we'd met at the bar. Each word was crisp, sharp. I must have caught her a least a little off guard if reigning in the anger betrayed by her voice was more of a priority than maintaining her cover.

"Oh, you know. We never got to finish our conversation." I smiled at her in a way that I hoped did not reflect the satisfaction I felt inside. The time had come; the snowy road under my feet was where I would complete my mission. It was where I would claim victory for the humans and rip vampires from the Obscure forces. I could taste the sweet kiss of my conquest.

Nika's long legs carried her forward, closing the distance between us with confident strides. I shrugged off my coat, letting it fall to the ground as I slid my hand into the back of my pants and grabbed hold of the ever-present restraints. You never knew when you'd need a pair of Obscure restraints, and it paid to be prepared. Sometimes it even saved your life. Nika clocked the movement but didn't bother to slow her approach. Cocky. I pulled the restraints forward with one hand and dipped the other under the front of my shirt to free the gun that had all but frozen to the soft skin of my belly. Still, Nika did not reduce her speed. Instead, she opened her mouth to show off large fangs, fully extended. She paused only a moment to tense her entire body before she flew at me with full force in the middle of the road, lifting us both from the ground on impact. One minute I watched her approach, and the next she was on me.

I used the contact to take a firm grip on one of her hands and maintain awareness of her body as my own was carried with her momentum. She was certainly not getting the drop on me. We both toppled to the ground and rolled, each vying for the position of power atop the other. She succeeded, straddling me and pressing down on my shoulders with a strength that was far too familiar. A flash of memory pierced my concentration, overlaying Nika's body with Luke's, his concerned eyes boring into me as he pleaded for me to calm down and listen to his explanation.

I screamed my rage at the memory, bucking underneath Nika enough to throw her off balance for just a moment. Long fingernails ripped at the skin of my arm as we rolled again, that time ending with me on top and one of her hands trapped under me. Pain radiated down my right arm and I risked a glance to assess the damage. The shirt was absolutely ruined, shredded to ribbons over flesh that was much the same. Blood tricked from the wounds, steady and strangely warm against the freezing cold of the snow and frosty air. Still, despite the carnage, my hand remained steady. The thrill of the hunt thrummed through me, warming me from the inside and dulling what should have been excruciating pain. Nika laughed between my knees.

Raising the gun between us, I pressed it into her chest with one hand, gripping the arm that wasn't pinned underneath my knee and attempting to restrict it with my other. The Obscure restraints clanged against a rock on the ground, still held in the hand that raised Nika's above her head. In order to slap them on her, I'd have to release at least the gun and then the arm secured under my leg. No good; it was too risky. Besides, I still wasn't entirely sure that I intended Nika to make it back to headquarters with me. The restraints would only be helpful if I intended to *capture* her. Realization of my plan bloomed across her face, fury—and perhaps and hint of fear—building in her eyes as she once again summoned her otherworldly strength to wield against me. Apparently, she'd underestimated both my skill *and* my intent when she picked the fight, and didn't seem to want to make that mistake again. One of her knees connected with my tailbone, thrusting me upward toward her head. I squeezed my finger over the trigger in response, knowing that I'd not land a fatal blow, but also unwilling to let the opportunity to wound her in any capacity pass me by. The boom echoed off the trees that stood as witnesses to the event unfolding, the intensity of the sound knocking several dense sections of snow from nearby branches. The mechanical echo blended with the soft thudding of shifting miniature snow caps. Even the power of the blanketing snow couldn't hide the sound of a fired bullet.

The combination of racket and dampening snow had apparently covered the approach of footsteps because, suddenly, and with a shock to my finely-honed senses, a second body collided with mine, throwing me off of Nika entirely. Nika jumped to her feet and hissed her intent in my direction, which was also the direction of my second attacker.

Next to me, also struggling to their feet between the impact and the uneven terrain, was the stranger from the bar—the same one who had threatened me in the parking lot afterward. Shit, did Nika have an accomplice? How had I missed that? My eyes widened involuntarily, mind whirling to reassess the situation. I could *not* afford to let Nika walk away, even if that meant that I didn't either.

The blissful realization swept through me—as my hand clenched around something hard—that training and instinct had kept my hand locked around the gun even as my body had soared from atop my target's. Though I'd never admit it, Michael's teachings and incessant, tough conditioning had saved my life yet again. I raised the cold barrel to the man before me, stealing a glance in Nika's direction to note that she was both bleeding from a shoulder wound and also staring threateningly in the man's direction, likely because it was 'Fighting 101' that the closer danger was always the priority. She, too, seemed to have paused to assess the situation since another player had entered the game.

Perhaps they weren't comrades after all. If that was the case, what was that guy going to benefit from saving her?

He held his hands out, palms forward, in a gesture that begged me to wait, to give him a chance to speak before I redecorated the ground behind him with blood and brains. "My name is Evan Wicker. I'm a warden, just like you. I'm not assigned to this mission, but I have a personal stake in it and I need Nika Volkov alive. I need the chance to question her before she's taken to HQ. That's it."

216

Well, shit. That explained why he looked vaguely familiar. Unfortunately, I was not in the habit of intentionally botching missions for the sake of anyone else's personal issues. Despite the fact that there was absolutely nothing amusing about it, I laughed in his face. "Do you know how many people she's killed? I'm not letting an absolute idiot take her and—quite frankly, *very likely*—lose her. You think I didn't clock you in the parking lot before you grabbed me? Jesus, I let you do it. I was curious what you wanted and you walked right into my hands." I shook my head in disgust as his eyes widened slightly and his brows furrowed. He was both insulted and confused. Good. I adjusted my grip on the restraints in my other palm, the cold making them uncomfortably sticky against my warm skin.

Suddenly, Nika rushed forward, eyes locked to Evan, whose attention had been on the wrong threat—me. Before I had time to swing the gun in her direction and lock onto even a half-decent shot, she'd crossed the distance and sank her fangs into Evan's neck, shielding herself with his body as he cried out. Hell. He was going to get the both of us killed. Christ, who had trained the moron? I briefly considered shooting through him, idiot that he was, since it wouldn't be that much of a loss for the New Government if he didn't survive, but seeing as how President was already quite furious with me over the number of Obscure deaths I'd been responsible for, it was maybe not a great idea to add a warden to that count as well. Even though he'd deserve it. Damnit.

I lowered the gun, charging forward as Nika ripped her mouth savagely from Evan's neck, intent on causing as much damage as possible. The wounds had looked deep even before the ungraceful exit of Nika's fangs. Jagged edges held pooled blood that bubbled up instantly inside the craters of flesh, dark and wet. Evan slapped a hand over his neck and turned quickly, snagging Nika's wrist with his other hand as she made to flee. Most vampires had extra speed at their disposal as a result of whatever made them a vampire to begin with, and I was surprised at the quickness in which Evan's hand shot out—a near match to Nika's speed. Either Nika was slow—whether that be due to her own blood loss or otherwise—or Evan was *fast*. The sudden weight made her steps falter, rubber banding her body just enough to bring her down hard on one knee. She wiped her free hand across her mouth, spitting red into the snow.

"Humans are disgusting." She glared at Evan, using their contact to pull him forward before lashing out with a backhanded slap that spun him around so quickly, I was sure he'd seen stars. He, too, went down, his form sprawled heavily across the road at Nika's feet.

I used her shift in attention to move forward as well, reaching her just in time to drop the gun, which had begun to freeze to my hand slightly, and pull my knife free of its home in my belly band. The blade glinted in the sunshine as I plunged it into the bullet wound in Nika's shoulder. She let loose a scream that I was sure had rattled the bones of any creatures lurking within miles of us. "Stupid vampire," I whispered in her ear, using our nearness to unleash a psychological attack on top of the physical one I'd been carrying out. "You've been paying attention to the wrong warden. How weak are you that I've been right under your nose, sitting in *your* bar this entire time, and you never even knew?" I left the knife embedded, releasing it to grab and swing forward the restraints. I felt her shift slightly, but didn't dare stray from my path. If I cuffed her, it would be that much easier to kill her afterward. Nika's teeth settled in the bend of my arm nearest her the moment my eyes turned away. Pain shot up my arm, slicing through my focus and melding with the agony radiating from the rest of my already-mauled body. I'd been able to push back the sensations until that point, until she'd bitten down to the bone and forced the broken receptors in my brain to reconnect. Nika rolled her eyes up in ecstasy. Our gazes met.

"I thought vampires didn't drink blood," I muttered at her through gritted teeth, abandoning the restraints in favor of ripping the knife from her shoulder instead. I made sure to twist it on the way out. Her mouth opened in a cry of pain, allowing me to slide free and reclaim my arm from her control and her teeth. I grabbed a fistful of her soft, luscious hair and yanked it backward, stretching her neck before me. She let out a choked laugh around the contortion of her throat.

"Blood is not what we seek from a bite," she croaked. A wicked smile spread across her lips. We both glanced over at Evan's form simultaneously, lying still in what was quickly becoming a small halo of red around his upper body. Nika's eyes found mine again, but when I met them, they swirled chaotically, shades of red and black swimming behind and through one another like oil droplets shaken in a bottle of water. Dizziness crept inside of me, a coldness beginning to spread outward from the wound on my arm, threatening to consume my entire body in the feeling of frozen numbness. Damnit. The theory was that all humans contained a small amount of magic in them in varying degrees, but never enough to do much with. Genetic mutation had supposedly been responsible for the birth of Obscure, who also held a varying amount of magic within them, but in hundreds of different flavors and a significantly higher concentration. Vampires, the lecherous bastards, fed off of that magic. Without it, they aged like a normal human and would eventually die of old age, just like we did. Ingesting magic kept them youthful, essentially healing the damage that age had done to their bodies. It also gave them the freakish abilities they possessed if they were powerful enough to hold all that magic inside themselves and feed off of it slowly. All it took was an open wound for them to invade the body and suck out every last bit of life-sustaining power.

While it wasn't fatal for humans, who survived mainly without any magic anyway—and was an entirely different story for other flavors of Obscure, whose entire being relied on their magic—it still left us weaker than before, and also made us more vulnerable to other types of magic. Our own human magic acted sort of like an immune system, filtering out the other flavors that were attempted to be thrust into us. Without it, we were defenseless against any of the Obscure, which made vampires even more dangerous than the others. With vampires removed from the war, even temporarily, the remaining Obscure had a much more difficult time overtaking us. That was the true secret behind targeting the vampires in order to cripple the Obscure.

The flip side of their power was that vampires in particular needed a great deal of focus for their own magical bullshit, and breaking that focus could save your life. A witch may be able to cast a minor spell with a whisper and a flick of the wrist, but vampire magic was only as good as the length of time they could channel it.

Nika reached up and caressed the side of my face with a hand. Though it was difficult, much like moving through a pool of molasses, I dragged my gaze from hers for just a moment, to her shoulder wound, which I noted was already mostly healed. It was frightening that she could still move so easily during the Obscure crap she was pulling, and even more terrifying that she was simultaneously drawing out my magic while healing herself with it, which told me all I needed to know about how powerful she was. My mind was made up.

I reached behind me slowly, fighting the sluggishness of my movements to sift my already cold fingers through the snow until I brushed against hard, frozen metal. It stung to touch, but I ignored the pain and raised the gun as far as I dared before firing a shot blindly. Nika's magical hold on me wavered for just a second. I seized the opportunity, drawing on the remnants of the magic she hadn't yet siphoned from me. I could feel it swimming through me, coursing back to its home deep inside, and I called to it. It came, weak and flickering, but it came. I shoved it forward, just as Nika had done when pulling it outward from me, and I imagined clearly in my mind's eye that I could sharpen it, spear her through the heart with it. I imagined webs of magic cocooning her insides and squeezing the last bit of life from every organ, slowly, painfully. The sensation raised goosebumps on my skin as the magic released from me, followed immediately by a creeping cold that reminded me enough of being siphoned that I shuddered against it. Nika recoiled as though I'd struck her, eyes wide and mouth suddenly puckered in an effort to either draw in air or speak. Or maybe scream. I couldn't truly tell which she was attempting to do.

The feeling of magic vanished from the air around us both, though the void of my own felt strange. Warmth returned incrementally to my wounded arm, but only on the barest levels, as I was pretty sure that the temperature in the air had frozen the bits that should have hurt.

I hadn't hit Nika with the second bullet I'd fired, it appeared, which was a shame even though I hadn't really been aiming, either. Her surprised face closed down as she jerked her head forward and free of my hold, making a face like a fish out of water.

"No you don't," I yelled, lunging forward. I tackled her in the back, pushing her face-forward into the ground underneath my weight. The restraints were suddenly in my hand—I didn't remember grabbing them—and I snapped one cuff on her wrist, pulling the entire arm harshly behind her back. I reached for the second arm just as she tried to turn and throw me off. With a growl, I pulled back a fist and rammed it once, twice into the side of the beautiful face that had turned to look up at me. Quickly snatching the other arm, I slapped on the second cuff and physically felt the strength drain from her as the restraints did their job. Her mouth continued to open and close rhythmically, her body jerking in tight movements under me. I wondered vaguely what exactly I'd done to her with my magic. I was, after all, only human. Was it possible that we could use even our small well of it as a weapon? Were we capable of fighting back on more than a physical level?

That would be monumental for our cause. And yet, with the dozens—if not hundreds—of people under the employ of the New Government, studying Obscure and formulating ways for us to best protect ourselves, it seemed odd that they'd not have explored that avenue. Which, when I stopped to think about it, likely meant that the power was mine alone. With President already keeping an eye on me, perhaps it wouldn't be such a good idea to bring up what I'd learned. That still left the question of what the hell it was.

Evan groaned behind us, shifted. I glanced back to see him struggling to sit up, pale as the crisp snow that fell in gentle flakes all around us. He kept a hand clamped to his wound, which still steadily streamed blood from between his fingers, though at a significantly reduced speed. Well, at least I didn't have to report his death. That saved me some paperwork.

My arm throbbed.

I yanked Nika to her feet as I got to my own, keeping a firm hand on both of her wrists behind her back. Restraints or not, I wasn't letting go.

"Please," Evan begged from his spot on the ground. "Let me take her before you turn her over. I have a cabin just down the road. You can even stay with us; take her right after I'm done. I swear." When I made no attempt to look at him or acknowledge his words in any way, he continued to beg, squirming in his spot for my attention despite how weak we both knew that he was. "She's not going to tell the New Government what I need to know. They won't even know to ask. Marie, please."

I glanced at him, my gaze cold and harsh. "That's Mare, to you."

He flinched, face falling. He knew what I intended to do before I raised the gun in my free hand and pushed the barrel against the back of Nika's head. One shot released. Then, when Nika's form crumbled to the ground, I added two more for good measure—one more to the head and one to the heart. You had to be careful with the older vampires; they had a nasty habit of coming back, I'd heard. Although I had no idea what I'd done to her before I had even fired the first killing blow, I wasn't willing to take any chances. Nika had been old, powerful, dangerous. She was no longer any of those things, and the vampires were about to be decimated. With Nika out of the picture, they'd scramble to find a new leader.

I wouldn't let them.

Evan made a sound much like a kicked puppy, but I didn't look at him again as I headed back toward my car, still idling in the middle of the road just a few yards away. That didn't, however, stop him from yelling at my retreating form.

"I know who you are and I see it now. *This* is why they've nicknamed you; why they call you NightMare. I didn't believe the stories, but they're true. They're all fucking true." His voice shook, though with anger or fear, I wasn't sure. "You're every bit as evil as they are."

I considered calling in Evan's injury, having the closest wardens head his way to bandage him up, but frankly he'd broken code and would be severely punished for it if anyone found out. It wasn't necessarily that I cared for his safety or whether he was punished—more that if I kept quiet about that particular secret, it may have ended up coming in handy for me later on. His injuries were severe, but if he truly did have a cabin nearby, then it was possible that he'd be able to make it back and bandage himself up. Either way, it wasn't my problem.

If he survived, he survived. If he didn't, well, that might just have been for the best anyway.

Chapter 38 - Mare

Instead of beelining for headquarters to rub in President's face that I'd completed her mission, I bandaged up the worst of my injuries and backtracked across the frozen and desolate lands in the direction of home. I thought hard along the way, warring within myself over Nika's death. It was clear that I felt not an ounce of remorse for killing the rogue vampire leader, but there were things about myself that I could no longer deny—such as the fact that I had enjoyed firing those last bullets into the murderer's body. Also the fact that I had, not for the first time, summoned an unknown presence within myself to gain the upper hand in a situation that could have otherwise turned out quite badly for me. It was unnerving, but not entirely surprising, as though the possibility had been a thought at the back of my mind all along, simply unrealized thus far. I'd need to ask someone about it … but who? Who could I trust with information that could very well put a target on my back?

A name flickered through my mind, summoning an exasperated groan just as quickly. It *did* make sense, I supposed.

Was that what Luke had been keeping secret from me? Was there something he knew about me that I didn't know about myself, and he'd been hiding it on my behalf?

The idea shifted the throbbing from the whole of my body directly to my head, the hard rattle of denials thrashing against the inside of my skull. It was welcomed, preventing me from forming any further irritating realizations. I considered ripping a piece of my shirt off and wetting it in the snow to drape across my head for the pain, but decided that living with the agony was doing me a whole lot more good than the alternative would have been.

As the miles ticked by under the purr and hum of engine and tire noise, the ice eventually melted away from the scenery outside and dead foliage traced my path in its place, almost as a reminder of what I had done.

President would be furious.

Or would she?

It was hard to tell. Frankly, it seemed that she would be angry with me based solely on principle, as it was becoming more and more apparent that she was not a fan of mine. That being said, I consistently completed her missions one after another, dragging forward hidden informants and knocking down the power structure of the enemy ranks. There was no denying that I was single-handedly turning the war in our favor; not even for President. Not too shabby for a retail-worker-turned-warrior. The problem remained that I was, apparently, making a name for myself, and not in a good way. What had Evan called me?

NightMare.

If word was spreading as quickly as he implied, it would soon become difficult to work effectively; I'd be identified on the spot by anyone with half a brain, and my time spinning Obscure into pawns of our war would be over just as quickly as it had begun. Plus, I didn't entirely trust the New Government anymore. President had been keeping too close an eye on me lately, questioning my every move for a reason that was not clear to me and not obvious to outsiders. It didn't sit right. In fact, it reeked of danger and the thought raised the hairs along my arms.

Well, it was a good thing that the new and improved version of me thrived on danger. What a coincidence.

The sun had vanished for the night, leaving a looming darkness overhead that beckoned my tired eyes to close. Reluctantly, I pulled into an abandoned parking lot, the building that once stood proud looking down on me with its broken glass eyes and mouth. Ominous, and just creepy enough that anyone else who may have happened by seeking shelter wouldn't want to give the place a second glance. Perfect. I nestled my car into the darkest corner, reclined the seat just slightly, and shut my eyes. Sleep claimed me instantly.

I woke just two hours later to the nagging feeling of someone watching me. My phone screen lit obnoxiously to a series of text messages, still incoming in rapid succession. With a groan, I smacked at it until it turned so that I could read the screen. They were all from Luke. I spied two of them as the previews rolled past in a wave of notifications: 'Where are you?', 'I need to talk to you.'

I considered responding to inform him that the only conversation I was interested in having with him was the same one he'd been avoiding for years. I didn't. Instead, I peered around in the darkness to try and locate the source of my unease. Nothing shifted in the shadows, not even a leaf in a light breeze. The parking lot, the building, and the shaded edges of the wooded canopy around the perimeter were all perfectly vacant and undisturbed.

It was as good a time as any to continue on, since it seemed that sleep had had its way with me and was no longer interested in holding me in its grasp. Apparently, not even if I begged for it.

Two hours was certainly not enough sleep for a normal person to function, but I would argue that I was not a normal person—not in any number of ways. With my seat inclined once more, I started the car and pulled back out onto the road. I may not have had sufficient sleep, but at least I'd arrive home several hours earlier than anticipated and could try again in the comfort of my own bed. The comfort of an apartment, and a world, that was safe from vampires for at least several weeks.

Longer, if I'd have my way.

It wasn't until another fifteen minutes had passed, and a flood of chaotic thoughts came crashing in, that I realized my headache was gone. The rest of me was sore and screaming for a hot soak, the entire sleeve of my right arm crusted with dried blood, but my mind was, apparently, fully recovered and ready for another round.

No, thank you, I wouldn't like another helping of disturbing realizations, but the offer was most appreciated.

I drove faster than I should have, checking diligently for a tail along the way, but I passed no other cars during my journey home—at least until I hit the outskirts of Redding where the buses still ran like clockwork, thanks to Randy and Carmen. I'd stuck to the back roads most of the way, avoiding any true cities—abandoned or otherwise—except where I had to venture in for gas, and it felt strangely relieving to finally be around familiarity.

At least, until I opened my apartment door to the image of Luke standing with his arms crossed in front of the flashing television screen that I'd left on when I locked up several days ago. Surely, I'd still been asleep in the parking lot, having a nightmare that I'd wake from any moment, angry and sweating with frustration.

But no. Luke was well and truly standing in my living room.

Apparently, he *really* wanted to talk to me.

Fuck.

Chapter 39 - Luke

My heart raced as footsteps approached. I could tell by the weight of the step, the slight drag of the left heel that it was Marie heading in my direction. Not that I really expected anyone to be breaking into her apartment in the middle of the day.

Well, besides me.

If they did, they'd be in for quite a rude awakening, especially with my mood teetering so precariously toward violence.

I pushed down the anger and worry that had been boiling in my gut since I'd arrived two days ago and found no trace of Marie. Of course she'd disappeared without a word. That was how she lived; with no regard for anything, even her own life. Truthfully, she had no reason to owe me a heads-up with her travel plans, which was precisely why I'd bunkered down to wait. If I couldn't go to her, I'd wait for her to come to me.

As the hours passed into double digits, I'd wound myself into a frenzy, finally breaking down to call and text like a madman—with no response, of course. Typical. She'd be annoyed by it, I was sure. Too bad. It couldn't wait. The fact that she'd ignored the messages entirely ground my nerves, though I soothed the hurt with the promise that, soon, within minutes, actually, it would all be over and there would finally be an answer to the question of whether Marie would still hate me once she knew the truth. The narrow-eyed stare she fixed on me as the door swung open and she tensed at the realization that she was not alone was nearly laughable. If she thought she was upset about that...

"What in the fuck, Luke? Ever heard of privacy?"

I stepped toward her, arms out in a defensive maneuver that I hoped would disarm her just long enough to get her to agree to listen. "I know. I'm sorry. But this is important."

She sighed, shoulders sagging enough to dump to the ground the bag that had been slung over one of them. I noticed how tired she looked, how she moved as if she was stiff and sore. Then I noticed the speckles of blood along her clothes. My brow furrowed in concern before I realized that it couldn't possibly be hers. The pattern was all wrong to have come from her own body. My expression loosened slightly on a deep, slow breath in and out. Then she reached forward with her right arm to dump her car keys onto the table and the dark spot of bruising against her inner elbow was on full display. Purple and blue streaks coated her arm, spidering from two neat pricks at the very center. She shifted again and the ruin of her upper arm swung into view.

Worry, fury, and disbelief sprung forward at once, catapulting my body across the distance so that I could grip her arm for a better look. It told me just how exhausted she was that she didn't protest the movement or pull away from my grip; she only winced in pain that she fought hard to conceal from me. That, alone, told me how severely she was injured.

"This is a vampire bite, Marie. What the hell are you doing messing around with vampires?"

Her eyes narrowed, lips pressed together briefly before her hard, cold eyes met mine from inches away. "Nika Volkov is dead. We have just enough time to subdue the vampires before someone else rises to power in their ranks... if we act quickly." Genevieve's face flashed across my mind at the news. Nika was dead? Jesus, was Marie telling me that *she* had killed Nika? She jerked her arm away from me, finally. "Now if you don't mind, I'm fucking tired. Say what you have to say and get out."

Behind me, the TV crooned into the silence that fell between us, the noise ever present in Marie's home since the war had begun. I needed to tell her. There was no way around it, but if she had graduated to killing Obscure to try and win a war she knew nothing about, I was no longer confident in what she'd do with the information I'd planned to deliver.

Frozen, allowing fear to slip inside me for the first time as I considered our future, the words refused to come forward. The truth glued itself to my tongue despite knowing full well that it would come out whether I was ready for it or not. I glanced at my watch. Peter's email had said 4:00 p.m., which gave me still three hours to find my balls and hand them to Marie, as I'd planned.

The reporter's voice rang from the screen, shrill and piercing as she announced a report of urgent, breaking news. The color drained from my face and I turned slowly to watch the horror unfold itself. It *had* to be about something else, *anything* else. Maybe it was about Nika—had they discovered that Marie killed her? The email had said 4:00 p.m.; I was confident of that. I'd read it three times on the way over.

Marie's attention was also fixed on the screen, likely thinking the same of Nika's murder. A small smile curled into the corners of her mouth. From my peripheral vision, I watched her run the fingers of her left hand gingerly over the bite on the opposite arm. Christ, she was in deep. Could I even get her out anymore?

The screen flashed again, the "breaking news" banner fading away to a black screen only briefly, before showing the frozen image of a man and woman sitting at a small, round table together.

Panic flooded my system. I turned, yanked on Marie's arm, pleading for her attention, for her to turn away from the screen, to me. I wasn't ready. *She* wasn't ready. "Marie, I—"

But she'd seen it. Her head swiveled back to the screen and she shoved at me with all her might, her angry voice biting off my words. I noted how weak she was, how I'd only moved several inches despite her attempt to gain space. She was angry, and she was vulnerable. She was definitely not ready… and yet, there was no other choice. Nothing left to do but try to salvage the situation, to keep it from ruining everything.

"What the fuck? What is this?" she yelled. Her voice was shrill with disbelief and something else, something deeper, more dangerous. Betrayal?

I tried again to rush forward and steer her away from the screen, to let the words come from me, the me right in front of her instead of the me on the television set.

"Let me explain. I—"

She shut me up with a slap. Frozen fingers snapped hard against my cheek, and that time there was force behind it. Anger flared her nostrils, her balled fists at her sides threatening that the next one would hurt much, much more. I withdrew inside myself, the waves of regret drowning me slowly and surely as I watched a recording of myself utter the words that Marie had wanted me to give her for so long; words that I had fully intended to give to her—in person. I thought I'd had another three hours to do it.

I was wrong.

"I come to you today as a representative of a faction of Obscure who wish to end the war. We want to collaborate with the humans and with the New Government to bring peace once more. Our hope is that, by giving information freely, outside of the confines of a New Government cell, the targeted attacks against us will end, thus beginning a truce of sorts." I took a deep breath, both in person and on screen. The one in person was held, stuck in my throat just as surely as the words had been just moments before. "I am here to willingly provide answers to any questions that I am capable of, and I will do so for as long as I need to, because I, Luke Therion, am a werewolf, and I want the killing to stop."

My terrified eyes flicked to Marie, who remained motionless, eyes glued to the screen, except for a whisper that escaped between tightly clenched teeth. There in her words, after all the grandstanding she'd done from the moment she walked through the door, was the pain she'd been holding back. Years of it.

"You son of a bitch."

Chapter 40 - Mare

Louder than before, my entire body launched forward to unleash physical blows as the verbal ones landed: "You *son* of a *bitch!*"

But Luke's arms were on mine before I reached him. The speed and strength he'd worked so hard to hide from me all those years was finally, reluctantly, on full display. Geraldine's words echoed in my head, the ones she uttered just before she ended her life to avoid being on the receiving end of the New Government's focus.

*You wonder why it's called a curse, but then it hits you. The undeniable urge for a **pack**. The magic, it wants you to be around... humans, your former pack. It taunts you and teases you with it, and if you don't oblige, there's unimaginable pain. It gets worse and worse the longer you fight it, until you just can't fight it anymore.*

Luke's grip on my wrists tightened briefly, a gentle squeeze despite the knowledge that he could likely crush my bones into dust if he wished it, before he released me and took a cautious step back. His voice was tender as it scraped from his throat. Raw.

"I wanted to tell you so many times. I was afraid that..."

The words hung, suspended above us as though they were a grand piano falling from the sky, plummeting to crush us at any second. I already felt like the proverbial bug squished under a sneaker.

"What, that I would leave you? I did that anyway," I growled at him. With the truth out in the open, I wondered suddenly what the information would change. Truthfully, that thought scared me more than the knowledge that I'd bedded and lived with an Obscure long before their existence was known.

Jesus, that explained so much. *So much.*

I puffed out a long breath, releasing some of the tension in my body as I did. Luke had been hiding something huge, something that would have changed the world as we knew it. Yes, he should have told me. Frankly, it may have better prepared me for the state of the world as it was, but there were still more questions that needed answers; questions that Luke wouldn't be addressing on TV, to reporters. There were more truths that needed to be unveiled. Truths about us. About me.

The question was whether Luke was finally being honest, or whether the information provided was merely a distraction from an even bigger truth that remained hidden behind his innocent smile and hurt eyes.

"Do you have any questions?"

It was so quiet that I barely heard it, just a released breath that hinted at words. The fragile truce between us would shatter under a single wrong move, and he knew it. We both did. I stepped forward, satisfied with the fact that he stepped back as I did, and locked my focus to every bit of him at once. I watched his breathing, saw it hitch almost imperceptibly at my advance. I took in his hands, loose at his sides but twitching nervously every few seconds. I drank down his gaze, so full of sadness that it nearly buried the spark of hope deep within. But it was there.

"Yes," I said slowly, carefully. "I do." With a hand raised and an accusatory finger pointed at my own chest, I took another step toward him. He didn't back up. "What the fuck am I?"

His eyes widened, breath quickened, and his hands jerked upward to place an invisible wall between us. There was my answer. I may have been a warden, a soldier fighting a war against—apparently—him, but he still felt it prudent to lie to me and play the role of protector. Whatever I was, I did not need his protection. Not ever again.

Fuming, I walked past him briskly, toward the door, which I held open as I gestured through it. I would not stand for his games any more. It was all or nothing, and he'd chosen nothing. He could take his secret-keeping ass anywhere else.

Taking his cue, Luke exited the apartment, lingering just long enough as he passed to let me see the emotions churning inside him before he shut it all down and disappeared down the hallway.

I wanted to say goodbye, to call after him to ask him to stay. It was a reflex, an urge I'd not known still existed within me, but I did not give in to it. He had been brave to put himself in that position, to give the world the secret that would make him a target. His life would be on the line every day, and a large, deeply buried part of me hurt for him, wanted to console him. Wanted to protect him.

But that was the old me, the one that focused on love and money instead of winning a war. A war which, frankly, I needed to get back to. Luke's confession would help us, but not as much as he'd hoped.

I still had a victory of epic proportions to report smugly, directly in President's shocked face.

Genevieve had said that humans being hunted by the Obscure was natural and expected; I begged to differ. It was time for a new Natural Order.

Chapter 41 - Luke

On all accounts, I had failed. I was supposed to protect her, to keep her safe and out of that world entirely. At first it was just my job, but then it was my life's purpose. My only desire. I dreamed and breathed and lived all things Marie Morrison, sure that our love was going to be enough for her to just *trust me.*

I had a plan to take her away from all of it—to hide her until it was safe again, just like I did before. But I failed.

She knew.

She knew.

Or, at least, she suspected. Same difference, really. It was only a matter of time before she discovered what else I'd been hiding, and then… then, the world would plummet into more chaos than anyone could ever imagine.

Anyone who feared Obscure had not yet seen what Marie was capable of.

I had failed.

AUTHOR'S NOTE

This series has only just started. Marie has only shown you the beginning of her world, Luke has barely hinted at the depth of his secrets, and Jesse—Jesse will leave you guessing until the very end.

Starting nearly fifteen years ago, this idea has been fed and watered and pruned and shaped until it finally resembled something that came from my heart. I have a deep connection with this story, which has roots in the very people who surround me. If you've related to the characters in any way, it's likely that they were written for you.

Thank you for befriending my characters and allowing them to take you on their journey. Trust me when I say that they have much more in store for you, if you're willing to accompany them. It means so much to me that you've given my story your time and dedication, and I hope that, at some point, it made you *feel*. The best compliment an author can receive is that of evoking emotion in their readers.

A special thanks to everyone who read my messy drafts and helped me to turn them into something worthy of public consumption. You're the real stars of the show and I would be buried in edits without you.

An extra special thanks to my magnificent other half, Jamie. I wouldn't have been able to do any of this without his support and encouragement. Also, he always managed to find time for the half-baked ideas I threw at him with zero notice. If that isn't love, then I don't know what is.

If you'd like to know when the next book will be released, please check my website: www.bhmillerbooks.com or find me on social media: @bhmillerbooks

ABOUT THE AUTHOR

B.H. Miller learned to love words during her six-year career as a legal assistant. She was raised just about everywhere within the United States, plus a brief stint in Italy, which gives her a unique, 'middle of nowhere' perspective. Her writing style showcases her admiration for the urban fantasy and contemporary fantasy genres while still giving her the opportunity to pose questions of morality. Currently residing in West Virginia, she can often be found sipping hot tea and browsing the vast depths of the internet for entertainment, when not otherwise engaged in video games or soapmaking.

Made in United States
Orlando, FL
05 January 2025

56608581R00143